OTTO PENZLER PRESENTS
AMERICAN MYSTERY CLASSICS

HEADED FOR A HEARSE

JONATHAN LATIMER (1906–1983) was a bestselling author and screenwriter. Born in Chicago, he began his career as a crime reporter for the *Herald Examiner*, working there until 1935, when he set out on a twisting road to Hollywood, which included stints as a dude rancher, a stunt man, and a publicist. In the late 1930s he began writing screenplays for MGM, producing the scripts for several classic noir films, including *The Big Clock* (1948) and the adaptation of Dashiell Hammett's *The Glass Key* (1942), which starred Alan Ladd. All the while, Latimer was writing fast-paced mystery novels such as *The Lady in the Morgue* (1936) and *The Dead Don't Care* (1938). After fighting in World War II, he returned to Hollywood, where he continued writing novels and became a staff writer for the *Perry Mason* show.

MAX ALLAN COLLINS is a Mystery Writers of America Grand Master and the award-winning writer of mysteries, comics, thrillers, screenplays, and historical fiction. His graphic novel *Road to Perdition* was the basis for the 2002 Academy Award–winning film by the same name. Collins cofounded the International Association of Media Tie-In Writers and studied at the Iowa Writers' Workshop. He collaborated with Mickey Spillane on several projects and is completing a number of the Mike Hammer novels that Spillane left unfinished. Collins lives in Iowa.

HEADED FOR
A HEARSE

JONATHAN
LATIMER

Introduction by
MAX ALLAN
COLLINS

AMERICAN
MYSTERY
CLASSICS

Penzler Publishers
New York

This is a work of fiction. Names, characters, places, and incidents either are the product of the author's imagination or are used fictitiously. Any resemblance to actual persons, living or dead, businesses, companies, events, or locales is entirely coincidental.

Published in 2022 by Penzler Publishers
58 Warren Street, New York, NY 10007
penzlerpublishers.com

Distributed by W. W. Norton

Copyright © 1935 by Jonathan Latimer
Introduction copyright © 2022 by Max Allan Collins
All rights reserved.

Cover image: Andy Ross
Cover design: Mauricio Diaz

Paperback ISBN 978-1-61316-281-1
Hardcover ISBN 978-1-61316-280-4

Library of Congress Control Number: 2021921417

Printed in the United States of America

9 8 7 6 5 4 3 2 1

INTRODUCTION

When I discovered hardboiled detective fiction in the early 1960s, I was a wide-eyed junior-high kid, on a voyage of discovery. There were no books of criticism about "tough-guy" fiction yet; there was no *Armchair Detective* or *Mystery Scene* or other fanzines to help chart my passage—at least none that I knew about.

All I knew was that certain paperbacks on the rack at Cohn's Newsland looked very interesting. They bore images that promised sex and violence and, I discovered gratefully, they for the most part delivered.

These grand gaudy covers conspired with the late 1950s/early 1960s TV private-eye boom to entice and incite my interest in what Jonathan Latimer once described as fiction devoted to "booze, babes and bullets." I had no signposts, no critics to guide me. I read Richard S. Prather and Michael Avallone alongside Raymond Chandler and Dashiell Hammet and there was no one to explain the difference.

However, four writers of private-eye fiction (based solely on my own adolescent response to them) rose to my personal pantheon of Tough Private Eye-dom. Two of them were the afore-mentioned Chandler and Hammett, and another was Mickey Spillane, the covers of whose books had been among the most persuasive in interesting me in the genre in the first place.

Gradually, through library research and the *New York Times* columns of Anthony Boucher, I began to realize that Hammett and Chandler were critically recognized in a field that was generally held in disrepute. I also learned, to my shock and dismay, that Spillane (particularly in articles circa the early 1950s) was viewed unkindly. Often, in fact, he was discussed more in terms of being a communicable disease than a spellbinding author.

This unhappy discovery has led to decades of defense, on my part, of one of the world's most popular writers (God help me if Mickey ever heard me refer to him as an "author"). It continues to this day, although the critical response has begun to shift in my (which is to say, Spillane's) direction.

Almost as unhappy a discovery was the absence of mention of the fourth writer in my Private Eye Pantheon—a writer who I considered to be of an importance equal to Hammett, Chandler and Spillane.

Jonathan Latimer wasn't discussed much at all.

And, while there has been a reassuring resurgence of interest in Latimer's work in the last several years, this unique practitioner of the hardboiled art remains woefully underappreciated.

If, in my childish enthusiasm (a quality I retain decades past adolescence, incidentally), I elevated Latimer to a position he didn't quite deserve, I would still unhesitatingly rank him just after Hammett and Chandler among the pioneers in the field.

And, with the exception of Spillane and Ross Macdonald, I

would have difficulty coming up with other names that would push him off the pedestal I've provided him.

When you read this book, you should understand why, though in truth Latimer has "dated" somewhat. He is not as timeless as Hammett and Chandler. But just as Spillane's early Mike Hammer novels remain a vivid if noir-ishly blurred snapshot of the 1950s, Latimer's Bill Crane novels endure as a bleary-eyed yet sharp-edged photo study of the 1930s.

I mentioned above that Latimer and his Bill Crane books are unique, and that was not hyperbole. For one thing, the Crane novels are probably the most successful melding of the hardboiled novel and the classic drawing-room mystery. Latimer's only rivals in writing the hardboiled drawing-room mystery are the much-celebrated Rex Stout and Erle Stanley Gardner.

But the Nero Wolfe yarns—despite Archie Goodwin's tough presence and crisp delivery—have always seemed to me more cozy than tough; armchair detective Wolfe, with his beer and orchids and attitude, is more precious than the hardboiled field would tolerate. And Erle Stanley Gardner's Perry Mason stories—with their crackling realistic dialogue, overwhelming interest in American business and greed—and/or adultery-driven murderers—have more in common with James M. Cain than Agatha Christie. (No coincidence that Latimer's extensive work on the *Perry Mason* TV series included both the best adaptations of Gardner stories and the most successful Mason pastiches, an opinion shared by no less an authority than Gardner himself.)

Headed for a Hearse (1935) is one of the best Bill Cranes (although every one of them is good, with only *Red Gardenias* (1939) falling off somewhat), and demonstrates handily why Latimer is the master of the hardboiled drawing-room mystery.

It includes a locked room puzzle right out of John Dickson

Carr, but it also includes scenes of vivid if understated violence of the Hammett variety. There are gut-wrenching scenes of daily life on death row, with convincing human portraits of both the wrongly convicted stock broker and a homicidal labor racketeer—scenes that, if not quite realistic, make for gritty melodrama. There is also much drinking and dining (food is described as lovingly and sensually as the numerous beautiful women), and an air of partying, moving from one bar, one restaurant, one penthouse, to another.

Along the way, as well, are drive-by shootings, gangland slayings, and stops at police headquarters. In the latter quarter of the novel, when Bill Crane decides to sober up and put his mind to the case, some frantic and hardnosed detecting—one part inspired drawing-room methodology (wait till you see how Crane locates a missing gun!), one part methodical gumshoeing (Crane tracking down the seller of another gun).

What is most remarkable about Latimer is his ability to merge a (superficially, at least) realistic crime story with the more overt fantasy of the drawing-room school, as evidenced by the Charlie Chan device of having all of the suspects gathered in one room (at both the beginning and end of the novel). For much of the way, Latimer has the suspects all serve as detectives; unlikely as this might seem, it suits the "ticking clock" of the structure. In only a few days, the innocent stock broker will be executed.

While the cast is large and, in drawing-room fashion, is largely made up of types, Latimer fills in each of them with realistic touches and human quirks. The women characters are particularly attractive, and not just physically. In particular, the relationship between Crane and a seeming throw-away character—a showgirl/gold-digger squatting in the framed stock bro-ker's apartment—takes on unexpected life.

All of this is delivered with casual brilliance—snappy dia-logue and sharp (pre-Chandler) imagery: a cup of coffee (food again!) is "excellent, as black as tar, as pungent as garlic, as clear as dry sherry, as hot as Bisbee, Arizona." Latimer has it both ways: he masters the style he mocks.

Like an early 1930s screwball movie comedy, only more overtly nasty and racy, *Headed for a Hearse* is a wild, funny ride. But the cynicism of Bill Crane and his ingenuously shady side-kick Doc Williams give this screwball comedy a dark underside. So does the drinking, which is not presented as revelry, but re-sults in collapse and hangover. The despair of the depression is ever-present, though never directly stated. The starkness of the death-row scenes, and the ultimate misfortune of the resolution of the wronged stock broker's situation, add to a sense of sadness under the brittle, sometimes absurd humor. This gives *Headed for a Hearse* life and resonance, making it a screwball tragedy, and none the less entertaining for that.

Why Latimer wrote a mere handful of these popular Bill Crane mysteries is a mystery itself, although perhaps not as much of one as the similar question about Dashiell Hammett and his five novels. Latimer, like Bill Crane, is first-rate about what he does for a living but is just cynical enough to not take himself or the world or life itself very seriously. Perhaps, that's why, when Hollywood reared its well-paying head, Latimer sauntered West to make his fortune and, in a sense, abandon much of his posterity.

One can see Bill Crane doing much the same thing; but it's typical of Latimer that in this novel, we rarely get into Bill Crane's point of view. Often, in fact, he's referred to with tongue-in-check formality (and distancing) as "William Crane." We rarely know what he's thinking or feeling; like the audience of a film, we witness the screwy spectacle from without. Perhaps significantly, the only extended passage within Crane's thoughts is when the detective wakes up with a particularly bad hangover—which immediately precedes Crane getting down to business.

Finally, a word about racism. Latimer's characters, as befits the times, often reveal racist attitudes at an alarming rate, by modern standards anyway. I think it's clear, when Latimer's union thug makes such remarks, that the author is reporting social attitudes, not approving of them. At the same time, there is a moment in the novel when Latimer the stingy omniscient narrator refers to a black character, repeatedly, as a "nigger." Those who find this offensive, and that should be most of us, must cut Latimer some slack, here. The use of rough slang, even in narration, is obviously Latimer working at maintaining a hardboiled edge. It is style, not racism. In retrospect, it might be an unfortunate artistic choice. But that is all it is. Looking past the offensiveness of ethnic-slur slang, we can see Latimer effectively invoking the melting-pot that America so overtly still was in 1935. And Chicago—which former *Herald-Examiner* reporter Latimer so colorfully portrays—was a prime example of that not entirely yet blended ethnic stew.

I would suggest readers grasp the context of when this story was written, and accept seeing racist moments as bitter elements in this bleary-eyed, sharp-edged photo study of the Windy City in the 1930s just another part of an exceptionally rich, entertaining novel.

—MAX ALLAN COLLINS

CHAPTER I

Saturday Evening

IN THE cell to the right, a man was still crying. It was past sundown now, and he had been crying since noon. He cried softly and persistently and querulously, without hope and without conviction, as does a small dispirited child at night.

Robert Westland, from the dim cavern of his own cell in the death house, listened to him. Except for the noise, the silken twilight was pleasant. The gloom thickened fast, as though someone were folding layers of muslin over a magic lantern, and semidarkness had already obscured the steel bars of the cell and cloaked the lewd white porcelain of the uncovered toilet. Swinging down the long jail corridor, cool air, moist and fragrant, pressed Westland's face, and he drew a breath through his nose and tightened his fingers on the steel bottom of his bed. From the jail kitchen came the odors of fresh bread and stewing beef and the sounds of cooks preparing supper: the clatter of pans and tableware, the clinking of china, the rush of water, heavy footsteps. . . .

After a time the man in the next cell ceased crying and

sniffed the air anxiously and wetly like a hound dog with a cold. There was a moment of fragile silence and then he muttered:

"I don' wanta die. Jesus Christ! I don' wanta die."

He began to cry again, querulously and without hope. The jail lights came on, flooding the corridor and pitching shadows, angular and grotesque, into Westland's cell. The light was harsh, and Westland rubbed his eyes and yawned. Bare feet slapped the floor of the cell to the left, and the man named Dave Connors thrust his blond head against the bars to the right of his cell's front and peered at an angle into Westland's cell.

"What the hell time is it?" he demanded.

He had a six-inch scar over his left eye, and he wore a pair of gray trousers without a belt. Muscles crossed his bare chest and bunched on his shoulders. He was a labor racketeer and he spoke out the corner of his mouth without moving his lips.

"I think supper's about ready." Westland swung off his bed and walked to the front of his cell, blinking at the corridor lights. "I hope it's good."

"This ain't the Blackstone." Three gold teeth shone in Connors' mouth. "But they ought to give us plenty of grub seein' we only got a week to eat it."

"A week is not so long," said Westland.

Blue eyes under frayed hemp brows came electrically alive. "You said it! A week's only seven days." Connors grinned again.

"Six days." Westland leaned against the hard bars. "The kindly State of Illinois says we shall be placed in the electric chair at 12:01 Saturday morning and as this is Saturday night, there are left only Sunday, Monday, Tuesday, Wednesday, Thursday, and Friday. That's six."

Sharply, a bell rang in the distance, and then silence cut it off. The man in the cell to the right continued to moan softly.

There was a distant noise of steel grating against steel, and a confused sound of voices.

"Supper," said Westland.

"The State says we gotta die on Saturday." Connors' fingers, on the bars, were brown and unyielding, as though a woodcarver had made them out of oak. "Why don't they wait until 11:59 Saturday night, or at least until sunrise like they do in books? The State don't seem to like us at all."

"No," said Westland, "it doesn't."

In the corridor the draft was quite cool now, and it moved faster and purposefully. The man in the cell to the right sniveled, and moaned:

"Jesus Christ, I don' wanta die! I don' wanta——"

Connors showed the three gold teeth in a snarl. "Shut up, you sheeny," he shouted. "Cut that out." He shook a massive fist. "Cut it out, d'you hear?"

The man emitted a startled snort, returned to his crying.

"I can't stand that guy," Connors said. "I ate at the same table in jail with him before I was sentenced. He's a dirty rat."

"He's been crying ever since they put us in these cells this morning."

"He's a rat." Connors' mouth curled contemptuously, drawing the right side of his face into vertical wrinkles. He looked at Westland. "Listen," he said, "don't get an idea I'm scared to die from the way I'm talking, see? I'm just joking, see?" He was a powerful man, and the flesh on his face was pale and firm.

"Sure, you're just joking."

"Y'understand, I don't like the idea of dying more than anybody else, but I ain't afraid."

Westland saw with surprise that Connors' lips were actually moving. "That's more than I can say. I'm scared to death," he said. "I didn't think I'd mind, but I'm beginning to now." The draft was cold on his arms and he rolled down the sleeves of his broadcloth shirt.

Connors said, "You're different from me. I been expectin' this for twenty years, and I'm used to the idea. I guess I got it comin' to me anyway. I knocked off a lot of tough ones during the alky-runnin' days, but you was raised to expect to die in bed with a lot of doctors hangin' around." He pushed blond hair off his square forehead. "I guess it's tough when you don't expect a rap like this."

The man in the cell to the right blew his nose and coughed. Two questioning toots came from a switch engine in the railroad yards south of the jail.

"I didn't expect it," said Westland; "and I still don't know what it's all about."

Connors' blue eyes, expressive in his oak face, were questioning. Coiling muscles pulled his shoulders into a shrug. "To my way of thinking, they ought to pin a medal on me for fogging those Canzoneri brothers, instead of the hot seat. I never seen a tougher pair of Dagos."

The corridor echoed uneven footsteps, magnified the clang of a steel door. It was the guard. His name was Percival Galt, and he walked unsteadily on stilt-like legs. Steaming food cluttered a tray held gingerly in his smudged hands. He smiled with the professional insincerity of a physician, exposing banana-yellow teeth. Halting in front of Westland's cell, he said:

"Come and get it."

This was a joke. The guard's protruding Adam's apple jerked convulsively with his laughter. This was a good joke.

"Steak smothered with onions," he added enticingly.

Connors shrugged his shoulders and disappeared into

the rear of his cell, but the man in the cell to the right shuffled forward. He was a small man, and his face was pallid under a spotty growth of brown stubble. He had a broken nose, his button-black eyes were small and close together, his mouth twitched as though he were mumbling a prayer. His name was Isadore Varecha. He walked to the bars, thrust his hands, palms upward, through them in a gesture of supplication.

Guard Galt's eyes, watching him, shone.

Isadore Varecha pleaded: "I am so hungry, mister." His twisted face was appealing, he slobbered onto his receding chin. His voice was an off-key voice, shrill and uneven.

The guard looked at him.

The steel bars let Varecha's hand pass through. "Please, mister," he said.

The tray clanged as Guard Galt set it on the cement floor. "That's the way to act." He lifted a tin pan of stew, a chunk of bread, and a tin cup of beige coffee, handed them, with a spoon, to Varecha, who was making animal sounds with his mouth.

Guard Galt's eyes were screened with yellow veins. He regarded Westland and said: "And you?"

"I'm grateful for anything I get," said Westland.

"You should be." Guard Galt handed him his food. "I don't know why the State don't starve you to death, anyway. It'd be cheaper."

Westland retired to his bed with the hot plate of stew. It didn't taste bad, and there were vegetables floating with the large chunks of beef. The bread was fresh, too, and he dipped a piece in the plate.

The guard had moved to the next cell. "Ain't you hongry?" he demanded of Connors. He was holding the food out temptingly.

Connors came forward and grasped two bars. Muscles

bunched on his back. "Either give me that food or don't," he snarled. "It don't make any difference to me as long as you get the hell out of here."

The easy smile was blotted from Guard Galt's thin face. He looked frightened for a second, then he regained his mocking manner. "Tough boy has a nasty temper," he said. His shadow, against the white corridor wall, bulked like a turkey buzzard, hunched and unsteady and black.

Connors' voice rasped, "Get out!" His bare shoulders rounded as he pulled down on the bars.

An unpleasant croaking seemed to come from the birdlike shadow. It was Guard Galt laughing. He controlled himself after a time and said, "Let's see you make me." He laughed again. He was going to have a good one to tell the boys in the guards' mess hall.

"Get out," said Connors again.

The guard's eyes rolled, inspected the cell door. It was locked. Then, his cadaverous face vicious, he slowly poured the warm, steaming stew out of the tin plate onto the cement floor. With mock daintiness, he dropped the bread into the mess and poured the beige coffee over it. He bared his teeth. "I can't help it if a prisoner throws his food into the hall." His bulging veined eyes were triumphant.

Rigid against the bars, Connors spoke without moving his lips. "Your mother was a nigger."

Guard Galt put the tin plate and the coffee container on the tray. "Stick your dishes in the hall when you've finished, boys," he said.

His departing footsteps diminished, halted while he swung open the steel doors at the end of the corridor, and then passed into silence.

Dipping the bread in the stew, Robert Westland ate carefully from the near side of his deep tin plate. He could hear Varecha licking his pan and making choked animal noises in his throat as he finished his food. When exactly half his own stew and half the bread was gone, Westland slipped from the bunk and walked carefully to the left front of his cell. Connors' hands still grasped the steel. A black shadow from one of the bars ran vertically down his face, concealing his left eye.

Westland asked, "Could you eat some of this stuff? I'm not so very hungry."

Anger pinched the gangster's eyebrows. He stared at Westland through his pale blue eyes. In the silence Varecha made sucking noises with his cheeks and teeth. Then, surprisingly, Connors said, "Thanks." His face relaxed. "You eat it. I ain't hungry at all."

"Come on," Westland said. "I really don't want it."

"Naw," said Connors. He appeared embarrassed.

"Hey, mister." Isadore Varecha leaned against his bars, his loose mouth quivering. "Mister," he said. His disheveled head jerked convulsively, and he kept glancing apprehensively over his shoulder. "I'll eat it, mister."

Westland took a tentative step toward Varecha, saying, "Somebody better eat it before it gets too cold."

"Hey!" Connors' teeth gleamed. "I believe you would give it to that rat, just to show me." He pushed a hand through the bars so that it was in front of Westland's cell. "I ain't as proud as all that."

Westland gave him the plate and the bread. "Thanks," said Connors. He tilted the plate slightly, pulled it between the bars. Varecha's licorice-drop eyes were hurt; tears formed in them and rolled down his sooty checks. He drew back in his cell, noisily nuzzled his own pan.

Half the coffee finished a few minutes later, Westland carried the tin cup to the edge of Connors' cell. This time the big man took the offering without comment. They understood each other, and in a way they were pals. Westland felt fine about this, and for a while he stopped wondering how much it hurt when they switched on the current in the electric chair.

Some time after midnight Westland awoke. Clammy air still moved along the corridor, and under his sleazy blanket he was cold. Isadore Varecha was muttering quite loudly.

"I don't . . . I don't . . . I don't . . . " he repeated indistinctly. Then his voice merged with an animal wail and ceased in a racking cough, as though he were vomiting.

There was a timelessness about the unblinking lights in the bare corridor and the waiting shadows and the silence and the eternally moving current of air and the inhuman sobbing and muttering and choking of Isadore Varecha, and Robert Westland's nerves suddenly uncoiled like the mainspring on a broken watch. He scrambled from his bed and beat frantically at the steel bars of his cell, his eyes staring at the white wall of the corridor.

"Wait a minute, buddy," said someone on his left. "That won't get you anywhere." It was Connors, and his chest was bare. He must have been standing there.

Robert Westland realized his hands were bruised, that the cement floor was cold on his bare feet. "It isn't right," he said confusedly. "They shouldn't do it this way. They ought to give you a chance."

Connors, his voice soothing, said, "You gotta take it the

way it is. You can't make the rules as you go along." His brows cast pale shadows over his eyes. "I been thinkin' a bit about it myself."

Unblinking lights blazed in the corridor. There was hardly any movement to the air, but soon it would be passing again, damp and chill.

Varecha muttered, "Don't let me die, God! I don' wanta die!"

Westland said, "These damn lights! Why don't they put them out?" He looked at Connors. "How can you sleep with them on?"

"I sleep on my belly, but you could put your towel over your eyes."

Varecha was tossing on his bed. "Don't let me die," he yelled. His voice rose to the jangling pitch of a faulty chalk on a classroom blackboard. "Don't . . . Don't . . . DON'T . . . !"

Connors' angry bass voice filled the corridor: "Shut up, you Polish sheeny. Shut up!"

Varecha choked, coughed, was silent for a moment. Then he began to whimper softly. "What's he in for?" asked Westland. The gangster shook his blond head. "I think he knocked off some dame."

"Like me," Westland said bitterly.

Varecha whimpered pianissimo.

"He didn't get so much publicity," said Connors. Tiny muscles crinkled the skin at the corners of his shadowed eyes. "I would've had a lot more myself but for you."

"I read about you," said Westland. "It seemed to me a restaurant was a pretty public place to shoot those two fellows."

"They were a couple of New York torpedoes hired to fog me. Some guys wanted to muscle into my union—the Coal Wagon Chauffeurs, Local 241—but they had to get me out of the way first. I heard about the torpedoes an' decided I better get them before they got me." His right hand appeared to be pushing someone away from him. "How'd I know there'd be a lot of dicks in the joint at the same time?"

"One of the policemen shot you, didn't he?"

"Yah, after I dropped my gun, the yellow bastard."

Westland said bitterly, "At least they got you for shooting men."

Light from the electric bulb changed the pupils of Connors' wide open eyes from blue to ash gray. "Listen," he said, "I didn't think you were guilty."

"You're about the only one."

"I figure this way—a guy will never fog his wife." Connors' blond head moved negatively from right to left and back. "He might choke her or beat her to death, but he'd never shoot her." He pushed an invisible someone away again. "Besides, your case was too open and shut. It looked like a frame to me."

"I don't know why anybody would want to put me out of the way."

"Maybe not." Connors' mouth was close to Westland's left ear. His voice was a low rasp. "Anyway, if you'd had the right mouthpiece, he'd got you out." Westland started to protest, but Cononrs continued: "Yah, I know you got the best money could buy, but what does a society guy like you know outside of the brokerage racket? You get an expensive lawyer and he thinks you're guilty and he lets you go the chair." Connors' voice was earnest. "Now you take a mouthpiece like Charley Finklestein. He'd prove you were in Milwaukee on the night of the killing, and he'd get everybody except the mayor to swear to it."

Westland interrupted. "How about the people who saw me going into her apartment?"

"They wouldn't worry Finklestein. Some would change their stories, and those that didn't would disappear. He'd fix things so's the jury would give you a vote of confidence, instead of the chair. Of course, it would cost a lot of jack, but it'd be worth it."

"I guess it would." Westland blew on his injured hands. "But why didn't Finklestein get you off?"

"Even Finklestein couldn't alibi six coppers."

Westland's feet and legs were extremely cold. He felt sleepy and less nervous. "I guess I'll turn in," he said.

"Sure," Connors said. "A guy's gotta sleep."

Westland awoke with a realization he had been having bad dreams. His head ached sullenly; his left arm, under his chest, was numb. There were voices in the corridor.

"Throw some water on his face," he heard a man say.

Westland rolled over in the bunk, sat up. Dazzlingly illuminated, the corridor was like a Klieg-lighted set in a macabre German motion picture. Two men, blue coated and with brass buttons on their sleeves, stood in front of Varecha's cell, their backs toward Westland. They were looking at something on the cement floor; their India-ink shadows, heads down, splashed on the wall opposite the cells. Westland walked to the front bars.

On oiled hinges Varecha's door swung open, gave way in front of Guard Percival Galt. He bent with a tin cup in his hand, dashed water onto the face of Isadore Varecha, sprawled on the corridor floor. Westland goggled in horror at Varecha's face. It was the face of something dug from the earth, monstrous and corrupt. The skin was blue-black; the eyes were fixed open and unseeing; saliva and blood, together the color of ethyl gasolene, drooled from a lipless mouth; the black hair gleamed wetly.

Westland asked, "Is he dead?"

The taller of the two men in uniform had a pleasant face. "He'll come out of it," he replied. "He tried to hang himself with his trousers." He had more brass buttons than the other man.

Guard Galt returned from the cell with another cup of water. This time he washed away the trickle of blood. He said importantly, "It's a good thing I made my round when I did, or he'd have done it."

The blue was lighter in Varecha's face. He began to breathe hoarsely, with difficulty. His legs twitched and trembled. "Carry him into the cell," said the tall man with the most buttons.

The other men lifted Varecha roughly by hands and heels and took him through the door. Westland felt sick to his stomach. He kept saying to himself, I don't want to die either, not if it's like that. The man with the buttons looked at him questioningly.

Westland said, "Listen, I must see the warden in the morning." His voice was uneven. The man studied him with noncommittal eyes, and Westland added, "I must see him, I must. . . . "

"I'll tell him," said the man. His voice was calm. "I'll tell him first thing in the morning. You better get some sleep."

The other man came out of Varecha's cell, and Guard Galt locked the door, and all three of them left without speaking. Westland laid on his bunk, but the light shone in his eyes, and he did not sleep.

CHAPTER II

Sunday Morning

WARDEN BENJAMIN Buckholtz' shoulders brushed the sides of the corridor as he waddled towards Robert Westland. He was an immensely fat man; a living cube as wide as he was high and, so it seemed to Westland, as thick as he was wide. He wore a blue uniform with more brass buttons than even the tall man of the night before, and he was freshly shaved and powdered, and his hair was slicked down on his head. There were dimples as big as half dollars at the ends of his pouty mouth.

By taking progressively smaller steps, he managed to halt in front of Westland's cell. He said, "Good-morning. I hear you want to see me?" There was a handful of fat on each of his jowls.

Behind the warden smirked Guard Galt, his mouth full of saffron teeth. "Look what I have for you, Mister Westland," he said with artificial gayety. "Look." He held up a green-and-white wicker basket of fruit.

Westland ignored Galt. "I'd like to see you alone, Warden."

Warden Buckholtz said, "Sure." He unlocked the cell door, took the basket from Guard Galt, handed it to Westland. There was a ruffle of fat on his wrist. "Galt, you wait down at the end of the hall." He squeezed into the cell, his breath coming in short puffs.

Westland set the basket on the floor, plucked an envelope from under a bunch of purple grapes. The envelope was grimy from having been opened by someone. Inside, a note on blue paper read:

Dearest Robbie:

I have never felt so tender toward you, my darling, nor so confident of your fineness—nor ever before realized how terribly important you are to me.

I feel we will have things straightened out soon, and you will be with me, darling, consoling me, and taking away the hurt and the pain of this awful business. . . .

Emily Lou.

There was a faint scent of lavender about the paper. "Your girl?" asked the warden. The bunk groaned under his weight. "My fiancée," said Westland.

The glass panes in the corridor skylight shook in an abrupt gust of the autumn wind. Splotches of light dimmed and brightened in the corridor as thin clouds scudded past the sun.

"Warden," said Robert Westland, "I think I can save myself yet, if you will help me."

Warden Buckholtz' face was inscrutable.

Westland said, "I am not asking for much." He unfolded a piece of creased paper. "First read this."

Thrusting the paper into a sulphur-colored beam of light, the warden laboriously read:

*I don't know who gave it to your wife, but I know you
didn't. I thought they would turn you loose, but you must have
had a bum mouthpiece. I didn't want to take a rap for what
I was doing in the building that night, or I would have al-
ibied you before. If you can fix it so I don't have no trouble,
I'll tell the D. A. what I know. I don't like to see an innocent
man suffer. You can get me through Joe Petro, 901 S. Halstead
Street—just ask for M. G.*

Warden Buckholtz blinked his small eyes. "When did you
get this?"

"Two weeks ago."

"Probably a crank." The warden's fat hands turned the paper
over, smoothed it against his knee. "Lot of 'em around."

Westland rubbed a palm against his aching eyes. "I don't
know." He spoke breathlessly. "But I want to find out. It's my
only chance."

"Why didn't you go after the guy when you got the letter?"

"I didn't care then. I wanted to die, I guess." Westland paced
the floor. "But last night I changed my mind. That little Jew next
door trying to hang himself and yet so afraid to die, it made me
afraid to die too—at least in this way." He halted in front of the
squatting warden. "This place gets me too, it's so horrible and
impersonal."

"Now, now," said the warden. "We do everything we can to
make you comfortable."

"You've got to help me," said Westland. "It's my only chance."

The warden fished an envelope from his packet, pulled from
it a decayed cigar stub. This he thrust between his thick lips.
"What do you want me to do?" He found a match in his vest
pocket.

"I've got to find out about this letter and do whatever else I can to save myself," Westland said. "I'll have to see a lot of people."

Steel-blue smoke issued from the warden's mouth in quick puffs. He shook the match, tossed it into the toilet, and said, "That's very irregular. . . . " His voice rose questioningly.

Westland said, "I just want to talk to some people each day, that's all. I'll talk to them in my cell, or any place you like."

Complacently, Warden Buckholtz sucked his cigar. "I don't see how I can do it. It's against the rules and my job's none . . . " There was that rising note in his voice again.

Westland sat on the bed beside the warden. "I'll make it worth your while. It's my only chance, and I'm willing to pay."

With thick fingers, Warden Buckholtz spun the cigar in his mouth. "A fellow once offered me two hundred bucks to let him escape." His voice was ominous with memories of what he had done to that fellow.

"How about ten thousand dollars?" Westland asked. "Just to let me see a few people each day?"

Puffy lids widened around the warden's eyes. He bit his cigar, straightened his back, asked, "What was that?"

"Ten thousand dollars."

Warden Buckholtz nodded. His ears hadn't deceived him. He extracted the cigar from his mouth. "Cash or check?" His manner was cautious but friendly.

"Cash, of course."

The warden's cigar hit the porcelain toilet seat, caromed to the floor. He plucked another, new and black and thick, from the outside coat pocket over his heart and offered it to his prisoner. Westland said, "No, thank you." The warden undid the red-white-and-green band, had trouble getting it unstuck from his thumb, but finally rubbed it off on the bunk. "You ain't going to say anything about this?" he asked.

"Not to a soul."

"When do I get it?"

"I'll have one of my partners bring it around tomorrow morning."

"Ten thousand?"

"Ten thousand."

The warden heaved himself to his feet. In the corridor the sun was bright yellow. "Wait a minute," Westland said. "I want to see an attorney, Charles Finklestein, today. Will you get him for me?"

"Charley Finklestein?" The warden had hold of the steel door. "I'll get him on the phone right away." He swung the door shut, rattled the key. "Right away."

His pants were shapeless over his departing posterior.

The afternoon had passed slowly. The sun was low; the light was no longer unbearably bright in the corridor; the draft in the hall was cooler. Isadore Varecha slept in his cell. He had not cried at all during the day, but his silence was almost worse than his sobbing. He had appeared from the back of his cell to accept breakfast and dinner with the air of a brutally whipped dog, and the rest of the time he lay outstretched on his bed in a trancelike sleep, his thin gray face, with its broken nose and twisted lips, as unhuman as a mask in a cheap waxworks. His neck was muffled with a livid bruise.

While Westland waited for Finklestein, Connors had a visitor. He was a priest, an elderly man with pink jowls and an impressive manner. His skirts swished against his legs as he halted in front of Connors' cell.

"David Connors?" he asked in a mellow voice.

Connors advanced to the bars. "Yeah," he said. "What do you want?" The priest's face was solemn. He said, "David Connors, do you know you are to die in five days' time?"

Connors said, "You're not telling me anything."

"I have come to prepare you to die," said the priest. His left hand held a silver crucifix.

Connors said, "You have like hell." He thrust his square muscular face against the bars. "Get out of here."

The priest was startled. "Come, my boy," he said, "you don't know what you are saying."

"Get out of here," Connors repeated.

The priest said, "David Connors, you'd be breaking your mother's heart if she could be hearing you."

"I never had a mother," said Connors. His voice was defiant and frightened.

"What! You deny your mother?" The priest's voice rang with horror. "The mother that bore you and suffered pain for you?" His fingers tightened around the crucifix. "What kind of a son are you?"

Haze had obscured the sun, and the light in the corridor was like watered milk. The priest's face was red; he breathed noisily.

"Get out of here," said Connors.

The priest raised the crucifix, his brows met over his nose. He opened his mouth, paused, closed it; his anger died. He turned his back on Connors, walked towards Robert Westland. "Are you a Catholic, my son?" he asked.

Westland said, "No, Father."

The rhythmic swish of the priest's garments became indistinct as he neared the far end of the corridor.

Charles Finklestein looked like a small but fierce chicken hawk. With a silk handkerchief, he fanned dust from a chair in the small musty office marked, on the glass door, Assistant Matron. Finally he sat down opposite Robert Westland, handed back the letter from the mysterious "M. G." His ash-colored eyes were alert.

"You see," Robert Westland said, "there might be a chance."

Finklestein spoke slowly. "You mean you ain't guilty?" he asked. Light glinted from the thin gold rims of his spectacles.

"That's just what I mean."

"Hmm." The attorney was doubtful. "Isn't it kinda late to start a job like this?"

"It's my only chance. I didn't care before, but I have decided I don't want to die after all."

Finklestein said, "A lot of people feel that way." His smile exposed strong, uneven teeth. "I don't know. It's certainly a million-to-one shot. You better tell me about the evidence against you first, then I'll be able to decide——"

"You might as well believe I am innocent right now," Westland said. "I wouldn't be doing this if I wasn't."

Finklestein said, "I don't know." It was quite dark in the room, and he walked over to the wall switch and snapped on the light. He was a trim, dapper man, and he wore a diamond the size of a dime on the third finger of his left hand. Returning to his chair he said, "You better tell me about the case, anyway."

"You know the general story—the papers gave it enough space." Westland's head throbbed. He put his hand against his temples, leaned his elbows on his knees. "My wife, Joan, was found shot to death on April 28th in her apartment at 191 East

Delaware Place. She and I were living apart. They broke the door down and found her."

Finklestein asked, "Who's they?" He took out a pencil, a notebook.

"Well, according to the testimony at the trial, my wife's maid, June Dea, tried to get into the apartment around nine-thirty in the morning. The door was locked, so she called the manager, Gregory Wayne, to find out if Mrs. Westland had gone out and left a message for her. Wayne discovered from Tony, the elevator boy, that my wife hadn't gone out, so he came upstairs and pounded on the door, too."

"Didn't he have a passkey?"

Westland said impatiently, "I'll tell you about the key later." He rubbed the back of his head. "After Wayne had pounded for a while, Mike Sullivan, the house detective, and Theodore Pulsinski, the janitor, came up. They were standing around, trying to decide what to do, when Bolston arrived on the scene."

"Who's he?"

"Dick Bolston? He's one of my partners in the brokerage business. He took over my wife's stock account after she and I separated two years ago. I thought it would be best for me not to handle her money, so I asked him to take care of it. He'd had a business appointment with her for ten o'clock." Finklestein scrawled on the tiny pad of paper as Westland continued: "Dick told the others of his appointment, and they decided to break in." Westland's voice faded into a whisper. "She was lying on the living-room rug, a bullet through the back of her head."

Finklestein asked, "Who broke down the door?"

"Sullivan, the house detective. He was the first one in the room."

Finklestein's pencil tapped the paper five times. "There were four others behind him?" he tapped the paper again. "I figure those present included your partner, the janitor, the manager, the maid, and Tony, the elevator boy?"

"That's right," said Westland.

The pencil scraped against the paper. "Go on."

"Sullivan wouldn't let anyone touch the body, and the manager called the police."

Finklestein said, "You might just as well call a herd of elephants."

"I don't know exactly what the police did after they got there, but anyway they arrested me at the athletic club while I was playing squash. It seemed that Joan has been killed with my gun, a Webley automatic which I'd used when I was in the British army."

"Wait a minute," said the lawyer. "How'd she get shot with your pistol?"

"I don't know. They never found the damn thing."

"This is getting interesting." Finklestein jerked his chair to the table. "You mean this jane—pardon me, I mean your wife—was found in a locked apartment, shot to death, and there was no pistol there?"

"Something like that. The police came to me and asked me if I had lost my Webley. I said I had it in a drawer in a cabinet in my apartment. But when they looked, it was gone. That's when they booked me for murder."

"How'd they know you had a Webley in the first place?"

"My other partner, Ronald Woodbury, told them. He didn't even know Joan was dead at the time."

Finklestein asked, "How many partners have you got?"

"Just Woodbury and Bolston. The firm name is Westland, Bolston and Woodbury."

"How'd this Woodbury know you had a Webley?"

"We served together in France. He had one, too."

"How'd they know it wasn't his gun that shot her?" Finklestein shoved his glasses up his hooked nose. His voice came in barks.

"They didn't have to know." Westland looked indignantly at the attorney. "He wouldn't have any reason to kill my wife; none in the world."

"How'd they know it was a Webley at all?"

"Ballistics experts. They proved the bullet came out of a wartime Webley."

"And they got you because you couldn't produce yours?"

"The prosecutor said it was obvious I had concealed my gun to escape detection."

Finklestein shook his head. "What else did they have?"

"They had plenty. Probably the worst thing was the key. When I lived with Joan we had a special lock put on the apartment door, one of the kind that doesn't snap but has to be turned with the key. We had only two keys made. I had one, she had the other. When we separated, I didn't give her back my key."

Finklestein asked, "That's why they had to break down the door, because the special lock was fastened?"

"That's right. And I had one of the keys, and hers was found with some of her other keys on a table beside the body. Since the door had been locked from the outside, it was obvious that my key had locked it—after she had been shot."

The lawyer's teeth gleamed. "That's easy. Somebody had a duplicate made."

"No." Westland shook his head. "That's the big puzzle. There weren't any duplicates. The maid, June, had been trying for a year to get Mrs. Westland to have a duplicate made for her, but

Joan wouldn't do it. She kept jewelry and bonds in a safe in the apartment. She said she wouldn't have any duplicate keys floating around; she wanted to be able to sleep securely at night. Only about a month before the murder she spoke to me about my key. She said she was worried about the bonds and jewels and wanted to know if I had had a duplicate made. If I had, she said, she'd change the lock. I told her I hadn't."

Outside, blue street lights appeared. The room's two narrow windows were streaked with a gray substance. Over the right one hung a cobweb, its ends twisted and sooty.

"How about your key?" asked Finklestein. "Couldn't someone have pinched it and had a duplicate made?"

Westland shook his head. "Not a chance. I keep it in a leather case with three other keys, and the bunch is never out of my sight."

"You had the key after the murder?"

"Yes, I had it."

"Her apartment then . . . aren't there any other doors, or some windows . . . ?"

"That's the only door. There is a small package entrance in the kitchen, but it isn't big enough for a man to get through. I know, because we had it measured. The windows are just twenty-three floors from the ground."

"Maybe the guy lowered himself into the apartment below with a rope?"

"The windows were all locked from the inside."

"The hell you say!" Finklestein rubbed the bridge of his nose with a finger tip, pushed his spectacles in place. "This sounds like a story by that fella—what's his name—Van Dyke? You got a woman dead from a pistol wound. The gun's missing, the keys are all accounted for, the door and the windows are locked from the inside, and there ain't any other way to get out." His rubbing finger made a white line where the bone ran on his nose.

Westland said, "Sometimes I think I really must have done it." He drew a cigarette from the breast pocket of his shirt, lit it with a kitchen match. He flipped the match into a dusty brass spittoon.

"Go on," said Finklestein. "What else did they have on you?"

"You knew that I was in her apartment just before she was murdered?"

"I read it in the papers, but you better tell me about it, anyway. I want you to act as if I didn't know anything."

"It's pretty funny why I was there."

"Funny?"

"I mean strange." Westland crossed his legs and clasped his left knee with his two hands, his fingers interlocked. "I told you my wife and I were separated. I had been trying to get her to divorce me, but we couldn't get together on a property settlement. We were on fairly good terms, but I was anxious to get free so I could marry a girl named Emily Lou Martin. The marriage was all arranged; it was only a matter of my getting free."

Finklestein said, "Sure, but how about that visit?"

"On the night of the murder, that was Sunday, Emily Lou, at least I thought it was Emily Lou, telephoned me and said my wife had talked to her that afternoon and had warned her to stay away from me. She said my wife had called her a 'scheming slut.' Emily Lou was quite upset, so I decided to go over and have it out with Joan."

"What time was this?"

"About eleven-thirty. I was reading in bed when Emily Lou telephoned."

"And you went over to your wife's apartment that night?"

Westland squashed his cigarette butt against the table and dropped it in the spittoon. "It took me about twenty-five minutes to get over there." He automatically lit another cigarette. "I took the elevator up to her apartment, and we had a terrible quarrel. She denied having spoken to Emily Lou, and I called her a liar. I got pretty excited and made a damn fool of myself."

"And the elevator boy heard you?"

"Yes." Westland's eyes rounded. "How'd you know?"

"They always do," Finklestein said. "Go on."

"I stayed about forty minutes and then I calmed down and apologized—I think I would have killed myself if I hadn't apologized in view of what happened later—and we parted on a friendly basis. I ran the elevator down . . . "

Finklestein interrupted him. "You ran the elevator?"

Westland explained, "The boy quits at midnight, and the elevator works automatically after that." He continued, "I ran the elevator down to the lobby and went home."

Finklestein rubbed his hands on his silk handkerchief. "Did anybody see you on your way home?"

"Nobody."

"What time did you get home?"

"It must have been close to one."

"They found the body about ten the next morning?"

"That's right," Westland said. "And at the trial, the coroner's——"

The diamond glistened on Finklestein's upheld hand. "I know, I know. The coroner's physician testified that the body had been dead just nine hours. Those boys are magicians." He adjusted his glasses violently. "They can tell you just when a guy died, while an ordinary specialist don't even know whether he is dead half the time."

"There wasn't any doubt about her being dead."

The attorney asked, "That all they had on you?"

"No. They found a letter from me in her purse. In the letter I said: 'If you don't divorce me, I'll have to get rid of you.' By that I meant, I'd divorce her if she didn't divorce me, and it sounded pretty bad when the prosecutor read it to the jury."

Finklestein groaned. "I'll say it must have."

"Then they found her will, leaving all her money to me."

"Oy!"

Westland spoke apologetically. "I guess she hadn't bothered to change it after we were separated."

"How much did she leave?"

"It wasn't much, only thirty thousand dollars."

Finklestein was dusting off his hands again. "Thirty thousand dollars looks like a million to a three-dollar-a-day juror." He stuffed the handkerchief in his coat pocket and wrote on his pad. "Is that all?"

"There was that telephone call from Emily Lou," Westland said. "I told the police about it, but they found she hadn't called me at all that evening."

"She hadn't called you at all!" The lawyer pressed his hands to the sides of his head. "Say, this thing is going to drive me goofy."

"If you're puzzled, think how I felt," said Westland. "The State puts Emily Lou's uncle and aunt, with whom she lives, on the stand, and they testified that she hadn't used the phone all that evening. The only phone in the house is by the living room, and they would have heard her."

"Maybe she went out?"

"No. She stayed in all evening. They testified that they played cards and listened to the radio and that Emily Lou was with them." Westland smiled at the attorney's wry face. It was his first smile in months. "But there is something even more bizarre than that. During the trial I suddenly recalled that the Emily Lou of the telephone had used bad grammar in talking to me. I attributed it to excitement at the time, but later I realized that it couldn't have been Emily Lou talking after all. I remembered that her voice had sounded a little queer."

"So I suppose you told all this on the stand?"

"Of course."

Finklestein groaned again. "So the prosecutor got a chance to say that you had hoped your girl would lie for you, and when she wouldn't, you had been forced to change your story." He shook his head sadly. "I don't ever talk about other lawyers, but if I did, I would have to say yours were lousy." He made a note on the pad. "That's all?"

"I think so. . . . " Westland scowled. "No, I guess there is one more thing. The man in the apartment below testified he had heard a noise like a shot as he and his wife were having a cup of tea before going to bed. They both said it was around twelve-twenty. Their name is Shuttle."

"And you had admitted you were in the apartment with her from a little after twelve until almost one?"

"Certainly. Why should I have lied about it?"

"You must have been just about the best witness the prosecution had." Finklestein pushed up his glasses. "You'd think a guy with a hooked nose like mine could keep his glasses up, wouldn't you?" He put his elbows on the table and peered at Westland. "Who would want to see you put out of the way?"

"As far as I know—nobody."

"How about your money? Who gets it?"

"Part of it goes to Emily Lou—two thirds—and the rest to my cousin, Lawrence Wharton. You mustn't tell Miss Martin, she doesn't know." Westland lit a cigarette. "Then there is ten thousand to my man, Simmons."

"How much are you worth?"

"I think about three hundred and fifty thousand now. I have spent almost a hundred thousand defending myself." He rubbed his forehead. "Of course, that doesn't include personal property and some real estate."

Finklestein's fingers, pushing against a cheek, almost closed his right eye. "Any reason for either of your partners to get you out of the way?"

"No. It might even hurt the business." Westland blew smoke out of his nose. "Although, God knows, it's been bad enough for the last five years. If I didn't have a private income, it would have been damn tough. I'd have had to root instead of taking it easy."

"Then you haven't been very active in your firm?"

"No. I've kept some of my accounts, but I have been half retired."

Abruptly the lawyer pushed back his chair, stood up. "Either you were unlucky or you were framed." He snapped his thumb nail on his teeth. "My guess is you were framed." He bent over Westland and said, "Look, legal advice won't be any good."

Westland said, "Then you won't assist . . . "

"Sure I will. You've got me convinced. But there is only one way to get a reprieve now. The Governor ain't goin' to listen to a lot of rumors about new evidence." The attorney shook a finger at Westland. "We have to get the real murderer."

The room was cooler now. Light slithered through the crack under the warden's door.

Finklestein continued, "Only four days left, so we'll have to hump." With short nervous steps, he paced the floor. "I'll send to New York for the smartest detective in America. And in the morning, as you suggested, we'll have a meeting here of everybody connected with the case: your partners and Miss—" he consulted his notebook, still on the desk—"Martin."

Westland objected. "Why bring her here?"

Finklestein held up his hand. "I want to see her. Besides, she can be of help. I may send her after that M. G. who wrote the letter. A lady can always get in touch with a man quicker than another man, particularly if she is pretty."

Westland said, "She's pretty all right."

"Another thing," the lawyer said: "I'll be your outside commander, but I think you had better hear all the reports." A thought shadowed his face. "The only trouble will be the warden."

"I've got him fixed."

"Fine. Fine. Then I'll see you first thing in the morning. I'll get the others." Finklestein picked up his notebook and opened the door to the warden's office. Squeezed into a swivel chair, Warden Buckholtz was apparently asleep. His face hung in peaceful folds, and a ribbon of smoke rose from his cigar on the edge of his golden oak desk. Finklestein paused at the door, looked back at Westland. He seemed embarrassed. "Naturally I expect some . . . emolument for this. . . . " His voice died away.

"Of course," said Westland. "You name the fee."

Finklestein's eyes sparkled back of the glasses. He rubbed

his hands. "I'll tell you what I'll do," he said. "I always was a gambling man. I'll take fifty thousand if we set you free and nothing but expenses if we don't." He left the door, moved to wake the warden, saying: "That's sporting, ain't it? Fifty grand or nothing . . . "

" . . . but expenses," said Robert Westland smiling. He stood up, brushing the seat of his trousers with his hands. His head felt much better.

CHAPTER III

Monday Morning

IN JAIL they make you get up early. It was absurd. Time would pass much faster if they would let you sleep until noon, but instead they ring an electric bell at 6 A. M. This means breakfast will be ready in fifteen minutes. But today Robert Westland was glad, for once, of this bell. He was glad not because of breakfast but because it made the day longer.

After he had washed in cold water, he pulled on his trousers and thrust his arms in his shirt and lit a cigarette. The smoke was warm and fragrant in his throat. His hands were cold, and he put them in his trousers' pockets. The part of the jail reserved for the solitary death cells was clammy, like a mausoleum, and always the strange damp current of air passed along the hall. He lifted the basket of fruit which Emily Lou had sent him, carried it to the front of his cell and peered in at Isadore Varecha.

"Hi," he said, holding out the basket. "Have some fruit?"

Varecha was sitting on his bed, his legs crossed under him, tailor fashion. The swollen flesh around his neck was navy blue. His small eyes gleamed suspicion.

"What's d' matter with it?"

"Nothing. I have just got too much." Varecha considered this reason for a moment: its logic appealed to him, and he came to the front of his cell. "T'anks," he said. His hand was chapped rawly under an encrustation of dirt and soot. He took a russet pear. "Have some more," urged Westland. He handed the little man a cluster of velvety hothouse grapes. "T'anks," repeated Varecha. He regarded the grapes with awe.

Connors had been watching them from the other side. He selected a pear and a tangerine. "Much obliged," he said. In the half light of early morning his face looked as though it had been hacked out of Indiana limestone. "These'll make the Java taste better."

Robert Westland took a peach and put down the basket. The sour-sweet juice made his teeth feel clean. "Breakfast ought to be along any time," he observed between bites.

Connors said, "Yeah, and that lug of a guard." His jaw muscles were like piano wire. "I'll get my hands on him one of these days."

"Don't let him bother you," said Westland.

They ate thoughtfully for a time.

"Where'd you go last night?" Connors asked.

Westland told him about the letter and about Finklestein and his plan to save himself.

"Joe Petro?" Connors wrinkled his forehead. "I think I know the guy. He's a fence. He runs a restaurant just to fox the coppers. I never bothered with that sort of stuff myself."

"We're going to try to find this M. G. in the morning."

"I hope you get a break." Connors spoke sincerely. "This is no way for a guy to die."

A few minutes later Percival Galt, the guard, appeared with breakfast. He spoke with the aggravating cheerfulness of a radio announcer. "Good-morning, everybody." His Adam's apple bobbed up and down. Beard grew in patches on his long horsey face. His dirty thumb was in the oatmeal and milk when he handed Westland his dish, but he slid Connors' food to him with his foot along the wall, carefully keeping out of the gangster's reach.

"Looks like you're holding a convention," Warden Buckholtz declared between gasps as he led Robert Westland to the Assistant Matron's office. He paused, one hand on the doorknob, his fat face coquettish. "You won't forget me?"

Westland placed his hand over the warden's and pulled open the door. There were a number of people in the room. He saw Richard Bolston's blond head. "Dick, will you come here a minute?" he called.

Bolston walked over to the door. His brown Harris tweed suit fitted smoothly across his broad shoulders, and an Irish linen handkerchief with a brown edge peeked negligently out of his breast pocket. He was a big man, half a head taller than Westland, and handsome. He was about thirty-five. Westland whispered in his ear, and Bolston drew a pigskin-covered check book from his hip pocket.

Warden Buckholtz lifted a pudgy hand. "Cash."

Bolston's blue eyes were inquiring. He looked at Westland, who said, "I guess you'll have to send it over this afternoon."

Warden Buckholtz bowed, cheeks hanging away from his jaw bone. "I ain't worried about you gentlemen," he asserted. He waved them into the room.

In the solemn light of the November morning the room seemed packed with indistinct figures. Westland hesitated at the door, blinking his eyes. Someone had raised a window, and the air was new and damp and faintly textured with an odor of fish, brought west by a wind from Lake Michigan.

Ignoring the others, Westland crossed directly to the table on which Emily Lou Martin was perched, her silken legs crossed. She was wearing a swagger coat of honey-colored summer ermine over a red wool sports dress. A yellow feather nodded jauntily from her brown felt hat. She slid from the table, ran to Westland and threw her arms about his neck. "It's so sweet to see you," she said. "So sweet." She kissed him on the lips.

Westland put an arm about her waist, swung to face the others. There were two strange men standing by the windows. He looked inquiringly at Attorney Finklestein.

"This is William Crane, an investigator," the lawyer said. "And his assistant, Mr. Williams." He coughed behind his hand. "They flew from New York this morning."

Westland shook hands with them. Crane said: "How d'you do?" He was a tanned, youthful man, and he wore a brown tweed suit like Bolston's, but his was lighter and looked as though he had slept in it. Williams was a dapper man with bright black eyes and a black mustache. He announced: "I'm pleased to meet you, Mr. Westland." There was a dead white streak in his hair, over his right temple.

Finklestein said, "I have some bad news for you, Mr. Westland." His voice was oily. "Colonel Black, who heads the agency these men work for, is searching for a missing Shakespeare folio in England and can't help us. Mr. Crane is his second in command, but I had hoped Colonel Black . . . "

"I am sure Mr. Crane is equally capable," Westland said.

Crane nodded in humorous agreement.

Over in the corner, talking in undertones, was Westland's

other partner, sleek Ronald Woodbury, and Westland's cousin, Lawrence Wharton.

"Hello!" Westland exclaimed. "Look who's here."

Wharton was thick and middle-aged. His face was red from wind and whiskey. He played polo and golf. "By gad, Bob!" he said. "What's this all about?"

Woodbury said, "Glad to see you looking so fit, Bob." He was handsome in a Latin way: dark, slender, and sophisticated.

Westland answered Wharton, "I don't know myself." He glanced around at the others. "Attorney Finklestein has the key."

Someone pounded heavily on the door. Bolston, who had been standing beside it, turned the knob. Warden Buckholtz' purple face loomed in the opening. "Two more," he said heartily.

A young woman and a gray-haired man squeezed past him into the room. The woman was slender and tall, much taller than Miss Martin, and her hair was dark. She was exotically beautiful in the South American manner. Her skin was pale and lovely; her eyes were sultry behind blue mascara; her scarlet lips promised passion and scorn. She was Westland's former secretary, and her name was Margot Brentino, and her father was a vice president of the Bank of Naples, Chicago branch.

The man was the chief clerk in Westland's brokerage office. He was a bent, unassertive old man, and people rarely remembered his name, which was Amos Sprague.

Westland shook hands with both of them and introduced the detectives. Miss Martin nodded coldly to Miss Brentino.

"That's everybody." Finklestein slammed the door to the warden's office. "Now, if you will all please sit down . . . "

Crane helped Miss Brentino to a chair. She used Caron's Sweet Pea perfume. He sat down on the sill of one of the open windows with Williams.

Finklestein said, "This seems queer to have everybody come here, but Mr. Westland and I need your help."

Everyone except Williams looked at Westland, who was seated beside Miss Martin on the table. Williams' glossy eyes were fastened upon Miss Martin's seductively rounded knees.

Finklestein continued. "Mr. Westland has received a letter which makes us believe that we can still prove his innocence." He produced the letter. "I'd like to have everybody read it."

He gave the letter to Woodbury, who handed it to Miss Martin. She read it, trembled with delight. "Why, honey," she said, "this means they will have to free you." She squeezed Westland's arm.

"We'll have to find M. G. first," said Westland.

Bolston took the letter from Emily Lou Martin. Wharton looked over his shoulder as he read it. Finished, Bolston grasped Westland's hand. "That's great news," he said. His hair was the color of sawdust. "It's the first break you have had since this thing started."

"By gad, Dick!" Wharton's voice shook the windows. "I never *was* quite sure you were guilty." Conscious of the others' startled glances: "I mean, dammit, that all that evidence didn't convince me." He shook a finger at Finklestein. "A man who sits a horse the way he does, sir, doesn't kill his wife."

The letter, passed to the others, was finally returned to Finklestein by old Mr. Sprague. Westland was silent amid the hubbub of congratulations. As the noise waned, Finklestein said, "Please." He waved the letter in the air. "We have some work to do."

Miss Brentino pressed a slender finger against her lower lip. The red polish on her nail was lighter than the pomegranate shade of her lips. "I think I know the man mentioned in the letter," she said. "He runs an Italian restaurant on Halstead Street. He used to be a friend of the Capones before repeal." Her lovely mouth curved downward at the corners. "He is not a nice man."

"Nice or not, we will have to see him," Finkelstein said. "But before we decide how, I want to tell you why you're all here." He spoke toward Lawrence Wharton. "I think Mr. Westland has a chance of freeing himself, a thousand-to-one chance, of course, and I'm sure you will all want to help him."

Wharton, under the attorney's eye, blew out his red cheeks irritably, said, "Of course, man. Get on with it."

Finklestein continued, "This is an extraordinary case. A detective would have a hard time solving it in the limited time we have left." He bowed to William Crane. "No offense, Mr. Crane?"

"No offense," said Crane.

"But there is another way of going at this case." Finklestein paused importantly. "It's unorthodox; it's wild; but I'm going to try it. I'm going to ask you to be the detectives."

"Us!" Wharton's rough voice was incredulous. "What's a gentleman know about Sherlocking?" He glared at the attorney through bloodshot eyes.

"It would take a detective several days to get the background of Mrs. Westland's murder. By that time, just as he was ready to begin work on the case, Mr. Westland would be . . . "

"In his grave," said Westland.

"Honey!" Emily Lou Martin exclaimed reprovingly. She slipped her arm under Westland's, pressed her smooth cheek against his shoulder.

"Cut it out, you dope," Crane whispered fiercely to Williams, who reluctantly removed his eyes from Miss Martin's knees.

A pair of hand-stitched gray suède gloves dangled from Ronald Woodbury's hand on his gold-headed cane. "You mean, Mr. Finklestein, that we might be able to catch the actual murderer?"

"Exactly." The attorney polished his glasses with a silk handkerchief. "Every one of you knows every detail of the crime. We have here one of those who found the body." He aimed a finger at Bolston's blond head. "You, Mr. Woodbury, have an automatic pistol like the one used to kill Mrs. Westland. You, Miss Martin, can help us find who telephoned Mr. Westland and posed as you on the night of the crime." Finklestein paced up and down the small room, hands clasped behind his back. "But most of all, one of you should be able to tell us what the motive for the lady's murder was. Was it to get rid of her? Was Mr. Westland accidentally involved in the affair?" He paused dramatically in the corner by the door. "Or was the murder of Mrs. Westland deliberately planned to put Westland out of the way?"

Finklestein was presenting a good performance. He rumpled his sparse hair with both hands, then shook his finger at his rapt audience.

"If the object was to get Westland out of the way," he asked, "why didn't the murderer just kill him?" He held out both hands as though he was appealing either to Jehovah or to a jury of twelve citizens. "One of you has the answer to that question."

After thirty seconds of silence, Woodbury demanded, "You mean you think one of us is—the guilty party?"

"No, no! Nothing of the sort." The attorney warded off the question with the palms of his hands. "I mean that you people are closest to Mr. Westland, his friends and his employees, and if the murder was planned to entangle him (I think it was) then you should have some clue as to why it was done." He halted his pacing in front of Westland. "You don't think a stranger would go to all the trouble to murder this man's wife to frame him, do you?"

Woodbury shook his sleek black head. "Not if we accept your major premise that Mrs. Westland was murdered to get rid of Bob."

Emily Lou Martin's trim body jiggled on the table. Her aquamarine eyes were roundly wide. "What are we to do?" She crossed her knees and pulled her red skirt down over them.

Crane cast a warning glance at Mr. Williams.

"Let me go over the evidence which incriminated Mr. Westland," Finklestein said. He produced his notebook. "There are four particular things we have to investigate.

"First, there's the keys. There are only two keys. Mrs. Westland's was found inside her apartment, and Mr. Westland had his. Yet, the apartment was locked either from the inside or from the outside after the murder was committed. We have to find out how the murderer got in and out.

"Second, somebody should try to find out what's become of Westland's pistol and who could have stolen it to shoot Mrs. Westland. That'll give us a clue if we do.

"Third, we should look into that telephone call purporting to be from Miss Martin. If someone imitated Miss Martin's voice well enough to fool Mr. Westland, she must know Miss Martin pretty well.

"Lastly, there's the shot. The man in the apartment below said he heard the report of a shot at twelve-twenty that night and Westland admits he was in the apartment with his wife then. We have to look into that."

Richard Bolston squared his broad shoulders under the brown tweed coat. "This is getting interesting. Why didn't we start after these things long ago?"

"That's my fault, Dick," Westland said. "I've been taking this thing lying down until yesterday."

Wharton said, "By gad! There's somebody you overlooked, Mr. Attorney."

"Who?"

"Westland's man, Simmons." The effort of speech made Wharton's face turkey-red. "He ought to be able to tell us something about that shootin' iron." He heaved his bulk savagely back and forth in his chair until he had swung about to face William Crane. "Not bad for an amateur, hey?"

"We'll go after Simmons," said Finklestein. "Glad you thought of him." Miss Martin asked, "But what are we to do?" Finklestein said, "First we should find that M. G. in the letter. We better get hold of him before we alarm the real criminal by our investigation."

Richard Bolston stood up. "I'll be glad to look for him." He was built like a prize fighter: broad shoulders tapering to a narrow waist. "I can get him if anybody can."

Finklestein raised his hand. "I have a better idea. I imagine M. G. is some sort of a criminal, a prowler, probably, and it won't be easy for a man to get in touch with him. But—" Finklestein simpered at Miss Martin—"if a lovely lady should ask for him, she'd be certain to find him."

Westland said, "I won't have her wandering about in that district—not for anything."

Emily Lou pouted.

"I'd like to look for him," said Miss Brentino. Her voice was exquisitely modulated, her accent slightly foreign. "I'm not afraid—that is if you think I'm pretty enough?"

"Neither am I," said Emily Lou.

"Wait," said Finklestein. "Why not let both ladies go?" He

continued before Westland could interrupt, "They'll be perfectly safe. I'll send Mr. Crane and Mr. Williams as escorts."

"What's the matter with me?" Bolston demanded. "Or Woodbury? Or Wharton?"

"Dammit, yes," said Wharton.

"These men are trained detectives," Finklestein insisted. "Once Miss Martin contacts M. G., they'll never lose sight of him. How would one of you gentlemen follow him in case he refused to talk to Miss Martin?"

Woodbury said, "He's right, Bolls."

"I don't like the idea," Westland said.

Crane slipped off the window sill. "They'll be safe enough. One of us will be with them all the time."

Finklestein said, "Now look. Here's the way we're going to operate." He adjusted his glasses with both hands. "All reports are to be made to Mr. Westland here. The warden is willing to let us see him once a day. He is going to be a detective in his own case." He paused for a second. "Of course, we are to help him with any theories we evolve." He wiped his hands with the silk handkerchief. "I am to be outside commander, and you are to take assignments from me. Is that agreeable?"

Everyone said it was.

Finklestein examined his thin gold wrist watch. "It's nearly time for lunch," he announced. "I suggest Mr. Crane arrange with the two young ladies to dine at Joe Petro's. The rest of us will wait for the results of their search." He folded his handkerchief and pushed it in his breast pocket. "You might be thinking about the case, however, even if you aren't doing anything in a physical way."

Surprisingly, old Mr. Sprague spoke. "It'll be brains, not brawn," he said, "that will solve this matter."

Wharton opened the door. "You can reach me in Lake Forest." He stepped into the warden's room. The warden was not there.

Emily Lou Martin lingered behind the others. She kissed Westland. "Everything is going to be all right, dear." Her yellow feather tickled Westland's ear. He ducked his head, kissed her, said: "I hope so." They walked hand in hand to where William Crane was waiting in the warden's office.

CHAPTER IV

Monday Noon

WILLIAM CRANE was solicitous on the broad steps of the Criminal Courts Building in front of the jail. He held Emily Lou's fur-covered elbow, guided her down each step. Her hair was more red than brown in the pearl-gray daylight.

"How'll we get to this fellow Petro's place?" he asked.

"We'll have to go in a cab." Tears pooled in her eyes, trickled down the soft hollows between her nose and her cheeks, leaving delicate green smudges of mascara. She daubed at the moisture with a linen square and smiled forlornly at William Crane. "I try to be brave, but I just can't help it," she said. "The odds are so great."

Crane said, "It is a long shot. But it's better to do something than to sit back and wait."

They reached the sidewalk and looked about for Williams and Miss Brentino. It was only a few minutes after noon, but the sky, blanketed with sleazy gray clouds, was somber. The air was chill, no wind blew; it seemed as though they were standing in a gigantic electric ice box.

Miss Martin shuddered. "I'm frightened. I feel as though something terrible was going to happen."

"It's just the cold," William Crane said. "Some lunch will do you good."

Williams was admiring a huge tan convertible touring car parked against the curb. "It's an English Bentley with a Rolls-Royce body," he announced with awe as they approached. He made a circular motion with his right thumb toward the radiator. "It's the fastest semi-stock car in the world. I seen one like it on Long Island last month. I'd almost trade my old Chevy in for one."

"That's Mr. Bolston's car," said Emily Lou. "I wonder where he is?"

"I don't see him, but there's Woodbury down the street a way," Williams stated. "He's talking to that black-haired dame."

Woodbury and Miss Brentino had their heads close together, as if they were whispering, but they drew apart quickly when the others came up.

Emily Lou said, "You look like conspirators."

Woodbury spoke to Crane: "Just some office business. Miss Brentino has been acting as my secretary since Mr. Westland . . . "

"Sorry to interrupt you," Crane said, "but we ought to get going on that letter."

Woodbury agreed. "You should. Why don't you let me go along? I could drive you down to the restaurant and, besides, three men would be safer than two."

"I don't think they would," said Crane. "The more men, the more suspicious Petro will be. That's why we're taking these young ladies." He looked into Miss Brentino's liquid black eyes. "You'll be perfectly safe."

"I am not afraid."

Williams shouted, "Hey!" A yellow cab swerved in, halted beside the curb with a scream of rubber on cement. Williams opened the door with a flourish. They got in; William Crane between the women and Williams on one of the metal pull-down seats.

"Nine hundred and one South Halstead Street," Crane told the driver.

As they jerked away, Woodbury called, "Good luck."

Miss Brentino waved at him through the rear glass.

It was only a five-minute run to the address. Crane tossed the driver a fifty-cent piece and said, "Keep the change." Chest-high green-and-white awnings ran around the glass windows of Petro's restaurant. Inside, the upper halves of Italian men drinking beer at a mahogany bar could be seen. William Crane opened the front door. There were linen-covered tables in a back room. Crane held the door while the others went in. The air in the barroom was strong with the smell of bourbon whiskey and stale beer.

"Can we get something to eat?" Crane asked the frowsy bartender.

"Why not?" said the bartender.

Splintered boards creaked under their feet as they went into the back room. The Italians at the bar stared at the two wom-en. At one small table, a tubercular blonde and a swarthy man wearing a green fedora hat were holding a passionately angry conversation. Crane picked a table as far away from the couple as possible.

As Williams was helping Emily Lou out of her fur coat, a waiter with a snap-brim hat on his head came out of the kitch-en, stared at them in surprise for a moment, then went back through the swinging door. "What the hell," said Williams, "maybe we better put our hats back on." He smiled at Miss Martin. "Someone's liable to shoot us if we don't."

"If we put our hats on, they'll take us for newspaper reporters," Crane said. "I'd rather be shot."

The waiter reappeared and distributed four glasses of water. He was unshaven; his eyes squinted, and the lobe of his left ear was missing. He still wore the snap-brim hat. "Whacha want?" he demanded. He looked suspiciously at Williams.

"Bourbon," said Williams.

"How would martinis go?" William Crane asked the ladies. Both said they would go very well. "Three dry martinis and a bourbon," Crane said.

The waiter's face was composed. He opened his mouth. "Three olives and a Kentucky straight," he shouted. He held himself rigid in an attitude of listening. In the distance, the bartender roared, "You betcha, comin' right up." The waiter's face relaxed. "You goin' t' eat?"

William Crane's suggestion of antipasto, green noodles and mushrooms, and endive salad was accepted by everyone, even the waiter. The latter was turning away when Williams observed: "He wears a hat because the Indians scalped him during the Fort Dearborn massacre."

The waiter halted, said, "What was that, buddy?" His dark face was surly; a snarl twisted his lips.

"Nothing," Williams said hastily. He took a drink of water. The waiter went out through the swinging door to the kitchen. "I seem to talk too much," Williams observed.

"You not only seem to," Crane observed, "but you do."

After the drinks, the antipasto tasted fine. There were salty anchovies bedded on a firm slice of tomato; scarlet peppers soaked in wine vinegar; thin bologna sausages; fat white shrimps; transparent slices of ham; and celery stuffed with cottage cheese; all going perfectly with the crusty Italian bread, the unsalted butter, and the peppery Chianti from a wicker-embraced bottle.

Emily Lou ate with a good appetite. "I never tasted anything as nice!" she exclaimed. She looked like an excited high-school girl with her disordered red hair and her lively blue eyes. She looked as though she ought to have freckles. "You all don't mind if I make a hog out of myself, do you, Mr. Williams?" She spoke with a Georgia drawl.

Williams was enchanted. His sly, bulging eyes expressed adoration. "Lady," he said, blotting cherry-colored drops of wine on his lips with the napkin, "you just go ahead and eat."

The wine tasted as though it had been sprinkled with cayenne. It tasted dry and clean, and each time, after he had swallowed some, Crane's mouth felt puckery, as it would have after he had sucked on a lemon, only there was not that feeling of wanting to cry. He sipped his wine, and looked at the two women.

He thought he had never seen two women with such large eyes. Miss Brentino's were more remarkable; perhaps because there was nothing else in her face to detract from their uniqueness. Her lips were exquisitely shaped, full and crimson and sullen, but they moved little even in speech. Her skin was unrouged. Her face was a pale ballet mask which, Crane thought, might have been made by Benda of Dolores Del Rio, but back of it there were alive those magnificent, duskily luminous eyes.

It was different with Emily Lou Martin. Her blue eyes were quite as large, but they were only a part of a face alive with movement. Dimples winked on her cheeks; her smiling lips disclosed small, perfect teeth; she even wriggled her nose.

When they had finished the green noodles with mushrooms, William Crane asked the waiter if the boss was around.

"What's a matter?" the waiter demanded. "Somethin' wrong with the food?" He placed one hand on the table, crushed a piece of bread.

Williams pushed back his chair, stood up. "I think I'll kill this guy," he announced. He laid his napkin beside his plate. Crane caught his arm, saying to the startled waiter, "Bring Mr. Petro here." The waiter backed away, and Williams subsided in his chair.

"Would you really have killed him?" Miss Martin asked excitedly.

William Crane said, "I thought I told you to leave your rod at home."

"I just slipped it in my pocket." Williams patted his coat. "It's kind of a habit. . . . "

A big Italian stood beside the table. He had a pockmarked face and crafty eyes, and his neck was too big for his shirt, so that three quarters of an inch of skin showed under his red tie where the collar failed to meet. "I'm Joe Petro," he said. He wore a violet shirt.

"My name's Crane," William Crane replied. He introduced the others and pulled up a chair for Mr. Petro. After a compliment on the food, Crane said, "We are looking for a friend of yours."

Mr. Petro shrugged his bulky shoulders. "I have many friends."

"This one wrote Miss Martin's fiance a letter. He signed it M. G."

The Italian's pudgy hands slapped his chest. Brown flesh bulged around a tight diamond ring. "Oh, sure, I know that letter. Mannie wrote it to him."

"Mannie who?"

"Mannie Grant." Purple eyelids fell over sunken eyes. "Why should I tell you his name?"

"Miss Martin would like to talk with him."

Miss Martin's eyes were innocently wide. She said, "Can't you find him for me, Mr. Petro?"

"I don't know." Petro eyed the white skin above her breast. "He's a ver' hard fellow to find. I don' know if he wants to see you now." He stared hard at Williams. "How do I know you ain't G-men?"

"Do I look like a G-man?" Miss Martin asked. She laid a hand on Mr. Petro's violet shirt sleeve. "I just know you are going to help me, Mr. Petro. I can see you are the kind of a man who would go out of his way to help a poor helpless girl."

The restaurant keeper scratched his ribs. Perspiration had made half moons under his arms. "I tell you what I do," he said at last. "I fix it up. You know the Café Monmarte?" Miss Martin said she did. "You go there tonight for dinner. Mannie, he'll be there too. Then, if he wants to speak to you after dinner, when he look you over, he can."

Miss Martin pouted. "Can't we see him sooner than that?"

"No, ma'am. That's the very best I can do."

William Crane asked, "How will he know us?"

"He will know these women anywhere, the Titian and the black Da Vinci." Mr. Petro raised his hands, palms upward, to a group of pink-and-gold cherubs on the ceiling. "I am at soul an artist, and I will describe their beauties so Mannie will know them."

In getting on his coat, Williams said to Mr. Petro, "I don't like your waiter."

"Don't mind him; he's just a punk," said the artist-proprietor.

On the sidewalk outside Crane arranged to call for Miss Martin and Miss Brentino at seven-thirty that evening.

The current of damp air flowed remorselessly along the shadowed corridor. It was almost evening again, and the cells were in a soft semidarkness. From his narrow cot, Westland watched the subtle changes of light in the corridor, thinking of his case abstractly and quite oblivious of the sobbing of Isadore Varecha. He thought of the days he had left—Tuesday, Wednesday, Thursday, and Friday—and he felt an impersonal impatience with the shortness of the time. The puzzle could be solved, he thought, but perhaps not quickly. He hoped Attorney Finklestein had started work on whatever evidence had been obtained from the "M. G." of the letter. He felt a curiosity about the man, and he wondered what he had been doing in the apartment building on the night of the murder. He wondered if he had seen the real murderer. If he had, he thought, it would simplify things. The man's testimony would at least obtain a reprieve for him, and then it would be merely a matter of building up evidence against the real murderer.

Reflected from the gray evening sky, the light in the corridor was the color of wood smoke. Footsteps, quick and nervous, echoed from Connors' cell: one, two—one, two, three—one, two—one, two, three—as the gangster paced a rectangular course. Isadore Varecha broke the even cadence of his crying with a convulsive cough.

The real murderer! Westland's mind refused to picture anyone for the role. He knew it must have been someone close either to him or his wife. Either the murderer had wanted to get rid of her and he had been accidentally implicated, or the murderer had killed her to get rid of him. It seemed unlikely that anyone would have a motive to kill her because her money went to him, but his mind boggled at the alternative. Why didn't the murderer, he wondered, simply kill him if he wanted him out of the way?

Varecha was sobbing noisily now, and his throat rattled like a dying man's as he gasped for breath.

Connors pressed himself against the front of his cell. "You goddam sheeny," he yelled, "I'm going to kill you if you don't shut up." His eyes were wild.

Astonished silence hung briefly over Varecha's cell. Then he returned to his minor-key crying.

Westland tried to picture his cousin Lawrence Wharton as the plotting murderer; then, in succession, broad-shouldered Richard Bolston; suave Ron Woodbury; his chief clerk, Amos Sprague . . .

Was one of them a murderer?

Gold letters on the opaque glass door read:

Westland, Bolston & Woodbury
Members: New York Stock Exchange
New York Curb Exchange
Chicago Board of Trade
Chicago Curb Exchange

Attorney Finklestein turned the chromium knob. A saucy phone girl arched her penciled eyebrows, paused in her gum chewing. The steel clamp holding her ear phones made a valley in her brown bobbed hair.

"Is Mr. Bolston in?" Finklestein asked.

"Mr. Bolston?" The girl acted as though she was hearing the name for the first time. "Mr. Bolston?" She chewed reflectively on her gum. "It's pretty late for him."

"I don't care if it's past his bedtime." Finklestein tapped his gold-headed cane on the chromium rail beside her black metal telephone switchbox. "I asked you if he was in."

The girl put her saucy face up to the hanging speaker. "I'll see. What's the name?"

"Charles Finklestein."

"And what's it about?"

Attorney Finklestein pushed against the rail like an enraged bantam rooster. "I'll tell him you asked," he said, "and if he wants you to know, I'm sure he will be glad to tell you himself."

The girl flicked a switch, moved her red lips against the black mouthpiece, then said brightly, "Mr. Bolston will see you, sir."

French windows pinpointed with lights from other office buildings austerely decorated two sides of Bolston's room. Yellow roses bowed from a silver vase on his large walnut desk. Attorney Finklestein's feet sank in the deep green rug.

Bolston walked around the desk and shook the lawyer's hand. "What's up?" he asked. His brown tweed suit smelled of peat smoke.

"Crane just telephoned to tell me they hadn't been able to contact the fellow who wrote the letter yet." Finklestein sat on the arm of an overstuffed chair and leaned on his gold-headed cane. "The fellow's name is Mannie Grant and Crane thinks he is some kind of a burglar. He and the girls are to meet him at dinner tonight at the Café Monmarte. If he likes their looks, he's going to come over to their table."

"I hope they get hold of him," said Bolston.

"You bet! His evidence sounds important. But I think we better get busy on some of the other angles." The attorney tugged his notebook from a pocket, thumbed the pages. "Where's Mr. Woodbury?"

Bolston lifted a cradle phone and said, "Mr. Woodbury, please." The phone clicked, and Bolston said, "Ron, could you come in for a minute?"

Finklestein repeated to Woodbury what Crane had told him. He listened without comment.

Finklestein resumed, "It's up to us to get going on this business, and there's plenty we can do." He looked at his notebook. "We're working on the four important pieces of evidence against Mr. Westland. Pieces one, two, and three are the keys, the missing pistol, and the telephone call which didn't come from Miss Martin.

"Fourth is the shot. A family named Shuttle, in the apartment below, heard it. They said it was around 12:20 A.M., when Westland admits he was in his wife's apartment, but I think there is something phony about it. I wish you two would look into it. Could you go over and talk to the Shuttles tonight? Maybe their clock had stopped or something."

"We'll be glad to," said Bolston.

Pocketing his notebook, Finklestein rose from his chair. "Tomorrow morning then," he said jauntily. "I'll be seeing you in jail."

CHAPTER V

Monday Night

BRASS BUTTONS gleamed as the Negro doorman slammed the taxi door and escorted them along the red rug under the canopy. Miss Martin and Miss Brentino left the two men as they stepped inside the Café Monmarte, disappeared through a door marked: "Dames." An orchestra throbbed in the distance. The cloakroom girl smiled at Williams, handed him his check.

"Watch out for those French chorus girls," she said.

"They better watch out for me, honey," Williams replied.

A gangplank with a silver rail extended upward in the direction of the music. Canvas with blue portholes painted on it to represent the side of a ship, stretched on either side of the opening. Black letters on a life ring spelled, Normandie. A tall woman in a gray gown with purple orchids on the left shoulder was having trouble with the gangplank's bottom step. She stumbled, fell into Crane's arms, and asked, "Have you seen my husband?" She smelled of jasmine.

Crane said, "No."

"Good!" The woman struggled out of his arms and lurched toward the door marked, "Dames."

"This seems to be quite a place," said Williams.

Miss Brentino appeared first. Her rounded ivory shoulders contrasted with her supple black satin evening gown, cut extremely low over smooth breasts. Her figure was slender, but still voluptuously feminine; her face, with its curving jaw line, was exquisite; her hair was as glistening black as a crow's wing. Her large eyes were mocking. William Crane felt she was the most beautiful woman he had ever seen in his life.

Miss Martin, behind her, was quite pretty and wholesome in a soft green evening dress which accentuated her red hair. She wore a white ermine cloak, a square-cut emerald ring.

"You have a reservation?" the plump headwaiter asked at the top of the gangplank.

"Mr. Williams' party," Crane said.

"Ah yes." The waiter's manner became ingratiating. "Mr. Williams of New York."

Behind him, they edged between crowded tables. The orchestra was at the far end of the gaudily decorated room. Many couples were dancing on the oval floor, their faces only half visible in the soft indirect light. The music was unobtrusive, stringy.

For a second a waiter blocked their passage. At a table to their right a chemical blonde with carmine fingernails and a naked back was holding a glass of whiskey to the lips of a stout man in a gray suit.

"Come on, Daddy," she urged, "have anozzer teeney dwink."

The stout man pushed the glass away. "Baby, I got to think of my wife and kidneys."

Silver and glass gleamed faintly on an empty table beside the dance floor. The fat headwaiter pulled out the chairs quickly and said to Crane, "Will this be all right, Mr. Williams?"

Crane said, "This is Mr. Williams."

"It's all right," Williams admitted, "but see that we get plenty of service."

Two waiters held the chairs for the ladies while the headwaiter accepted four menus from an assistant. He reverently laid these in front of the four. "Will you have cocktails?"

Williams ordered two bacardis without grenadine for the ladies, Scotch-and-soda for himself, and a dry martini for Crane. "Make 'em all double ones," he said expansively.

They agreed on hors d'æuvres, clear soup, lobster thermidor, soufflé potatoes, and French chicory salad. Miss Brentino and Miss Martin both insisted they would rather have sparkling Burgundy than champagne. Crane ordered two bottles of Chauvenet Red Cap put in ice buckets.

The fat headwaiter repeated the order with satisfaction to his assistant. "If there's anything else you would like to have, Mr. Williams," he added, "we will procure it. Mr. Gavin, the manager, said we were to take good care of you."

Williams waved a negligent hand. "O. K. If we want any little thing at all, I'll let you know."

While they were eating the hors d'æuvres Crane watched the orchestra to see what sort of a place this was. He saw very quickly that it was a high-class place because the orchestra was terribly bored. In a low class place the orchestra works hard, but it does not seem to enjoy playing. In better places the orchestra works hard and seems to enjoy playing. But the really high-class place orchestras do not work hard, and their members are very bored and sometimes play with their eyes half closed, as though they wished they were asleep or somewhere else, which, no doubt, they did.

When Crane saw the first saxophone player had his eyes

closed, he knew it was a good place, and he prepared to enjoy the food.

They were finishing the soup when Miss Martin leaned her shoulder against him. Her perfume was sweet and heady. She said, "I'm so thrilled. Do you think that Mr. Grant will actually meet us?"

Crane said he didn't know.

Without warning, the music stopped. Brilliant lights illuminated the room. The dancers, blinking, searched for their tables as though they had suddenly awakened from a dream. In voices loud and excited, the women called to friends, talked animatedly to escorts. The men walked stiffly, squared shoulders holding out starch-covered chests, chins held high by rigid collars.

"I don't know what Grant has to tell us," Crane said, "but his testimony will be damned essential—" he was a little drunk, but he managed to get the "essential" out pretty clearly—"if we want to get Mr. Westland out of his jam."

Emily Lou closed her eyes. "We just have to. . . . "

The chicory, which they ate in the American style with the lobster course, was as crisp as new currency. The French dressing was freshly made; it no more than suggested a garlic nubbin and was miraculously without sugar. They drank a great deal of the sparkling wine.

"I can read Italian," Miss Brentino remarked, "but not French." She was looking at the wall across the empty dance floor. "What does that sign say?" Her low voice made shivers run up and down Crane's back.

The sign was on the front of the elaborately painted representation of the Hotel des Deux Anges. Crane translated, "Rooms by the day or hour."

He added, "I think that hotel is a little wicked."

"It's modern," said Miss Brentino. Her face was reposed, almost cold and almost sullen, but Crane felt there was passion in her curved lips. He said, "I could go for you in a gigantic way—in fact, I do."

Her liquid eyes were mocking. "You mean: 'Rooms by the hour'?" she asked.

"I wouldn't care," he said earnestly. "For you I'd even take one by the day." He drained his wineglass.

"I'm sorry." Her face was suddenly unguarded. "I like detectives, but my spare time is all booked."

"Woodbury?"

She nodded.

Williams was telling Miss Martin of dope smuggling in San Francisco. "So I grabbed the Chink by the pigtail like you would a cat," he was saying, "and I trun him so far out in the bay they had to send a coast guard cutter after him."

Miss Martin saw the other two looking at her. "Mr. Williams has had the most exciting life," she exclaimed. "He's been telling me how he stopped dope peddling in California. He had to kill four men. . . ."

"Aw, they don't count." Williams adjusted his butterfly tie. "They was just Chinamen." He pretended embarrassment.

They finished with cheese and toasted water crackers. Crane had brandy; the ladies, cointreau; Williams took Scotch and soda.

As he seated a small man and a buxom blonde with too much paint on her face at a small table directly across the floor, the fat headwaiter bowed to them. The orchestra filed back onto the low platform. A spotlight experimentally flashed on and off the dance floor.

"I guess they are going to have the floor show now," Williams said. The blonde, who had white feathers all over the upper portion of her dress, seemed to be giving him the eye. He winked at her. She looked away. The orchestra began to play, "When You and I Were Young, Maggie," in tango time. Williams said indignantly: "Christ! They'll be making a rumba out of the 'Rock of Ages' next." After the piece was finished, a round little Jew with a cane came out and sang, "I Kiss Your Hand, Madam," the way Al Jolson would a Mammy song. Finally, in a recitative chorus, he intimated the girls about to appear were the beauty queens of Paris, that only to see them would make the Americans say, "Ooo, la! la! Some keeds, eh?"

When the girls kicked out onto the dance floor amid a blare of trumpets, William Crane saw they were French, all right. Or, at least, they were formed along more liberal lines than American chorus girls. While the band played noisily, they marched solemnly around the floor in gorgeously colored costumes which got scantier and scantier and scantier until a plump black-haired girl appeared with nothing on except some white fur mittens. These she used in the manner of a fan dancer with a fan, but the effect was startling. She walked, quite pleased with the sensation she was making, by Crane's table, stopped, daringly waved one hand at the party and said:

"Allo, Meester Weelums."

Williams was not too drunk to blush. "What the hell!" he said.

Both the girls giggled. "A friend?" asked Miss Brentino.

"I swear . . . "

Crane asked, "Say, who are you, anyway? Maxie Baer?"

"All I did," Williams said, "was to have the chief of detectives get our reservations here for us. I worked with him on a lot of jobs in the old days, but I never saw that girl in my life." He gulped some water. "Not that I wouldn't . . . "

"Now I see why we've had all the attention," said Crane. "I was beginning to think you were a millionaire playboy."

The parade had finished and two men in the blue costumes of French railway porters were tossing a man, cleverly made up to represent a stuffed figure, about the floor. They threw him in the air, they dropped him, they twisted his arms, they slapped him; but the dummy remained inert until they turned their backs. Then he kicked one of them. Finally, in a rage, they seized the dummy, thrust it in a box, slammed the lid and goose-stepped out with it.

Hollow handclapping filled the room. The orchestra slowed to a moaning tune, and a player, his eyes closed, drooled blue notes from a cornet covered with a silvered derby. From the side danced a red-headed girl in checker-board rompers. Powder had been dusted on her bare legs; her face was painted like a gaudy German doll. Blue veins squirmed on her dead white thighs. She looked at Williams, sang:

"I can't give you anything but love, ba-hay-bee
That's the only thing I've plenty of, ba-hay-bee. . . . "

Four men in well-fitting evening clothes strolled down the gangplank at the far end of the room and paused at the bottom to watch the girl in the spotlight. The dark eyes of one of the two younger men surveyed the room, paused for a second at Crane's table in bold appraisal of the two girls, and then passed by. Finally he nudged the stockier of the two older men, and three of them started towards the dance floor, leaving the other younger man behind. A warning palm upraised, the fat headwaiter stepped in front of them, but the thick man elbowed him out of the way. The three continued their leisurely progress along the edge of the dance floor their backs making somber patches in the square of light on which the redhead in rompers was singing:

"Diamond bracelets Woolworth
doesn't sell, ba-hay-bee."

The three men in evening clothes halted in front of the small table occupied by the big blonde with the feathers and her companion. The small man was eating; he looked up; surprise half-mooned his eyebrows; then with absurd haste he attempted to scramble to his feet. The thick man pulled a blue-black pistol from under his arm and shot him in the face. The blonde yelled with horror, her feathers ballooned as she dropped sideways out of her chair. The bullet went low and tore away part of the small man's jaw. He clapped both hands to the wound, bent over forward, dripping blood on the tablecloth between his fingers. The thick man shot him twice through the top of his head.

A scream skyrocketed from the mouth of the redhead in the checker-board rompers. One of the men shook a warning finger at her.

"Shut up, tutz," he said, "or I'll tear them panties off you."

The redhead froze into outraged silence. The orchestra was stopping one instrument at a time, the tempo getting slower and slower as on an unwound phonograph. Finally only the drummer, his eyes fixed on the dead man, moved an unconscious foot on the pedal of the bass drum.

The young man who had stayed by the gangplank threaded his way through the silent tables towards his companions. A square-jawed man with a large party started to rise as he passed. The young man narrowed his dark eyes; the square-jawed man sat down.

Williams had his revolver in his lap. "The bastards!" he was saying. "The bastards!"

"Wait a minute," Crane kicked him under the table. "Do you want to get us all shot?"

The men, with the young man from the gangplank, walking backward, marched to the kitchen doors. A waiter scuttled out of their way like a frightened crab. The first man stopped to hold the swinging door for the others, then, still not hurrying, he disappeared.

As though someone had turned on a radio, the room was engulfed with sound. Women spoke shrilly . . . chairs scraped . . . "I'll be God-damned!" a man behind Miss Brentino's rigid figure kept saying. Two waiters pulled the big blonde from under the dead man's table and carried her towards the gangplank. There were dust circles on the white feathers. A ring of men and women formed around the corpse; other diners made for the gangplank. The red-headed singer had her hands over her breast. "My Gawd!" she said in a strident voice. "Ain't nobody going after them?"

Lips were the only touch of color on Emily Lou Martin's face. Her eyes were terror-stricken. She said, "I think I'm going to be sick."

Miss Brentino said quickly, "Come on." She led Emily Lou away, one bare arm around her waist.

Crane and Williams went over to look at the dead man. He was lying with his face pillowed in his arms, like a schoolboy fallen asleep over a Latin grammar. The tablecloth had soaked up most of the blood. Presently someone threw another cloth over the body.

A dowager with jade earrings asked the plump headwaiter, "D'you know who he was?"

The headwaiter adjusted the cloth to cover the bloodstains. "His name was Mannie Grant."

CHAPTER VI

Tuesday Morning

His DISCOLORED teeth projecting in an ingratiating smirk, Guard Percival Galt said, "Here's Mr. Westland, Warden." He gave a convulsive jerk of his body, a sort of epileptic bow, and hurried away.

"Everything all right, Warden?" Robert Westland asked.

With a porcine grunt, Warden Buckholtz heaved himself from the swivel chair behind his mahogany desk. The dollar dimples appeared on his cheeks. "You bet," he said. "Your partner, Mr. Bolston, paid me last night on his way home." He waddled to Westland and laid a pudgy hand on his shoulder. "Your partner's a mighty fine fellow."

Westland dipped his shoulder from under the hand. "Anybody with ten thousand dollars is a fine fellow."

Warden Buckholtz was deeply hurt. "That's no way to talk when I'm just trying to help you." He shook his head sadly. "I have to protect myself in case something should happen to me."

"Sorry," Westland said. "I'm edgy today."

The warden inclined his body towards the Assistant Matron's office. "Some of your friends are already there."

Emily Lou Martin was wearing a gray squirrel coat with a plum-colored orchid pinned on the front. Westland said, "Dear!" He kissed her and then glanced around at the others. "Where's Dick and Ron?"

Attorney Finklestein snapped open the lid of his gold watch. "They'll be along any minute now."

Westland looked at William Crane, who was sitting with Williams on the window sill. "What's the news? Did you catch up with M. G. ?"

In the jail yard naked trees shivered in the wind. An angry black cat's-tail of smoke lashed back and forth above the kitchen chimney. Someone had brushed the cobwebs from the room's windows.

Crane shook his head. "He was dead when we caught up with him." He described the events of the preceding day.

"It was so exciting," Emily Lou exclaimed. "We nearly got shot."

Westland clasped her arm protectively. "I shouldn't have let you go." His eyes were anxious. "I won't let you do anything like that again."

Williams gazed maternally upon the man and the pretty red-haired girl. "He's a real sport," he whispered to William Crane. "That guy's death probably means a casket for Westland, but all he's worried about is his gal."

"By gad, Bill," Cousin Lawrence Wharton exploded, "don't be too hard on the gel. How'd anybody know that fellow was going to get his last night?" His red face challenged contradiction.

Attorney Finklestein pushed his gold-rimmed glasses closer to his eyes. "Then you don't think his murder had anything to do with our investigation?"

"Preposterous!"

Westland asked, "How would anyone have found out that we wanted to get hold of him?"

"Plenty of ways," Crane said.

Miss Brentino, seated beside Amos Sprague, smiled at him. She was wearing a floppy brim sand-colored felt hat, a tobacco-brown Chanel suit with a red and yellow silk scarf, tied Ascot fashion, around her neck.

"Damn it!" said Wharton. "This is deuced far fetched. That Grant was a horrid little thief, and those fellows live in danger of their nasty lives all the time." His bulldog face was purple. "He simply got it last night."

Crane said, "They don't kill horrid nasty little thieves that way."

Wharton was wearing gray-checked knickers with blue golf socks. He faced the detective. "Young fella, are you trying to tell me that I don't know what I'm talking about?"

"That's the general idea."

Wharton said, "You're a dem fool."

"It seems to me you are pretty anxious to have everybody believe Grant's murder was a coincidence." Crane balanced on the sill. "You haven't a personal reason for wanting us to think so, have you?"

Wharton clenched his fists. Williams, standing at the side, got ready to bust the old geezer on the conk with the handle of his automatic pistol. Westland seized his cousin's arm. "Now, Larry," he said soothingly, "calm yourself."

Wharton allowed himself to be led to a chair. "The bla'guard as much as said I killed that fellow," he muttered.

"Mr. Crane meant that we must look at every possibility," Finklestein announced; "didn't you, Mr. Crane?"

William Crane said, "Sure."

"There isn't much we can do about that shooting, anyway," Finklestein said. "It's up to the police."

"It was a gangster job," said Williams.

Crane said, "The man we're after didn't do that killing. He may have hired those fellows to knock off Grant, but they wouldn't know who hired them; it would be done through a third party, and even if they did know and they were caught, they wouldn't talk. We'd better stick to our own business and let last night's shooting alone."

"Is it so easy then, to hire killers?" asked Miss Brentino. Her make-up—mascara, powder and lipstick—was theatrical in daylight.

"I believe you have hit something, Miss Brentino." William Crane turned to Finklestein. "Anybody can't go out and hire some torpedoes. It looks as though our murderer, if he arranged last night's show, has some underworld connections."

"I guess you're right." Finklestein thrust out his lower lip. "Mr. Westland, have you ever had any contact with the underworld, with gangsters or kidnapers or men like that?"

"Never—at least, not with anybody except my bootlegger before Repeal."

"Have any trouble with him?"

"Not the slightest. We got along very well. I even sold him my Lincoln roadster."

"Was the car O. K. ?" Williams asked.

"Shut up," said Crane.

The door to the warden's office opened. Bolston, in a suit of gray Scotch twist, Woodbury, and a fusty middle-aged man entered the room. The closing door shut out the warden's gross and curious face. "This is Dr. Shuttle," Bolston said. "He and his wife heard the shot that killed Mrs. Westland."

Finklestein pulled out his notebook, fingered the pages.

Dr. Shuttle looked like a Western Congressman or an unemployed Shakespearean actor. His face was a graph of wrinkles. His hair, dyed the color of tarnished brass, hung over his ears. "This is very embarrassing," he said; "but these gentlemen were so insistent." His black silk tie was fastened in a loose bow; gold spectacles hung from a black ribbon around his neck.

Westland said, "That's all right. I don't hold any grudge."

"I only did my duty," Dr. Shuttle stated with dignity.

Woodbury was immaculate in a blue business suit, snugged almost effeminately at the waist. His slim hands were carefully manicured. He sat down on the edge of Miss Brentino's chair, and the two of them, poised and dark, reminded Williams of a photograph he had once seen in the Mirror of a Spanish duke and his wife who were visiting New York.

Bolston said, "Bob, I think I've got something." His face was a healthy pink, his blue eyes were clear. "I want you to think carefully. What time was it when you left your home on the night of your wife's murder?"

"A little after eleven-thirty. I had been reading in bed."

"What time was it when you reached Joan's apartment?"

"A little before twelve."

Finklestein, peering near-sightedly at the figures in his notebook, nodded.

Bolston asked, "How long did you stay there?"

"About forty minutes."

"Then you left before one o'clock?"

"My clock said one when I got home."

"All right." Bolston thrust his hands in his pockets. "Do you recall the date of the murder?"

"Why, sure." Westland's eyes rounded in surprise. He lifted his hand off Emily Lou's arm. "It was the morning of April 28th."

"The day before was April 27th. Does that mean anything to you?"

"No."

"At midnight on April 27th Chicago changed from standard time to daylight saving time."

Westland was puzzled. "Sure, but what of it?"

"Didn't you set your clock ahead?"

"Why, yes. Before I got in bed."

"That is—before you went to Joan's apartment?"

"Yes."

"All right." Bolston straightened his broad shoulders. He looked like an Arrow collar ad. "All your figures are on daylight saving time."

Bolston turned to Dr. Shuttle. "Now . . . " Crane slipped around the wall on tiptoe, Indian fashion, and jerked open the door. Warden Buckholtz was kneeling there, his palms forward in an attitude of prayer. His right eye was where the keyhole had been. Ponderously he overbalanced, fell forward clumsily on his thick hands. Crane helped him to his feet, tenderly dusted him off. "Won't you join us?" he asked.

Warden Buckholtz finally managed to speak. "I wanted to see if my guard was in with you, but I didn't want to disturb you." He squeezed backward through the doorway. "He must be in the jail." The closing door blotted out his jowls.

"Maybe that's where the news we were searching for the late Mr. Grant got out," Finklestein said.

Crane leaned against the knob. "He won't get any more."

"Now, Dr. Shuttle," said Bolston, "what time did you and your wife hear the report?"

Dr. Shuttle fumbled with his pince-nez glasses. His voice trembled nervously as he said, "Exactly twelve-twenty by our clock."

"At the trial you gave this testimony in order to help the State prove Mr. Westland was in the apartment at the time."

Dr. Shuttle's posture was dignified. "I merely told the truth."

Bolston leaned towards him. "What were you and your wife doing up at that time?"

"Drinking tea."

This drew a general laugh. Dr. Shuttle pursed his lips with an air of injury.

"What time did you finally go to bed?"

"Not until nearly one-thirty." The doctor twirled his glasses on the silk ribbon. "You know I play the organ." Williams' sudden giggle turned to a cough under Dr. Shuttle's indignant glance. "Sir! I have given recitals before the nobility of Europe." He addressed Bolston. "My wife and I always sit up after I have given a recital. It takes some time for my artistic frenzy to wear itself off. My nervous system is pitched very high."

"You had given a recital?"

"Yes, in Orchestra Hall." Dr. Shuttle thrust out his chest and stomach. His back arched inward like yew bow. "You apparently did not recognize my name. I am Dr. Frederick Shuttle, the church organist."

"I should have." Bolston's white teeth shone. "I have often heard your name mentioned." The skin over his cheek bone was firm and pink like salmon flesh. "But, Dr. Shuttle, we are very much interested in when you set you clock ahead."

"But I told you that at the apartment. I set the clock ahead when we went to bed."

Bolston spoke slowly. "Then you heard the shot at

twelve-twenty Central Standard Time. By Westland's time, that was one-twenty, or more than twenty minutes after he had reached his own apartment."

There was a momentary silence. A sparrow, on one of the skeleton trees in the court, chirped. Dr. Shuttle looked apprehensive.

Westland gripped Bolston's arm. "That's damn smart, old man."

Dr. Shuttle began, "I only told the truth as . . . "

"That's all right," said Westland.

Miss Martin exclaimed, "I think it's splendid. Now all we have to do is to tell the Governor you couldn't have been there when Joan was killed and . . . " She had hold of Westland's left hand.

"Just a minute." Attorney Finklestein was waving his notebook. "We aren't out of this yet. Even if Dr. Shuttle heard the shot after Mr. Westland said he left, that won't do us any good." The attorney's diamond glittered. "Mr. Westland can't prove he did leave his wife's apartment when he says he did, even though we know he did, and he'd have to be able to do that before the Governor would even listen to us."

Bolston was crestfallen. "I thought I'd hit on something pretty good."

"It helps. It all helps." Finklestein closed his notebook. "But we got to keep on going. If we could only get hold of someone who saw him leave."

"That's where Grant might have come in handy," Woodbury observed.

"I think it's mighty fine of Dick, anyway, and mighty clever too," Emily Lou said. "That shows us Robbie couldn't have done it."

Miss Brentino spoke casually, without inflection. "You knew that anyway, didn't you, dear?"

Hurriedly Westland said, "What do you think we ought to do next, Mr. Finklestein?"

"I'd like to look into that locked door business. We're certain there were only two keys. Mr. Westland had his, and the other was found with Mrs. Westland inside the locked apartment, but the murderer must have gotten out some way. I think Crane and Williams and I ought to look the place over." Finklestein patted his lips with the silk handkerchief, knuckles held outward so the diamond would show. "But the important thing is the motive. If we could find out why Mrs. Westland was murdered, we'd have a good start." The handkerchief was hand initialed "C.F." in green thread.

Amos Sprague had been sitting quietly in a corner. "I think I can tell you the motive tomorrow, Mr. Attorney." His laugh was a barnyard cackle, but his bright eyes under craggy white brows were grim. "Tomorrow, Mr. Attorney."

"What do you mean, Amos?" Westland asked.

"I can't tell you now, Mr. Westland, 'twould be too soon." The old man nodded his head as though he had been stricken with palsy. "But I can tell you it involves millions." His falsetto cackle rose. "Millions . . . millions . . . millions."

Finklestein's gold watch snapped open. "It's almost time for lunch again," he said. He pocketed the watch, pushed his notebook in his hip pocket. "Bolston has disposed of the time of the shot, anyway."

As the others were filing out, William Crane asked Bolston, "How'd you happen to think about changing time?"

"I don't know. It just popped into my head that the last

Sunday in April was the day you shifted. So I asked Shuttle about it."

"Well, it was a damn smart piece of work." Crane hurried out of the room, caught Finklestein at the top of the steps. "Like to have lunch with Williams and me, counselor?" he asked.

"Sure." Finklestein was watching Woodbury and Miss Brentino. Arm in arm, heads close in conversation, they were descending the steps. "Seem pretty intimate, don't they?" the attorney said.

Crane watched the sweeping curve of the woman's half presented profile, her narrow hips, her slender legs below the Persian lamb coat. "I wouldn't mind being intimate with her myself," he said.

Attorney Finklestein said, "That makes it unanimous."

CHAPTER VII

Tuesday Afternoon

THEY HAD lunch at Ricketts, just off the Boulevard on Chicago Avenue. They had martinis, and Williams had a crêpe suzette for dessert. "It tastes pretty good," he said; "but what have you got after you eat it?"

William Crane said, "You wouldn't be able to get out of that chair of yours, Doc, if you ate another of those pancakes—you probably can't now."

Williams looked at their ash-blond waitress, allowed one lid to curtain momentarily a wicked eye. "I'm a spry fellow for a G. A. R. Vet." He pretended lumbago pains wouldn't let him straighten up in his chair, eyes on the waitress. His coat caught on the chair back, exposing a black leather holster with a pistol in it under his left arm. The waitress giggled. She did not see the weapon.

William Crane said, "I thought you were going to leave that cannon at the hotel?"

Doc Williams said apologetically, "I feel just like I was naked without it."

"Don't worry about the pistol," Finklestein said. He finished the last of a bowl of preserved figs. "I'll spring him if the police get him."

"I wish the police would get him. I'm not worried about that." Crane was having coffee, no dessert. "I'm afraid the damn thing will go off some time and shoot me."

Finklestein paid the bill. Williams rubbed his sleek brush mustache with the napkin, still watching the pretty waitress. "What's your name, baby?" he asked.

The waitress had dimples. "Gladys," she replied.

"I'll be coming up to see you sometime, Happy Bottom."

The girl's eyes were almost perfect circles. "How did you know they called me that?"

"I'm a detective," said Williams.

When they reached the Boulevard, Finklestein suggested, "Let's go round and see Westland's man, Simmons. We might as well walk—it's only a few blocks to Westland's apartment."

Sidewalk shop windows framed women's apparel—sturdy tweeds, fragile evening gowns, soft silver fox skins, mink coats, pastel underthings that looked as though they had been loomed by a spider. Straight from the northeast, damp from the Lake, a flagellant wind whipped blood into the cheeks of passers-by. Suddenly upflung skirts disclosed shapely thighs, and flesh and garters: pink, white, and black. Into the wind the populace walked with bowed heads as though a day of prayer had been proclaimed. Down wind they ran, leaning backward, with short jerky steps, Chinaboy fashion.

Williams, looking at a display of shirts with tab collars in the window of Saks' Fifth Avenue, nudged Crane. "Look who's in there."

It was Miss Martin. She was standing in front of a counter, holding up a tie with regimental stripes to the light. Beside her was Richard Bolston, two other ties across his arm. He saw Crane and Williams, smiled a greeting and motioned them to come inside. Crane shook his head, pointed a finger at Finklestein's retreating back, and said the word "Work" with his lips. Bolston nodded that he understood.

Crane was pleased when they reached Westland's apartment on Astor Street. His right cheek bone ached from the cold, and his hands were numb. They took the automatic elevator to the eighth floor, where Simmons answered the doorbell. He was a nervous middle-aged man with sharp features, and he wore a black suit with a stiff collar. He looked like a school teacher.

"I'm Mr. Finklestein," said the lawyer. "Didn't Mr. Bolston call you this morning?"

Suspicion faded from the man's eyes. He drew open the door. "Come in."

The 28 x 30 living room was chaste in apple green and ivory. Venetian blinds, cloaked with Brewster green satin drapes, screened the two tall windows overlooking the street. Above the virginal black-and-white marble fireplace hung a brilliantly colored Parisian cafe scene by Toulouse-Lautrec . . . three prostitutes soliciting a bearded gentleman drinking emerald absinthe from a tall glass. The rug, tailored around the black composition hearth, was pale gray, and the modern furniture, chairs and a huge divan, were covered with material which looked and felt like sun-bleached gunnysack. A black and silver directoire lamp with a parchment shade stood on an end table.

"We're interested in Mr. Westland's pistol," Finklestein said. He took off his tan topcoat, jerked it away from Simmons. "Never mind; we won't stay long." He tossed the coat over one of the brown chairs. "Where'd he keep it?"

"In this cabinet, sir."

Two jade elephants trumpeted at each other on the cabinet top, and along the front were a series of gold handles for the drawers. Simmons opened an empty drawer. "That's where it was."

Crane asked, "When did you see the pistol last?"

The man hesitated, sucking in his thin lips over his teeth. "I saw it the afternoon of the murder."

"You did? Did you tell the police about it?"

Simmons glanced uneasily from Crane to Finklestein.

"It's all right," Crane said. "We don't like the police any better than you do."

"Well, to tell you the truth, sir, I didn't. I didn't think it would do Mr. Westland's case any good."

"You were probably right," Finklestein said.

Crane ran his hand across the rough material covering the davenport. "Were you in all the rest of the afternoon, after you saw the gun?"

"Yes, sir. I didn't go out at all."

"Westland had dinner at home?"

"Yes. He had dinner alone and then, after Mr. Woodbury had gone, he went . . . "

Finklestein and Crane exchanged glances. "Woodbury?" asked the lawyer. "What was he doing here?"

"He came over after dinner to talk over some business matter. I didn't hear what it was. He only stayed for a few minutes."

Crane asked, "Did many people know Mr. Westland kept the pistol in the drawer here?"

"Oh, yes, sir. He had a story about it—about using it to attack a German bombing plane when his machine gun failed him. He'd show the gun when he told the story; it had a silver plate with his name on it."

Finklestein asked, "Did Mr. Westland leave Wood-bury alone in the room at any time while he was here that evening?"

"You mean—" Simmons' fingers nervously pulled at the cuffs of his dark suit—"you mean Woodbury is the murderer?"

The attorney raised a hand. "Nothing of the sort." Light glittered from the diamond ring. "We are just checking on every possible angle."

Simmons frowned in concentration. "I don't . . . yes! He did leave him alone. He came out to the kitchen for some extra soda after I had served the drinks." He added in explanation, "You see I had gone to bed."

"Good." Finklestein's palms rubbing together made sucking noises. "Now we're getting somewhere."

Crane asked, "Have Woodbury and Mr. Westland always been good friends? No quarrels or troubles over money or anything?"

"Oh no, sir. They've always been on the best of terms ever since I started to work for Mr. Westland right after the war. You know they served together in France."

Doc Williams had been sitting in one of the brown chairs, his hat tilted over his eyes. He never took off his hat indoors except in the presence of ladies. "I got a question," he announced. "Do you mind if I got a question?"

Everybody said they did not mind. "What I want to know is, did that red-haired babe call him like she said she did?"

"I couldn't tell you that. Someone called him and he went out soon afterwards."

"Did you hear him come back?" Crane asked.

"No, sir. I had gone to bed. My room is in back of the kitchen—I wouldn't be apt to hear anything."

Finklestein lifted his tan overcoat from the chair. He looked dubiously at the cabinet with its gold-handled drawers. "I don't suppose there'd be any fingerprints?"

Crane said, "I imagine Simmons has polished that since Mr. Woodbury was here that night."

"Yes, sir." Simmons' thin school-teacher face was anxious. "Did I do wrong?"

"You couldn't have known about prints," Crane assured him. He jerked his head at Williams.

Finklestein allowed Simmons to help him on with his coat. He said, "I guess we better pay a little attention to Woodbury."

Simmons said, "If there's anything I can do . . . "

"Just don't talk about what we have asked you." Crane was trying the doors of the cabinet. They worked smoothly and without noise. "Where was Mr. Westland arrested?" he asked suddenly.

Simmons appeared surprised. "He was at the athletic club. The police called here on the telephone and I told them where he was. I didn't know anything was wrong then."

"What was he doing at the club in the morning?"

"He played squash every weekday with a professional at eleven o'clock."

The attorney was turning his hat in his hands. "We've a lot to do this afternoon——"

"Wait just a second." Crane was still testing the cabinet drawers. "I'd like to get the background clear in my head. Simmons, did they hold Mr. Westland after they got him at the club?"

"Yes, sir. They took him to the Detective Bureau on State Street to question him about the letter he had written to his wife—they found that in her purse, you know—but they were going to let him go even then until the coroner's office reported that she had been shot with a Webley automatic."

"How do you know they were going to let him go?"

"I was at the Detective Bureau."

"You were? Did they arrest you too?"

"No. You see, Mr. Bolston called me on the telephone to say that the police had gone to arrest Mr. Westland and that they would take him to the Bureau. He told me to go down there so I could help if Mr. Westland needed somebody to phone for a bond, or anything."

"Why didn't he go down himself?"

"He wanted to go to the office to secure money for a bond, and to get hold of Mr. Westland's lawyer. He came down to the Bureau about one o'clock and sent me home."

Crane winked at the impatient Williams. "What time did Bolston call you?" he asked Simmons.

"It was just eleven-thirty, sir. I happened to notice the clock."

"Now I have something important to ask you." William Crane moved from the cabinet to admire the antique brass and-irons in the fireplace. "Do you know if Mr. Westland had a duplicate made of the key to his wife's apartment?"

"I am sure he didn't. The poor lady had a fear of losing her jewelry and bonds in the wall safe. That's why they had a special lock put on the door in the first place. Mr. Westland's key was fastened on a ring."

Interest narrowed Finklestein's eyes. "Couldn't somebody have taken the key and had a duplicate made?"

"Not unless they took the whole ring, and Mr. Westland would have noticed that."

"Did anybody have a key to this apartment besides you?" Crane asked.

"Nobody—" Simmons looked faintly embarrassed—"except Miss Martin. She sometimes stopped off here in the afternoon after a shopping trip. Nothing out of the way, you understand."

"I understand." Crane moved to the door. "Don't say anything about this to Mr. Woodbury, Simmons."

The servant held the door for them. "I hope you can save him." He stood watching them until the descending elevator caused the floor to obliterate him, like a stage drop working upside down.

Wind shook the trees with convulsive jerks and roared around the corners of tall apartment buildings. Across the Boulevard the Lake tried to hurl itself over the stone breakwater, tossed defeated fountains of spray into the moving air. A whirling eddy of leaves and paper and dirt engulfed Doc Williams.

"Now I know why they call this the windy city," he said. "Where we going?"

"They call this the windy city because of the talkativeness of its early inhabitants," Crane replied. "And Mr. Finklestein knows where we are going."

The attorney was walking with short, quick steps. "I think we better stop and see Miss June Dea. She was Mrs. Westland's maid, and she works down the street." He eyed Crane through his gold-rimmed spectacles. "Looks as though we'd got onto something with Woodbury."

"It won't hurt to check him," Crane agreed. "But don't forget that Simmons gets ten grand in the will."

A butler in the Metro-Goldwyn-Mayer English manner answered the doorbell. "Miss Dea?" He eyed them haughtily. "I believe there is someone here by that name." He stood squarely in the doorway.

"Well, trot her out," said Williams.

"Miss Dea is one of the servants. If you wish to communicate with her, I suggest you do so at her own home."

Finklestein stuck his foot in the closing door. "We're from police headquarters," he said, "and if you don't change your attitude damn quick we'll run you in for obstructing justice."

Williams added, "How would you like a good paste on the schnozzle right now?"

Somewhat shaken, the butler disappeared into the dark hall. He left the door wide open, and warm air came out from the house. It felt pleasant on their faces and hands. When Miss Dea arrived she was good and mad.

"What are you flatfeet trying to do?" she asked. "Lose me my job?" Her hair was licorice black, and in her silk maid's costume she was pretty and pert, but not so very young.

She became more friendly when Finklestein explained they came from Westland. She said Mr. Westland was a fine man. She said she had always liked Mr. Westland.

Finklestein asked, "Where can we talk to you? We'd like to ask you some questions."

Miss Dea led the way along a wood-paneled hall, down half a flight of stairs, and into a light-walled kitchen. A large, elderly Irishwoman in a blue cotton dress and a white apron was peering intently at a boiling kettle on the electric stove. A sour-sweet mouthpuckery smell of cooking jelly filled the kitchen. The old woman regarded them with suspicion.

Miss Dea explained, "These are policemen."

The old woman's face did not change, but she bent over the kettle again, stirring the cherry-colored mixture with a spoon.

Crane explained to Miss Dea that they hoped to find some clue to the identity of the real murderer. "We are particularly interested in the special keys to the apartment," he added. "Are you sure Mrs. Westland didn't have more than one?"

Miss Dea shook her neat head. "I'm positive she didn't. She trusted me, but she wouldn't let me have a duplicate made because she was afraid I'd lose it. And there couldn't have been a duplicate made without her knowledge, because her key never left her possession."

Finklestein asked, "Do you think Mr. Westland might have had an extra one made?"

"I'm certain he wouldn't. He knew his wife's fear about her safe, and he promised her (I heard him) he wouldn't let his key out of his possession."

"How did she happen to let him keep his key anyway after they had separated?" Crane demanded.

"He'd had a specially constructed wine cellar built in the apartment with an automatic temperature control, and he kept some very valuable wines there. They agreed to let him use the cellar, as it would have cost him an awful lot of money to build another in his apartment. He used to come over and get a bottle or two at a time."

Finklestein asked, "Does he own this apartment, that he would go and build a wine cellar in it?"

"Yes, he does; Mrs. Westland's building was part coöperative."

Crane asked, "Is there any other way the murderer could have gotten out of that apartment besides the door?"

Miss Dea shook her black head slowly.

The old Irish cook had left the sour-sweet kettle and was

cleaning celery on the chromium sink. Her knife, over the noise of running water, made a crisp sound. She was cutting the celery into nice tasseled pieces with triangular bits of heart at the blunt end.

"Did you always arrive at Mrs. Westland's apartment at the same time in the morning, Miss Dea?" Crane asked.

"Yes, at nine-thirty. Mrs. Westland always slept late, and she didn't like to have me come before that."

"Can you remember just how you and the others went into the room after you broke down the door?" Crane looked longingly at the celery. "I mean in what order?"

"Well, the house detective broke open the door. He was the first in. The rest of us followed. I guess Mr. Bolston and I came in last. I remember Sullivan, that's the house detective, gave a sort of a snort when he went into the living room from the hall. We all ran in behind him, and there she was on the living room rug. She looked just like she was asleep, except for her pretty brown hair."

"Her hair?"

"It was all soaked with blood."

There was no noise of celery being cut now.

Crane asked, "Where does the hall go in the other direction?"

"It runs back to the bedrooms."

"Then wouldn't it have been possible for the murderer to wait in the bedroom until you were all in the living room and then simply stroll out to the elevator?"

Miss Dea wrinkled her pert nose. "Not a chance. Tony, the elevator boy, waited out in the hall. He stood in his car while the door was being broken down. And then, afterwards, he took the assistant manager, Mr. Wayne, down to call the police."

His fingers on the gold-rimmed spectacles, Finklestein said, "Well, that's damn funny. Are you sure the key to the special lock was there?"

Crane attempted to take one of the celery stalks. "No you don't," said the old lady. She cupped the pile of celery in her two hands, carried it to the Norge Rollator.

"The key was there all right." Miss Dea smiled at William Crane. "I saw it. It was with her other keys and some dimes and quarters beside her purse on the table. She was lying right under the table."

The cook, bending over the open refrigerator, made a wrapping noise with some paper.

"How about Mrs. Westland's jewelry?" Finklestein asked Miss Dea. "Was any of it stolen?"

"Everything was there. Even the pieces she had on."

Williams asked, "Where'd she get shot?"

"In the side of the head. It seemed to me that she hadn't seen it coming, as though she had been shot unexpectedly."

"I guess that's all," said Finklestein.

Miss Dea opened the kitchen door. "You better go out the back way; the butler's got ants in his pants." She smiled at Doc Williams. "I hope you catch somebody before poor Mr. Westland goes."

As Crane passed the pantry, the Irish cook held out a newspaper-wrapped bundle. "Here's something that'll be helpin' you," she whispered mysteriously, her right eye screwed up into a ferocious wink. "Me boy Ed's a policeman himself, in Deetroit."

Crane accepted the bundle gingerly. Outside it was quite dark, and each street lamp stood in a circular pool of light. The three halted in one of these while Crane undid the parcel. It contained half a broiled chicken. Crane took the leg and passed the rest to Finklestein. The attorney jerked off a wing, handed the breast to Williams. They munched reflectively and unembarrassedly as they walked along the Boulevard.

"Not a bad life," Crane observed, "a policeman's."

CHAPTER VIII

Late Tuesday Afternoon

THEY QUESTIONED Gregory Wayne, assistant manager of the building in which Westland and his wife had owned their apartment, in his Gothic office with the stained-glass windows, for some time, but it was no good. Mr. Wayne was forty, he had a paunch, and he was puffy about the jowls. He was convinced Westland had killed his wife.

"He must have shot her and locked the door himself," he said. "The keys for that lock couldn't be copied by an ordinary locksmith."

Like a bored and politely superior curate, he observed the amenities of question answering without enthusiasm. He was positive the apartment had been, except for the single door, locked from the inside. He had seen the window catches himself. He was equally sure nobody could have been hiding in one of the bedrooms.

"It's too bad Mike Sullivan, the house detective, has gone to Cleveland," he said, "or he'd verify the facts. Tony will also tell you that nobody could have come out. He could see the door from his elevator."

Crane shrugged his shoulders in response to Finklestein's inquiring glance. Wayne was just repeating Miss Dea's story.

"How about her key?" Finklestein asked. "You're sure you saw it?"

"Certainly I'm sure." The manager's tone was sharp. "I saw it lying on the table with the other keys and the change. The man from the coroner's office took charge of it after Miss Dea had pointed out it was for the special lock. The police, especially Deputy Strom, realized from the first that the apartment's being locked was important." Wayne placed soft hands on the red leather arms of his chair, lifted himself to his feet behind his desk. "Now, gentlemen——"

Crane said, "I'd like to give the apartment the once over."

The manager puffed out his cheeks. "I'm sorry, but a Miss Hogan is living up there. She wouldn't——"

"I understood the apartment was privately owned by Mr. Westland," Finklestein said.

"It is, but I rented it."

"So!" Finklestein shook a finger under the puffy man's astonished nose. "You rented it, did you? And now we have to get a court order to get inside?" The lawyer swelled like a pouter pigeon. "Let me tell you that when we do, we'll get a warrant for your arrest at the same time."

"I just thought—" the manager's fingers pulled at a button on his faintly purple suit—"I thought since it was not being used that it would be advisable to have someone living there . . . I mean to keep it in order. . . . " He succeeded in establishing a feeble smile on his plump face.

"You may lose your job here for that." Finklestein was very serious. "You call the lady and tell her we're coming up. If anything in that apartment is broken or missing it will be up to you to pay for it." He turned his back on the manager and winked at Crane and Williams. "We'll decide later what should be done with you, Mr. Wayne."

Wayne fumbled with an ivory cradle phone on the desk. "Get Miss Hogan." He held a moist hand over the speaking end. "I didn't suppose anyone would objec——" He removed the hand. "Hello, dear."

His voice melted. "Some of Mr. Westland's lawyers want to look in his apartment. They are coming right up." The receiver made a spluttering noise. "I can't help it," Wayne said in a louder tone; "they're in a hurry. Just throw something on." The receiver spluttered again. "I don't give a damn," Wayne said. "We'll be right up." He slapped the phone on the cradle.

Finklestein said, "You're not coming up. We've had enough of you. You better sit here and pray there's nothing missing."

They stepped out of the elevator and rapped at 2303, and the door was flung open by a sullen lady with orange-colored hair, scarlet lips, and blue-shaded eyes. Her voice was metallic. "You pick a funny time for a visit." She moved from the door; her brilliant red, blue, and green dressing gown fleetingly exposing a tapering bare leg the color of Boston coffee. "What d'you want?" Her jaws moved on a piece of gum.

Finklestein gave her his symphony concert manner. "Madam, we are indeed sorry to disturb you." He held his hat so the diamond ring caught the hall light. "We are conducting a final investigation of last spring's tragedy. It is essential we look over the apartment."

The woman's eyes did not miss the ring. "I suppose I'll have to let you nose around." She slouched towards the living room.

Gray terra-cotta walls rose from a mulberry rug—walls covered in two places by glittering coin tapestries from India, and in another with a flamboyant portrait of a Spanish boy thrusting huge purple grapes into his red mouth. At one end was an apartment-size Steinway; in the center, facing a fireplace of marble, was a chaste black-silk davenport. Plain chairs, two antique tables were the other pieces of furniture. On two sides were windows. Miss Hogan pushed a switch, flooding the room with indirect light.

She said, "They found her body by that table."

While the others waited, Crane, in the best Sherlock Holmes manner, went over the carpet with a small magnifying glass. He examined the faintly discolored spot where the blood had been, inspected the table by it with care. He felt around the sides of the davenport, lifted the cushions, pounded the back, slid part way under the bottom.

The woman's vivid lips curved scornfully. "The murderer must have got tired of waiting under there." She leaned a curved hip against the other, larger table.

Back at the small table again, Crane asked, "Have you got a pin? And some string?"

Miss Hogan frowned, said, "I guess so." She sauntered toward the hall.

Williams followed her with glistening eyes. "That fanny looks like the Follies, or high-grade burly-que," he said.

Crane sat on the floor. "Open the doors to the dining room, will you, Doc?" He pointed to the small glass-paneled sliding door at the end of the living room near the hall entrance.

Williams slid the doors open, looking down the corridor toward Miss Hogan's bedroom. The dining room had a red tile floor, a large unpolished table with wrought-iron legs: on the wall was a gaudy painting of a salmon-pink bridge over a too blue river. The swinging door to the kitchen was to the left, in the direction of the outside hall.

Miss Hogan returned and dropped a straight pin and a ball of brown twine in Crane's lap. She smelled strongly of lilacs. He caught another glimpse of her leg, wondered if she had anything on under the silk dressing gown.

"There is only one door to this place, isn't there?" Crane asked her.

"You came in by it."

"But there is an opening in the kitchen for packages?"

"Sure, but nothin' bigger than a monkey could get in there."

"That makes you fairly safe at night, doesn't it?"

Green-brown eyes behind the mascara were haughty. "I don't need doors to keep me safe at night."

Mr. Williams said, "This must be a sissy town."

"The lady is lovely," Finklestein said reprovingly, "but we are supposed to be working."

Williams stared boldly at Miss Hogan. "I could stop anytime."

Crane waved the twine at him. "Go open the door between the dining room and the kitchen and the place for the packages." He looked at Miss Hogan. "The lady isn't interested in us."

"Oh, I don't know," she said.

Crane went into the hall and looked at the front door. It fitted tightly in its frame, and there was no place at the bottom or top to poke any sort of a key through. The special lock had been plugged up, but he could see it was the kind you had to turn with a key to fasten. He came back and walked into the kitchen, where Williams was propping open the swinging doors. He told him: "You go out in the outside hall for a second, Doc."

The opening for groceries was head high and about one foot square. Nobody could get through it. When Williams got around to the other side, in the hall, Crane handed him the end of the twine. "Hold this." He unrolled the ball, passed through the dining room, and halted by the small table. He took a book, *Candide*, and drove the pin firmly into a crack in the table. He cut the twine from the ball, looped the end loosely around the pin. Then he took the line and pulled it up so that it was firm, but not tight enough to pull out the loose knot around the pin. He followed the line back to Williams, keeping it fairly taut. The girl and Finklestein wonderingly followed him. He took a latchkey, threaded it on the cord, and let it coast down to where the cord turned against the dining room wall to go into the living room, holding his hand by the grocery entrance. The key would not go around this turn and he gave the cord a swing. The cord slipped off the pin, and the key tinkled on the tile floor.

"Hell!" Crane said. "That won't work."

Williams came around through the hall. "Come on, Master Mind; tell us what you're doing."

Crane wound the piece of cord on the ball. "I thought maybe you could slide the key from the grocery place in the kitchen to the table and then jerk the cord from the pin and through the key so that the key would stay on the table." He pulled the pin from the table and handed it and the ball of twine to Miss Hogan. He could see she had on, at least, a pale yellow brassiere. "Every flossy detective story has a trick like that in it. You can just see the murderer working patiently out here for hours after the murder, trying to slide the key back on the table and having the cord slip off the pin. Maybe somebody asks him what he's doing and he says, 'I just knocked off a lady in there and I want to make it appear as though somebody else with a key locked the door from the outside.'"

Finklestein said, "Maybe he had a trained monkey that carried the key back for him. A monkey could get through the grocery opening."

Mr. Williams nodded. "Or a seal he sent up through the drain in the bathtub.

Miss Hogan put a hand on her right hip. "Say, what asylum did you guys escape from, anyway?"

"Don't tell on us," Crane said. "It's the first time we've been out in years." He sat on the black silk davenport. "Miss Hogan, suppose you wanted to make the police think this place had been locked by Mr. Westland's key from the outside. You have either to leave the key on the table and get out some other way than the door, or you have to go out by the door and then get the key back on the table in some way without unlocking the door again. How would you do it?"

"I couldn't." Miss Hogan shook her orange head with decision. "I bet you Mr. Westland's key locked the door. I read about it in the newspapers, and I thought all the time he done it. You can't trust them rich playboys."

"How do you know you can't?"

"I've had some gentlemen friends in my time."

"I'll bet." Crane thought it must have cost them plenty, too. "But, Miss Hogan, we are working for Mr. Westland, and we have to assume he is not guilty."

"You won't be working for him long." Miss Hogan pulled her robe tight across her slim buttocks. "Not unless you find out something in a hurry."

"It doesn't look as though we are going to get anywhere here," Finklestein observed.

Crane said, "Williams, you go and see if there's a chance of getting out by the bedrooms. I've got a feeling there's some way of beating this business."

"The fellow couldn't have used the windows because they were locked from the inside," Finklestein said. "And there's only one door."

Miss Hogan moved out of the room behind Williams, again exposing her slim, tanned legs.

Crane's eyes followed her. "If I want to do anything I better get out of here. I wonder how the hotel clerk got her."

"Depression." Finklestein looked at the lighted boulevard from one of the windows. "She'll toss him over as soon as some real dough comes along."

"I go for a gal like that," said Crane. "You always know just where you are. You know you have to sleep with one eye open to keep from having your throat cut. Then, when she double-crosses you, you're not as surprised as you are when a nice girl does."

"You don't think a girl—maybe that Miss Brentino—crossed up Westland?"

"She's pretty chummy with Woodbury, she told me so herself; and he could have taken Westland's gun if Simmons is telling the truth."

"What would be the motive? Why not just knock off Westland, if you want him out of the way?"

"I don't know," Crane said wearily. "I wish Colonel Black was here instead of in Europe. I'm a hell of a detective: thinking makes my head ache." He pushed himself out of the davenport. "I wonder if that old clerk, Sprague, was talking through his hat when he said he'd tell us the motive?"

"He doesn't look all there to me. I think he was just talking."

Mr. Williams came back with Miss Hogan. "No way out at all through the bedrooms," he reported.

"I suppose we'd better scram," Crane said. He pinched the sullen-eyed Miss Hogan's cheek. "I'll be seeing you, sweetheart."

She said, "Not this century, I hope." She looked at Finklestein with a friendly expression as he went into the hall. "If I can ever help you, Mister . . . "

"Finklestein," said the lawyer.

After the door closed, Crane said, "Whew, you must be eupeptic to win that tambo's heart so quickly."

The lawyer brushed a piece of lint from his camel's hair top coat. "I get around," he admitted.

Robert Westland had received another basket of fruit from Emily Lou, and after a dinner of chipped beef on stale bread, and coffee, he passed it to Varecha. The candy peddler had cried only a little all day. He selected a green pear.

"T'anks," he said. His smile revealed black teeth. "Onc't I sold fruit myself." His neck was a purplish abrasion.

Connors, taking a handful of grapes, said: "You and the little Heeb are gettin' pretty chummy, ain't you?"

"I feel sorry for the fellow," Westland said. "He ought to be in a hospital instead of in here."

He put the basket on the floor, shivered in the chill draft from the corridor. He wondered again how the gangster could bear the cold without clothes above the waist.

"Listen," said Connors. "I've been thinking about that Grant. They didn't just happen to pick that time to knock him off. They got him because they were afraid he was going to spill something they didn't want spilled."

"I think you are right, but what are we to do? We haven't time to chase the fellows that killed him. Only three days left. . . . We have to get something that will help me."

Connors spoke from the corner of his mouth, not moving his lips. "If you got the guys who hired those killers, you'd have the guy that gave it to your wife."

"That wouldn't do any good. We might be able to link him with my wife's murder ultimately, but in the meantime I'd be . . . "

"I get the idea. You havta get hold of somethin' that will prove you're innocent."

"Sure. If I can get a stay, I'll have more time to get hold of the real murderers."

Connors secured an apple, sank his teeth in it. "It wouldn't hurt to look into that shooting, anyway. It was a pro job, I'll tell you that. I got some friends that'll be glad to listen around to see what outfit done it."

Another bite carried away half the apple. "You'll find it's some guy who's interested in seeing you out of the way."

"But, my God, I never had anything to do with a gangster in my life. Why would they be interested in me?"

The wind breathed steadily on Westland's neck. From the distant Burlington yards came the puffing of an engine moving a heavy train.

"You see that I get a note out to my pals," said Connors; "and we'll see what we can find."

Finklestein had left them downtown, saying he had some important work to do. They went to their rooms at the Hotel Sherman and washed and spent about an hour drinking Canadian rye with White Rock.

"This is the damnedest job I ever had," said Crane as they were leaving their rooms for dinner. "I never wanted to get drunk so much in my life, but I don't dare." He turned the key in the lock. "In an ordinary case you've got a lot of time, a year if you need it, but here you have to have everything by Friday. I think I'm going daffy."

Williams said, "I wish the Colonel was here."

A sleek Italian in a pea-green suit joined them in waiting for the elevator. When the steel doors swung open, he pushed roughly past them and stepped inside. All the way down he glowered at them. He smelled of perfume, and his dark face was heavily powdered. He pushed past them again on the way out.

"I don't like that guy's looks," Williams observed conversationally as they walked past the coin machines in the lobby.

Crane said, "He didn't like ours, either."

They walked over to a steak place on Dearborn Street. After the waiter had taken their order, Williams said, "I wonder what Finklestein's doing that's so important?"

"I've got a good idea." Crane took a nickel from his pocket, walked over to a phone booth by the cashier's cage, and called a number. "Miss Hogan's apartment," he said. In a minute he spoke again. "This is the State's Attorney's office, we must speak to Mr. Finklestein." There was another pause. "Mr. Finklestein?—I suggest, Mr. Finklestein, that you have the decency to pull the living-room blinds."

He returned to the table, as pleased as if he had solved the Westland case.

CHAPTER IX

Tuesday Night

THEY DECIDED after dinner to talk to Deputy Strom at the Detective Bureau. It was not so windy outside, and a quiet fall of very dry snow had begun, as though someone was cutting up an ostrich boa with a pair of nail scissors. Already the streetcars glided silently along covered rails, automobiles moved cautiously on the white pavement, and State Street, subdued and clean, was quite pastoral. As they walked south they stared admiringly into the windows of the great department stores.

William Crane was thinking about Westland. "We don't seem to be getting anywhere fast," he observed gloomily.

"I don't know," Mr. Williams said. "I still don't think it would be a bad idea to keep an eye on Woodbury."

They walked under the elevated structure and into the honky-tonk district south of Van Buren Street. They passed a penny arcade with a shooting gallery; a burlesque show with "Fifty New York Cuties"; another show which, according to a red sign, "Daringly Exposed the Vice of a Big City with Seven Living Models"; a tattooing establishment and a pawn shop.

"Look," said Mr. Williams: "if you ever get tattooed, don't let the guy put your girl's name on the job."

"I don't ever want to get tattooed."

"Well, if you ever do, have somethin' like a broken heart, or the Statue of Liberty, or one of them doves with a bunch of grass in its mouth put on, but no names. You never can tell when you're going to change your girl, an' let me tell you them marks is hell to take out."

They were nearing the Detective Bureau, and the street was dim. On their right were junk and coal yards, surrounded by dirty board fences. Across the street was a row of brown, four-story tenement houses. They passed only an occasional person.

"I had a babe named Mary onc't," Williams continued, "and I had a guy over in Hoboken put a mermaid with Mary wrote under it on my chest. That was O. K. until I hooked up with an Italian girl named Angela. She wouldn't have anythin' to do with me until I got the 'Mary' taken off. She said it wasn't religious, but I still don't see why she was so upset."

Crane said, "Maybe she didn't like to commit sacrilege and adultery at the same time?"

Mr. Williams looked over his shoulder. "Christ!" He put his arm around Crane's waist, tripped him. Both fell heavily on the sidewalk. There was a quick irregular sound like a broomstick being pushed very fast along a picket fence, and a touring car with black side curtains went past at thirty miles an hour. A man was leaning out of the front seat, shooting at them with a sub-machine gun.

The snow was ice cold on Crane's face.

Williams pulled his revolver out of the tangle of his overcoat and returned the fire in quick flashes. Back of them, under a yellow street light, a spruce nigger in a derby hat and a tan overcoat watched pop-eyed. The man with the machine gun fired a last burst at them and disappeared inside the tonneau. Crane ducked again, and when he raised his face from the snow the car had gone and the nigger was flopping around in the gutter like a hooked black bass in a rowboat.

Crane unsteadily rose from the cement, fumbled for his hat. The nigger slithered halfway up on the sidewalk, making swimming motions with his legs and arms, and then slid back off the curb into the street. He moved in convulsive jerks when Williams bent over him.

"I'm not going to kill you," Williams said. "Where'd it hit you?"

The nigger's eyes were as big as poached eggs. He pointed at his leg. Blood oozed from the trouser bottom, was bright and thick on the snow. Williams put his gun away and slit the trouser leg with a knife.

The nigger moaned, said, "That's my bes' suit."

"You don't want to bleed to death, do you?" Williams took a polka-dot silk scarf from the colored man's protesting neck, and wound it around the leg above the wound. He and Crane each took an end, pulled it tight. Then he knotted it.

A truck pulled up beside them. "What's the matter?" asked the driver. The truck was marked "Bachelors' Friend Hand Laundry." Below this was printed: "Why Get Married While We Are in Business?"

Williams said, "This jig got hurt. Hit-and-run driver." He showed a nickle badge. "You take him over to St. Luke's Hospital."

The driver's face was fat and young. "Yes, sir." He helped them lift the nigger into the front seat, drove off rapidly.

William Crane said, "We better get the hell out of here."

"You said it! If the police find us here, we'll have to do a lot of explaining . . . "

"I was thinking of those guys in the touring car."

"Those mugs!" Williams' voice was scornful. "I wish they would come back. They can't shoot worth a damn."

"Thank God for that!"

Walking very fast on the crunchy snow, they were within half a block of the Detective Bureau when Williams seized Crane's arm. "That slick dago in the elevator!" he exclaimed. "The one with the green suit!"

"What about him?"

"He's been tailing us. I thought there was something funny about the gee. That's how those artillerymen in the car caught up with us. He gave them the office."

"But why'd they want to shoot at us?"

"I'm no super-sleuth like you; I never even went to college," Williams said; "but I'll bet it was the same gang that bumped off Grant. We got 'em worried."

Many feet had stamped the snow to mud in front of the swinging glass doors of police headquarters. Mist covered the thick panes.

"They wouldn't be scared, if they knew how little we know," said William Crane sadly.

Inside the police building there was a smell of perspiration.

A thick left arm around Williams' shoulders, Lieutenant Ernest Strom, Deputy Chief of Detectives, shook hands vigorously with William Crane.

"Any friend of Doc Williams is a friend of mine." He was a beer barrel of a man, blue-eyed and pink-cheeked, and his voice was like a train announcer's. "I'm glad to know you, Mr. Crane."

He led them back to a small one-windowed office, offered them seats and cigars. The brown swivel chair behind his desk creaked as he sat down. He lit a cigar and put his feet on the desk. His gray suit needed cleaning. "It's been a long time since I've seen you, Doc." He spoke around the cigar. "A damn long time." Williams said, "I've been in New York for the last five years. Private work."

"Are you making any dough?"

"Not bad."

"Good." Deputy Strom peered at Crane. "I used to work with Doc years ago. We broke open a lot of cases together, some of them damn big ones." Blue smoke poured from his mouth. "Doc, do you remember the Birkhoff diploma mill?"

"Do I? I still got a scar where that old guy stuck a paper knife in me."

The deputy's laugh shook the windowpane. "You always had a knack for almost getting killed." He looked at Crane again under straight brows. "But I don't suppose you're here to gab with me."

Williams said, "It's about the Westland case."

"Oh, ho! What about it?"

"You worked on it, didn't you?"

"Sure." The deputy's tone was less hearty. "That was my baby. What's happened?"

"Nothing." Williams turned half around to William Crane, who said: "We've been engaged to help Westland. We don't think he's guilty, and we're trying to save him."

Deputy Strom's blue eyes hardened. He seemed to be holding his breath. Finally he said, "Well, you certainly bit into something! You've got only three days to work for him, and the only way you can save him is to produce the real murderer—that is, if he ain't."

Crane said, "We're going to try. We got some pretty good evidence that Westland didn't kill his wife, but not enough to get him a reprieve."

"What is it?"

"First, let me ask you something. What have you got on that Mannie Grant case? You remember? The fellow who was shot in . . . "

"Sure I remember." Deputy Strom held the black cigar between two fingers daintily. "We got some pretty hot leads we're working on."

"Don't give us the old baloney," Doc Williams said. "We ain't newspaper men."

"What do you want to know about him for?"

Crane told him about the note and of the search they had made for Grant.

"H'mm." The deputy's blond brows almost covered his eyes. "You two guys probably ain't so popular with some of Grant's friends right now—at least, not if they knew you'd been trying to find him."

"But what about the letter?" Crane persisted. "Don't you think Grant saw something?"

"Say, every time there's a murder played up in the newspapers we get a bushel basket of letters like that. This Grant was a crank—like all the others. He was probably doped up the night of the murder and thought he was the one who shot her . . . "

Williams spoke to Crane. "Tell him about the difference in time."

William Crane explained what Bolston had discovered, and told the deputy of the change in Dr. Shuttle's testimony. "You see," he added, "it makes Westland's story stand up. He could have left when he said he did with his wife still alive."

"When he said he did . . . ." Deputy Strom shook his massive head. "Naturally, he'd say he left before his wife was killed. Who wouldn't?" Suddenly he peered at Crane's face. "What happened to you? Somebody sock you?"

Crane rubbed his hand against the part of his face which had been pressed against the sidewalk. "I slipped in the snow."

"You certainly smacked it."

"Listen," said Doc Williams, "we're trying to get some information out of you."

"I think you're up a blind alley, boys," the deputy said. "I know Westland's the man."

"But Grant's being shot? Don't you think that's funny?"

Smoke curled from the tilted cigar. "Just a coincidence. Yes, sir. Just a coincidence. Somebody wanted to bump him off and they happened to do it while you were looking for him." Deputy Strom's feet scraped as they slid from the table. "I'll tell you the truth, boys, we're working on something pretty good on that case right now. Grant was a jewel thief, an' he was in some pretty good jobs. We got a tip he crossed up some of his buddies in the big Walbaum jewel robbery in Miami. You remember? Last winter?" Finger and thumb caressed the cigar. "Of course I'm countin' on you boys to keep this under your hats."

"We aren't interested in anything except Westland," Crane answered him. "But we are interested in him. Do you suppose you could see if anybody else in the case has a record?"

"Who d'you mean?"

"Woodbury, Bolston and Wharton, and the two ladies, Miss Martin and Miss Brentino. And that clerk—Sprague."

Mr. Williams sat up straight in his chair. "You don't think that little Miss Martin—"

"It doesn't hurt to check everybody."

Deputy Strom said, "Why, all those people are on the up-and-up. I talked with them myself. They wouldn't——"

"Did you look them up in the Bureau of Identification?"

"No. Why should I? I had Westland cold."

"Well, would you mind looking them up now?"

The deputy grunted.

Crane wrote the names on a sheet of paper and gave them to a detective summoned from the outer office. "Make it snappy," Deputy Strom told the man. His blue eyes were alert as he looked at Crane. "If you've got it narrowed down to those six, it oughtn't to be so tough for a smart guy like you to get something on one of them."

"We haven't tried very hard so far. Haven't had time. All we know is that Woodbury might have taken Westland's pistol. He was in Westland's apartment on the night of the murder. That is, if Westland's pistol was actually used."

"Sure it was used. Major Lee, the ballistics expert, found out the bullet came from a Webley pistol of the type used in the war. An' the major's never wrong, let me tell you."

"Then why was the pistol hidden?"

"Because Westland knew it would convict him. He hid it."

"Yes, but if Westland didn't kill his wife, why would his pistol be hidden?"

Deputy Strom grinned with the side of his mouth unoccupied by the cigar. "You don't expect me to argue against myself, do you?"

The detective returned with the list of names. "Not a one in the files," he announced.

The deputy nodded his massive head in triumph. "You see. They're all in the clear."

Williams said, "It's too tough for me."

The door clicked behind the detective.

"Did you try to check on the telephone call Westland testified he received from someone pretending to be Miss Martin?" Crane asked.

"That was a lot of boloney." The deputy leaned back in the swivel chair. "First he said it was Miss Martin, and then, when she denied it, he said it was some woman pretending it was her. It's funny a guy wouldn't know his own girl over the telephone."

"It is funny."

"We checked on Miss Martin, anyway. She lives with her uncle and aunt up in Rogers Park, and they have only one phone in the house. It's in the hall by the living room. They were in the living room at the time Miss Martin was supposed to have called Westland, and nobody used the phone. I talked to them myself."

Williams said, "Maybe Miss Martin went outside."

"She didn't, though. She was home, too, that evening. The uncle and aunt are positive she didn't leave the house."

"What the hell," said William Crane. "It was somebody else who called him anyway."

The deputy said, "Nobody called him. He just made the story up."

"You don't seem to like Westland."

"I like him all right. I just think he plugged his wife." The deputy waved his cigar to indicate a minor thing like that wouldn't affect his personal interest in Westland. "Anything else you'd like to know?"

"The damnedest thing was the locked apartment," Crane said. "Don't you think there might have been some way for the murderer to have got out without a key?"

"The place was all locked from the inside. We looked it over carefully as hell, and every window was fastened," Deputy Strom replied. "The only way to get out was to use the door and then lock it from the outside. That's the way it was."

"Then somebody must have had a duplicate key."

"There ain't a duplicate key. There's just two. We know because the newspapers had photographs of the two keys and questions asking: 'Is there a third key?' The lawyers for the defense had them photograph the key because they knew Westland's only chance was to find someone who knew of a duplicate. If a keysmith had made a duplicate he'd have been sure to tell about it."

Williams rested his elbow on the desk. "That's about the only smart thing those lawyers did."

Deputy Strom shrugged broad shoulders. "What could they do? That guy did more to convict himself than the prosecuting attorney. He even admitted there couldn't be a duplicate key."

Crane asked, "Then how did the murderer get out?"

"That's easy. Westland murdered his wife and then let himself out with his own key."

"We always come back to Westland."

The deputy allowed the smoke to roll over his lower lip. "Why not?"

A young detective opened the door, thrust his head in the room. "St. Luke's has got a funny shooting," he announced. "A jigaboo was brought in with a bullet in his leg. He says he was plugged in a machine-gun battle between coppers and a carload of hoods a couple of blocks down the street. Like to go over an' see him?"

"Sure." The deputy heaved himself from the swivel chair. "Might be interesting." He struggled into his overcoat. "You fellows like to come along and see him?"

Crane spoke hastily, "No, thanks. It's time we were going."

It was only ten o'clock when they got back to their hotel room, and they decided to have a few drinks. They mixed the Canadian rye with water this time.

Crane took a fair-sized drink, then asked, "Did I thank you for saving my life?"

Williams spoke over the top of his glass. "I must have been out of my mind when I shoved you down."

"Well, thanks anyway. I wouldn't like to try to stop one of those slugs."

"Me neither."

Crane moved from his chair to the bed. He propped a pillow under his head and looked at the room with disfavor. "This isn't as classy as Mrs. Westland's apartment."

"No; there ain't any babes with orange hair in here."

"I wonder how he's making out?"

"Who? Finklestein?" Williams poured himself another drink. "I'll bet she's got that sparkler by now."

Crane rested on the pillow with closed eyes. His face, where he had struck the sidewalk, hurt a little, but not enough to prevent him from feeling comfortably drowsy. "That copper didn't think so much of our client's innocence, did he?"

"Sometimes I'm doubtful myself."

The red electric sign of the Palace Theater flashed on and off a block up the street, sending intermittent rays of light into the room. The snow was still falling, and now there was no wind at all.

Crane said, "I don't think he would have lied about the time. He didn't have to convince Finklestein or me that he wasn't guilty. We would have worked just as hard anyway." He reached for the glass of rye, carried it to his lips. "I think Bolston's discovery of the mistake in Shuttle's testimony proved Westland was out of there when the murder was committed."

"It may prove it to you, but not to the Governor."

"No, not to the Governor."

"Well, what are we going to do?"

"I'm damned if I know."

Williams slid his thumbnail across a red-topped kitchen match and lit a cigarette in the flame. "I got one idea." He inhaled, let the smoke dribble out his mouth as he spoke. "You got the list down to six. Why don't you find out where they all were on the night of the murder?"

Crane opened one eye. "That's a good idea. We'll start with Finklestein on that tomorrow."

"If he's still alive after that babe——"

Shrilly, the telephone rang. Crane jumped, pushed over his glass, deftly caught it as it rolled from the table. "I certainly got the jitters from that shooting." The phone rang again, and he lifted the receiver. "Hello! . . . Sure, come on up."

"Who was that?"

"Bolston. He says he'd like to talk to us."

Under his black Burberry, Bolston wore with distinction a wide-lapeled dinner jacket. He had an ivory-colored gardenia in his buttonhole. He sat on the straight-backed chair by the writing table and accepted a glass of rye whiskey and water. "I just finished a late dinner in the Loop," he explained, "and I thought I'd drop in and see if there was anything I could do."

"That's just the trouble," said Crane. "It doesn't seem as though there was anything we could do."

Bolston's carefully brushed blond head moved up and down. "It's a tough one all right, and it's costing Westland a lot of money to push this thing. . . . I paid the warden ten thousand, and Lord knows how much Finklestein is getting."

Williams said, "He can't take the dough with him, can he?"

"No, that's right. But he ought to get a lot of action for that much money."

"You mean," Crane said drowsily, "a lot more than we're giving him?"

"Well . . ."

"I admit we're not getting along very fast, but we're trying. Yes, sir, we're trying. If you've got any ideas, let's have them." Crane poured more liquor into his glass. It was his fifth drink. "You can't say we aren't putting in the hours. Take Finklestein, for instance. He's working right now."

Williams was stricken with an attack of coughing.

Bolston's tan face relaxed. "I'm not complaining, but I would like to see you pull this business off." He shook his head. "It's a terrible thing for an innocent man to go to the electric chair."

Williams said, "It's not so much fun for a guilty one, either."

"The only definite thing we have so far is what you found out about the time," said Crane. "We seem to hit a wall every time we try to figure out how the murderer got out of that apartment. We talked to Deputy Chief of Detectives Strom about it this evening, and there's no doubt the apartment was locked." He rolled into a sitting position on the bed and ran his fingers through his hair. "It makes a neat problem. The apartment is locked on the inside everywhere but at the door. The door has been locked by one of the two keys that will fit it. The lock couldn't have snapped shut, because it is the kind of a lock that has to be turned. One of the two keys is inside the apartment, and Westland has the other. Question: How'd the murderer get out without the key?"

After a time Bolston said, "Couldn't Mrs. Westland have killed herself and fixed things up to look as though she had been murdered? You know she never wanted her husband to marry Miss Martin?"

"How could she have disposed of the pistol?"

"I remember reading a Sherlock Holmes story in which the woman killed herself on a bridge with a revolver tied to a heavy rock. She fired the shot through her head and then the rock jerked the pistol out of her hand and into the pool. If it hadn't been for Holmes, another person, who had a mate to the first pistol, would have been hung as the murderer."

Crane said, "I thought of something like that, but I couldn't figure out where the pistol might have been hidden. The only place I could think of was under the couch, but it wasn't there."

"Well, it might be a variation of that stunt."

Liquid gurgled into glasses as Williams poured three more drinks. A newsboy in the street below was calling: "Read about the Million Dollar Fire. Two Dead. Read all about the Million Dollar Fire."

"Would Woodbury have any reason to put Westland out of the way?" Crane asked.

"Woodbury?" Bolston laughed. "Lord, no. They're the best of friends. Woodbury would have nothing to gain from a thing like that."

"Where was Woodbury on the morning after the murder?"

"At the office. I drove my Rolls from Mrs. Westland's apartment to the office, arranged for a lawyer and bond money with Woodbury, and then drove to the Detective Bureau."

Williams asked, "How do you park that big boat of yours downtown?"

"Oh, I don't park it on the street." Bolston exposed his teeth. "I use the garage at the La Salle Hotel, a block from the office."

Crane pursued his original line of questioning. "Wouldn't Woodbury get a bigger share in the brokerage business?"

"No. He might pick up a few customers, that's all. Westland wasn't very active, anyway."

"Yes, he said he had a private income. I suppose you have, too."

"Not I. All I have is what I make."

"Well, who would benefit by Westland's death?"

"I expect Wharton would be the only one. He's Westland's nearest relative."

"Is he hard up?"

"I think he is. Woodbury handles his affairs when Westland isn't there, but I heard he was pretty hard hit in a couple of things." Bolston smiled at Crane. "I don't want you to get an idea that I'm trying to make you go after him. I haven't the slightest suspicion of him, but I don't think it would do any harm to check on him."

"You don't know anything else about him?"

"He plays golf and gambles, and goes with that horsey Lake Forest crowd. That's all I know."

"No scandal about him?"

"Never heard any."

The room was hot, and William Crane raised a window. Air,

pouring through the opening, cooled his face and hands. Leaning out to look at the street he said, "I wish I could find out just where all of you were on the night of the murder. That might give me something to go on." Streetcars made muffled noises on the snow-padded rails.

"What makes you think it must have been one of us?"

"Who else would have had a motive for putting Westland out of the way?"

"I don't see that any of us would have." Bolston put his hands in his trouser pockets, thrust out his legs. His socks were a ribbed black silk with a faint trace of white in the vertical stripes. "Why couldn't someone have killed Mrs. Westland just to get her out of the way and at the same time fix the evidence up to implicate Bob? That would be the easiest way to throw the police off the trail. Maybe she had a lover who was tired of her, or she knew something about someone."

"Lovers don't usually kill their sweethearts when they get tired of them, but you may be right." Crane sipped the rye. "The whole thing is going to drive me crazy."

"Me too," said Williams. "Every time I think of that fellow in jail depending upon us to save his life, I get the shakes."

Bolston said, "If you'd like to find out where everybody was on the night of the murder, I'll be glad to help you."

"Do you know where the others were that night?"

"No—only myself."

"Where were you?"

"I haven't much of an alibi. I went to the theater, stopped for a drink at the athletic club, and then went home."

"Who went to the theater with you?"

"I went alone, but I drank with Peter Brady at the club. He drove me home about twelve o'clock."

"Are you married, Mr. Bolston?"

"No, but my Japanese valet will tell you I spent the night at home."

"All right. But who's Brady?"

"He's a lawyer. His office is at 160 North La Salle Street." Bolston was smiling. "I don't think you will have to check with him, though. Even if he did take me home, I'd still have had time to do the murder."

Crane said, "We'll probably find that most of you could have been there. But if we can absolutely eliminate anybody we'll be that much better off."

"I hope you have luck."

Crane questioned Bolston about the discovery of the body, but he told the same story as Miss Dea and the manager. On the Friday before the murder, Woodbury had given him a message from Mrs. Westland that she wanted him to come over on Monday morning on his way to work to look at some bonds. "Wanted some advice about investments, I guess." He'd stood back while the house detective broke open the door and then hurried in with the others. He didn't look around the apartment to see if everything was locked, he'd left that to the police.

Crane asked suddenly, "Did you pick up the pistol and smuggle it out to protect your partner?"

Bolston took a long drink from his glass. "Do I look that much of a fool?" He was amused. "I didn't see any pistol, and if there had been one, I couldn't have picked it up without being seen."

"No, I suppose not," Crane said. "Do you remember how Mrs. Westland was dressed?"

"Not very well. She had on a green gown—" Bolston was

apologetic—"but I can't tell you what else. You know I was terribly shocked."

"I know," Crane said. "I didn't expect you to remember much. I just wanted to know if she was fully clad and not in a pair of pajamas or something like that."

"I am sure she was fully clad." Smoothly, Bolston got to his feet. "I imagine her maid could tell you exactly what she had on." He slipped into his Burberry, caught his hat by the brim. "I've got to be going—hard day at the office tomorrow."

Crane asked at the door, "You'll drop in for the conference at the jail, won't you?"

"I'll try to be there," Bolston called from the hall.

Crane closed the door. Doc Williams, over his drink, said, "The guy's too busy to save his partner's life."

"What the hell!" Crane poured a nightcap. The bottle was nearly empty. "He's the only one who's been any help so far."

"Why didn't you tell him about Woodbury's chance to steal the pistol on the night of the murder?"

Crane said plaintively, "A detective has to have some secrets, hasn't he?"

"If that's the best we have, we better take up boy scouting." Williams finished his drink and opened the connecting door to his room. "I'm going to bed and dream about that orange-haired dame that ought to be in the Follies and those mugs who tried to plug us."

After William Crane had brushed his teeth and had climbed into bed and was about to switch off the light, Williams stepped into the doorway. He had on crimson silk pajamas with a monogram over his heart. He said excitedly, "I know who took those shots at us tonight."

"So do I," said William Crane. "Go to bed."

CHAPTER X

Wednesday Morning

SNOW OVERCOATED the jail yard and glistened in the butter-colored sunlight. From a cornice above a window in the Assistant Matron's office, water dropped, throwing a spray against the windowpane as it struck the cement outer ledge. The sky was the shade of faded overalls.

Westland's face was astonished. "If they'd go to all that risk to shoot you that near police headquarters," he said to William Crane and Doc Williams, "they must be getting pretty scared. It looks as though we were close to something."

"I don't know," said Crane. "I don't know whether the shooting has anything to do with you."

"But it must have. Nobody would want to kill you, would they?"

"No." Crane rubbed his sore cheek. "At least, not in Chicago—I don't know anybody here. But I think I have a pretty good idea. . . . "

"Look," Westland said. "You don't want to take any chances of getting shot. A friend of mine in jail here said he'd be glad to call on a couple of his friends if I needed any help. I imagine they'd be pretty capable fellows to act as bodyguards."

"Doc Williams can take care of me all right," Crane said. He stared through the window at a sparrow trying to tug a frozen piece of string from under a rock. "Still, I have a hunch we could use a couple of these boys for something else. Do you suppose you could get two for us this afternoon?"

"Sure. I'll speak to Connors and have the warden take out a message from him."

"Connors?" Williams asked. "Is that the labor racketeer who chased Al Capone out of the Truckers' Union?"

"I think so."

"Then his pals will be just the sort we need."

Crane asked, "How will he get in touch with them?"

"You call the warden about noon. He'll arrange a place for you to meet them." Westland glanced at the door. "Where do you suppose Emily Lou is?"

"She'll be along," Crane said. "We came a little early. We wanted to tell you about the shooting last night, but we didn't want the others to hear. You'll keep it quiet?"

"Of course." Westland appeared surprised. "But why——"

"Just being careful," Crane said. "I also wanted to ask you about your will. Does anybody know you are leaving your money to Miss Martin?"

"Nobody but my partners and the lawyer who drew the will. I'm sure they never mentioned it to anyone."

"And then about your wife——"

Warden Buckholtz opened the door for Woodbury and Miss Brentino. The warden was saying tactfully, "It don't look as though I was going to have the pleasure of you folks' company much longer." He closed the door, his face peacefully conscious of having observed the amenities.

"What about Bob's wife?" asked Woodbury.

Miss Brentino was dressed in a fine-textured blue wool suit, cut with military squareness over her shoulders, snug at the waist, and with a slight flare in the skirt. Her face was like a pale flower over her silver fox scarf. Crane admired her discreetly as he answered Woodbury, "I wanted to ask Mr. Westland how his wife was dressed when he visited her that night."

Westland said, "She was wearing a green evening gown. I remember it distinctly."

"Did you notice a pile of change on one of the tables in the living room?"

"Yes, there was some change on the little table. It was with some of Joan's keys."

Crane nodded. "I guess nothing had been moved, then, between the time you left and when they found your wife in the morning."

"That's right." Westland was still watching the door. "It seemed to me, when I heard the witnesses testify at the trial, that she must have been shot immediately after I left."

"My God!" Crane stepped away from the window. "You don't suppose somebody could have shot her with a silenced automatic from the corridor as you were coming out the door? That's the wildest yet, but——"

"She came to the door with me," Westland objected; "and besides, she was shot so closely that the powder burned her."

"It just doesn't make sense." Crane returned to the window. The sparrow was still working on the frozen string. "But I can't help that." He glanced at Woodbury. "We can do one thing, though. I want to check on the actions of everybody on the night of the murder. Do you remember what you did, Mr. Woodbury?"

Woodbury looked very French in his immaculate clothes. He was wearing a dark gray double-breasted flannel suit with a faint lighter gray stripe. A soft green shirt with a tab collar harmonized with an olive-green necktie. A handkerchief with a green initial peeped out of his pocket. He replied:

"I talked with Bob about one of his old accounts I had taken over—that was in his apartment—and then I took Miss Brentino to the Black Hawk. I picked her up about ten o'clock, and we danced until after two."

"Are times about right, Miss Brentino?"

Her pale face, with the darkly luminous eyes, was exquisite in the half light. "I don't know about the visit to Mr. Westland's apartment—" Her voice was flat, without inflection. "—but we did dance from ten to two at the Black Hawk."

Crane looked at her closely, and she met his stare with steady eyes. He thought, Boy, if I only had a little time to spend promoting that babe. He said, "I guess you two have an ironclad alibi."

She said, "Do you think we need alibis, Mr. Crane?"

Crane remembered an old police dictum. "An alibi is a handy thing to have," he said.

The door was swung open again, and Miss Martin, followed by Attorney Finklestein, entered the room. She cried, "Honey!" and flung herself into Westland's arms.

Finklestein's skin was lemon-colored, and his eyes were bloodshot. He sank into a chair and groaned, "Oy!" Williams noted with surprised approval that he still wore his diamond ring.

Miss Martin pulled herself part way out of Westland's arms and regarded his haggard face. "Have you any news?" Her great blue eyes under the delicately traced brows were wide and anxious. The white lace collar on her navy blue dress made her pretty face demure.

Westland shook his head. His color was bad, Crane saw: yellow pale, and his skin was without luster, as on the corpses in the cold storage vaults at a morgue. Westland glanced inquiringly at Finklestein, who sat, dejected, one hand pressed to his forehead.

"I've got nothing," Finklestein said. "What's Crane done?"

Crane said, "Nothing." His shoulders were cold from leaning against the windowpane.

The lawyer peered around the room. "We don't seem to have such a full house today."

Woodbury asked, "What's happened to Sprague? He was going to have something important to tell us."

"You ought to know," Crane said. "He works for you."

"I haven't been down to the office yet. Where's Bolston? He could tell us if Sprague came to work."

Westland was standing with an arm around Emily Lou's waist, half supporting himself. "Dick called the warden and told him he wouldn't be able to get here this morning. Some business he had to see about."

Miss Brentino's level voice was casual. "I'll find out about Mr. Sprague when I go to work."

"Then there's the red-coated huntsman," said Finklestein.

Woodbury was amused. "You mean Wharton?"

"Yeah. Where is he?"

"You can't depend on him to turn up anywhere," Westland said. "He may be breaking in a new hunter or training some dogs. He forgets everything when he's around a hound or a horse."

"Like some men with a woman," Crane observed.

Finklestein scowled, asked, "What have you got to amuse yourself today, Mr. Detective?"

"Plenty. I'd like to ask a few more questions, and then we'll get started."

Finklestein said, "It's about time."

"Oh yeah?" Williams looked at the lawyer through half opened lids. "I don't know what you're complaining about when you——"

"Never mind." Hands in his trouser pockets, heels against the floor, Crane balanced on the window sill. "Miss Martin, just as a matter of form, we have been trying to learn where everyone was at the time Mrs. Westland was murdered."

Westland's eyes were angry. "You needn't bother her with that stuff." He stepped toward Crane.

"Oh, I don't mind answering." Miss Martin smiled at Crane. "I know you have to check on everybody. I was home that night, from seven o'clock on."

"Were you with anybody?"

"Yes. My uncle and aunt. We played backgammon and listened to the radio and then went to bed about twelve-thirty."

"O. K." Crane said. "O. K. Another name off the list." He arched his back, pushed himself off the window sill onto his toes. "Now I'd like to get the details of that telephone call you thought came from Miss Martin. Was there really such a call, Mr. Westland, or did you make it up?"

Westland appeared angry and embarrassed. "Of course there was a call. Why do you suppose I went over to see Joan?"

"And you thought it was Emily—I mean Miss Martin?"

Her dull red hair pressing Westland's cheek, Miss Martin said, "Of course he thought it was me. I don't blame him for——"

"I did then," Westland said, "but I don't now. The voice on the phone used words Emily Lou wouldn't have used."

Crane squinted one eye. "You mean she—swore?"

"Of course not. I mean she said things which weren't quite grammatical."

"What did she say?" Crane was leisurely pacing up and down the room. "Tell us all you can remember of the conversation."

Westland's eyes closed, wrinkles creased his forehead. "It's been so long . . . Well, the phone rang and I answered it and a voice said, 'Robbie?' It sounded like Emily Lou, and I said, 'Why, hello, Emily Lou.'"

"Good," said William Crane interestedly. "Go on."

"Then she said, 'Honey, the awfulest thing has happened. Your wife just called me up and said she'd have me arrested if I didn't stop seeing you.'" Westland squeezed Emily Lou's arm. "I can't remember exactly what else she said, but she told me my wife had called her a 'slut.' I remember she said, 'She ain't goin' to get away with that.'" Westland shook his head at Crane. "I realized later that Emily Lou wouldn't have said that. The woman on the phone was excited, but she quieted down when I told her I would go over and see Joan."

Crane asked, "Whose idea was that?"

"Why, it was mine. I said, 'I'll get dressed right away and . . .'"

"She didn't say, wait until morning?"

"Why, no. I said——"

"How did the conversation end?"

"I said, 'Don't worry, Emily Lou,' and she said, 'I know I can depend on you, honey.'"

"Does Miss Martin call you honey?" William Crane asked.

"Certainly. Why not?"

"Quite proper of her." Crane jingled some coins in his pocket. "But I can't say it helps us."

"I don't know what you're talking about."

"Neither do I," Crane admitted; "but I still have another question left."

Finklestein asked, "Only one?"

Crane ignored him. He watched Woodbury, who was swinging his right leg from the table, out the corner of his eye and spoke to Westland. "Do you think your gun was in the cabinet drawer up to the night of the murder?"

"Yes, I am quite sure it was; at least, I saw it in the drawer on the day before the . . . death."

"Then it must have been stolen sometime during the evening, because your man, Simmons, saw it there when he was cleaning on the afternoon of the death."

Westland looked surprised.

"He didn't say anything about it for fear it would cause further trouble," Crane continued, watching Woodbury. "Now, Mr. Westland, did you have any visitors that evening?"

Woodbury's swinging leg halted abruptly.

"Nobody but Woodbury here," Westland replied.

Crane rotated his body at the hips, faced Woodbury. "You didn't take that pistol, did you?"

Woodbury's dark face was calm, but his leg was still held unnaturally in front of him. "Why would I take his pistol when I have one of my own just like it?"

"I don't know," Crane said. "I'm just asking you if you took his?"

"I didn't."

Crane continued to face Woodbury. "Were there any other visitors that evening, Mr. Westland?"

"No, but——"

"How about Miss Martin? Did she drop in any time?"

"Not while I was there."

Miss Martin's blue eyes were not quite so friendly. "I didn't go there at all that day."

"No offense," Crane said. "I'm just a young detective trying to get along." He glanced warningly at Williams, who had been admiring Miss Martin's shapely legs, and moved to the door. "Anyway, I've run out of questions for a while."

Finklestein followed him across the warden's burn-spotted rug and out into the corridor. He said, "Christ, I've got a hangover."

Williams, coming up behind him, asked, "How much that babe take you for?"

"Now," Finklestein said, "she's a nice girl."

"Nice and dangerous," said Crane.

Miss Brentino and Woodbury emerged from the warden's office and joined them. Miss Brentino put her gloved hand on Crane's arm. Her voice was liquid and full of tone shadows. "Did you ever think," she said, "that the voice most like somebody's voice would be that person's voice?"

Miss Martin was within five feet of them. Her eyes were narrowed, her brows no longer arched. "I heard you." Her voice echoed in the corridor. "You sneaking cat!" She advanced toward them, and William Crane retreated two steps. "You tried to make Mr. Westland when you were his secretary, but he preferred me." She trembled with rage. "Now you're trying to pay me back, but you won't get away with this either."

Miss Brentino's white face was composed. Her scarlet lips curved in scorn; her voice was expressionless again. "Don't be a little fool." She turned her back on Miss Martin's furious face and walked away, slim hips moving with tigerish grace under her tight gray silk dress. Woodbury followed her along the corridor.

In the street the air was crisp and the snow underfoot was springy like a rubber mat. A Yellow cab went by them unsteadily along the streetcar tracks, a broken link on a tire chain banging the left rear fender.

Finklestein shuddered, pulled his overcoat collar up against his ears. "I don't feel so good."

"You better pull yourself together," William Crane said, "because you've lots of work to do."

"We better do something pretty quick." The attorney pulled on a pair of ostentatiously hand-stitched pigskin gloves. "Did you notice Westland's face?"

"Yes, he's plenty scared." Doc Williams said, "I don't blame him."

"Look," said Crane. "We've got only three days and I can't waste time checking on all these people's alibis. But I think somebody ought to do it."

"Sure," Finklestein agreed without enthusiasm. "What do you want me to do?"

"Check with the Black Hawk and see if Woodbury and Miss Brentino were there—somebody might have spotted them—and then find out if Bolston's story that he drank at his club with a lawyer named Peter Brady at——"

"I know the guy: he's a corporation lawyer."

"Bolston hasn't got a complete alibi, but I'd like to see if he's telling the truth about Brady taking him home on the night of the murder." Crane signaled to another cab. This one didn't have any chains. "I'll take Wharton and Miss Martin."

Finklestein poked his head through the cab door. "How about Sprague?"

"That's right. You better take him, too. I'll call you around lunch time at your office."

Finklestein slammed the door. Rear wheels spun in the snow as the cab eased out into the street. The driver slid open the panel. "Where to, Mister?"

"Do you know where Deerpath Road is in Lake Forest?"

"Lake Forest?" The driver's hair was cut round in the back, and his neck was chapped from the cold. "Whooee! That's thirty miles—clear out in the country—clear up north."

"Well, drive as far as you can," said Crane, "and we'll take a dogsled the rest of the way."

"This is the joint," said the driver. The cab heeled over as the wheels cut through the snow in the gutter, and skidded to a standstill. The meter read $6.55 and there was a charge of .05 for one extra passenger. "D'ya want me t' wait?"

The country snow was as clean as Ivory soap flakes. Blue-green fir trees dotted the sloping yard in front of a stone two-story house.

"Sure," William Crane said. "We won't be very long."

"Take as long as y'like." The driver spat, and tobacco juice made a burn in the snow. "I ain't had a day in the country since my sweetie up an' married a policeman."

Just inside the house a dog barked angrily. Crane was about to lift the brass knocker a second time when a pompous serving man opened the oak door. The dog, a rusty black Scottie, growled and pretended to come out after them through the man's legs.

The servant raised his eyebrows.

"Mr. Wharton there?"

"Who shall I say is calling?"

Wharton appeared behind the man. He was wearing wool plus fours, baggy in the English manner, a dark-brown tweed coat, and a camel's-hair pullover sweater. "Hello, there." His red face was unfriendly. "What's up?"

The serving man withdrew into the house. A wood fire was bright in the many-windowed living room, but Wharton did not invite them in.

Crane said, "I wanted to ask you some questions."

"Couldn't you have phoned?"

"You can always hang up on the phone."

The Scottie became interested in a smell on the stone doorstep.

"What do you mean by that?" Wharton glared at Crane. "Look here, I won't have any of your bloody nonsense."

"I don't give a damn," Crane said. "I'm trying to help your cousin. If you don't care enough about him to answer a few questions, it's your affair."

Wharton's hand on the doorknob was undecided; then he said, "What d'you want to know?"

"First I'd like to know how well you knew Mrs. Westland."

"I knew her hardly at all—to speak to, of course, but that's all."

"You wouldn't know if she had any enemies?"

Wharton shook his head.

"When did you hear about her death?"

"Bolston told me at Westland's office. I had an appointment with Bob on the day he was arrested. I was waitin' for him when Bolston came in and told me about the murder."

"What time was your appointment with Westland?"

"Eleven-thirty." Wharton kept pulling the door to him and then pushing it away. "I got there a few minutes ahead of time and waited about forty minutes, until noon. I was gettin' ready to leave when Bolston came in."

"What time was that?"

"About two minutes after twelve. I'd just told Miss Brentino that it was noon and that I wouldn't wait any longer."

"Wasn't Woodbury at the office?"

"Yes, but my business was with Westland."

The Scottie liked the smell of Crane's tweed trousers, but he shied when Crane tried to scratch his ears. Williams was peering longingly at the crackling fire in the living room.

"Now, about the night of the murder," Crane said. "Can you tell us where you were between eleven and two?"

Wharton swelled visibly. "By gad, I don't see why I should tell you." His face purpled. "Are you intimatin' I'm one of the suspects?"

"Not at all," Crane lied. "I'm just going through a routine check."

"I'm damned if I'll tell you, anyway. It's a personal affair."

"Listen!" Williams pushed Crane aside. "If you ain't got an alibi, just say so. It'll save us a lot of time."

Crane said, "We're trying to help your cousin, and the only way we can is to find out the actual murderer. If you've got an alibi, we won't have to worry about you at all."

A gray squirrel came toward them across the snow like a ballet dancer, saw the Scottie, and darted up a tree. It began a scolding chatter. The cab driver appeared to be asleep.

"Dammit!" Wharton regarded them with anger and perplexity. "Can't you take my word for it?"

"Why the hell should we?" asked Crane.

"By gad! I——" Wharton paused, rubbed his mustache violently. "Bob's a clean-cut fella, and I'd hate to see him electrocuted. I'm a bloody fool, but I'll do it. I'll take you to somebody who knows where I was that night." He thrust open the door violently. "Carter! My coat."

The serving man appeared with a rough coat and brown hat. Wharton put them on, called to the Scottie, "Come on, Bogey." He paused on the steps. "Don't think I'm doing this for you, because I'm not. I don't like you."

Crane said, "Kraft-Ebbing will never have to write a case history of my passion for you, either."

Awakened from a refreshing nap, the driver sent the cab along the blanketed streets at a smart clip. Wharton guided them to a large Tudor residence on Green Bay Road, rang the bell for them. A neat maid in uniform opened the door and exclaimed, "Oh! It's Mr. Wharton," and led them into a beamed living room. Williams and the Scottie halted gratefully in front of a fireplace with two railroad ties smoldering on copper alloy andirons. Wharton and Crane stood and regarded each other with mutual distaste.

Presently a lady came down a curved stairway and unsteadily made her way toward them across brilliant Cossack scatter rugs. "Hello, Larry-Warry," she called in an incredibly harsh voice. She was a big woman, well on her way toward the fifties, and her large face was flushed and veined from hell-for-leather living, and she was cock-eyed drunk. She made the big table by the fireplace as an exhausted swimmer would a reef, and clung there, blinking at Williams.

"Hi there, handsome," she said.

Wharton offered shocked reproof. "Amy! So early in the morning?"

"You ol' rep'bate," said the lady, swaying dangerously. "I bet there's whiskey on your breath too." She leered at Williams again. "Whoos your little playmate?"

"These men are detectives," said Wharton severely. "They're investigating Joan Westland's murder."

"Murder? Murder?" The lady took a deep breath, swelling out her breasts, and shouted, "An-nah!"

Bogey, the Scottie, cocked his ears in polite surprise.

The trim maid appeared from a hall beside the stairway. "Whiskey," said her mistress huskily. The maid pivoted neatly and disappeared.

Wharton said, "These men are trying to save Westland, Amy. They're trying to check off the possible suspects." He enunciated clearly, as though speaking to a foreigner. "They want me to tell them where I was on the night Mrs. Westland was killed."

"Tell them, m'dear." The lady edged around the table toward Williams. "Wha's your name, handsome?"

"But it won't do any good for me to tell them." Wharton was beginning to shout. "They won't believe me."

The lady paused in her pursuit of Williams. "Dearie, how I know where you were?"

Glasses tinkled as the maid set a tray on the table. The statuesque lady poured stiff jolts from a bottle of Dewar's Ne Plus Ultra into four tumblers. "That's all, Anna." She squirted soda water from a siphon into three of the tumblers and picked up the other. "Here's how." She drained the glass.

While Crane and Williams sipped their drinks, Wharton continued, "You remember well enough where I was. That was the morning I had to go down to meet Westland in the Loop. You drove me down." He was shouting at her.

The lady laughed loudly, delightedly poured herself another drink. "I do believe you're tryin' to compr'mise me, dearie."

"You remember driving me down, don't you?"

"I'm too much of a lady to remember anything." She moved closer to Williams; he retreated toward the fire. "Still, if it'll do you any good, I did drive you down that morning." She blinked at Crane, screwed up her heavily rouged face. "I remember because I thought at the time it's amusin' Larry should have an appoin'ment"—she had a hard time with that one—"appoin'ment with Westland when he'd just killed his wife."

"Who'd killed his wife?" Crane demanded. "Larry?"

This released more laughter. "Larry married! Dearie, the woman who'd marry him would have to live in a kennel."

Crane turned to Wharton. "What does it prove if she did drive you down to the Loop that day?"

"Wait. Amy, don't you remember where I spent the night of the murder?"

"No," Amy said.

She was frowning, and her eyes were looking down toward her feet, and she didn't seem quite so drunk.

"Listen, Amy," Wharton said. "I want you to tell the truth, because it will help my cousin. I wouldn't ask you if it was just myself."

Her head was thrust down so that her chin touched her breast.

"Just tell them where I spent the night." She did not move, and Wharton continued, "Or call in Anna. She knows."

The woman suddenly swung into action, as though she had touched a shock machine in a penny arcade. "I won't call an'body," she shouted. "As far as I'm concerned, you slept in the stable that night." She picked up the silver and glass siphon. "You've got a lot of nerve tryin' to ruin a respec'able woman's reputation, Lawrence Wharton. But you're not getting me to alibi you. And you can get right the hell out of here." Surprisingly, she pressed the lever of the siphon bottle and sent streams of cold hissing water over all three of them. "Get out, do you hear? Get out! You dirty dogs! Get out! Get out!"

They fled, water running off their faces onto their clothes and beneath their collars, and the Scottie under their feet. They raced through the door and across the snow to the cab. The lady pursued them as far as the porch and from this elevation hurled the siphon at them. It splintered on the cement walk. The driver said, "Jesus!" and started the cab with a jerk.

Crane, the Scottie under his arm, sank back in the seat, out of breath from running and laughter. Wharton was really disturbed. "The demned fool," he kept saying; "the demned old fool."

Doc Williams thought of the Dewar's whiskey. "The hospitality was good," he observed, "while it lasted."

CHAPTER XI

Wednesday Noon

"THE CASE is getting daffy," Crane said. He finished his second bacardi cocktail. "I keep worrying about that poor guy in jail and thinking he has only five days, four days, three days to live and I haven't room in my mind for any really constructive thoughts about the case. Can't you get a reprieve from the Governor anyway, Finklestein?"

The attorney shook his head dolefully. "I talked to the Governor when he was here Monday night. He said he couldn't do a thing unless we got hold of some real evidence."

While the waitress was serving them with cherrystone clams on the half shell, Crane told him about the morning spent with Wharton and his lady friend.

"He was trying to give himself an alibi like Jack McGurn, the Capone machine gunner, did with his gal," explained Doc Williams. "You remember the blonde alibi? But McGurn married the gal later."

"That was the gentlemanly thing to do," Crane said.

Finklestein asked, "Then it looks as though Wharton's story doesn't stand up?"

"It wouldn't in court." Crane squirted lemon over a firm clam, thrust it and part of a Vienna roll in his mouth. "But I'm inclined to believe it. If the lady had said sweetly: 'Why, yes, Larry-Warry and I spent the night with a hammer breaking the Ten Commandments,' I wouldn't have believed her, but in my opinion Amy backed up his tale like a lady by tossing us out."

"Amy?" Finklestein looked curiously at Crane. "Not Amy Dunmar, the grain king's widow?"

"I don't know who she is. She lives in a big house on Green Bay Road and has good whiskey."

"That's Amy Dunmar. She's a dipsomaniac, and she's got more money than the U.S. Mint."

Williams was startled. "What's a dipsomaniac?"

"That's just a fifty-cent way," said Crane, "of saying she takes a little nip now and then."

"He's telling us!"

Finklestein said, "That gives a little class to our investigation, but it doesn't seem to help us much. What's next?"

"How'd you come out on your checks?" Crane asked.

Finklestein gingerly tasted his eggs Benedict from a brown pottery saucer. "Woodbury's story that he danced at the Black Hawk with Miss Brentino is out." He muffled his last word with a large mouthful of the eggs.

"Out! Why?"

"The Black Hawk was taken over by a Northwestern University sorority party on that night. The manager looked up the reservations for me."

"That doesn't look so good for Woodbury." Crane hated fruit salad, but he was eating it because he was afraid of getting fat. "How about Bolston?"

"Brady says he drank with him until about twelve-thirty, and then drove him home." Finklestein shook a roll at Crane. "But that doesn't clear him. He still had plenty of time to go over and kill Mrs. Westland."

"I know it. I just wanted to see if his story would stand up."

During the rest of the meal, which consisted of a number of Scotch-and-sodas for Crane and Williams, they discussed Miss Hogan, the lady with the orange hair. The detectives plied Finklestein with questions, but the lawyer was reticent. "Can't a man have any private life at all?" he asked.

Crane said, "There's nothing private about Miss Hogan."

"She got any friends like her?" Williams asked.

"Next time I see her," Finklestein promised, "I'll ask her."

"Ask her now," Williams urged him. "Let's don't have any suspense."

Crane left them discussing the probable immorality of Miss Hogan's friends, if any, and went into a phone booth. First he dialed Westland's home.

Simmons' voice was unfriendly. "Who is it?" he demanded.

"Crane."

"I don't know any Crane."

"The detective with Mr. Finklestein."

"Yes?"

"I wanted to ask you if Miss Martin came into the apartment at all on the day of Mrs. Westland's murder."

"She didn't."

"You're sure?"

"Yes. Good-bye."

The second call was to Westland's office. A fresh feminine voice said, "Westland, Bolston and Woodbury."

"Is Mr. Woodbury there?"

"I will connect you with his secretary."

Miss Brentino's voice was even and low pitched. She said, "Hello."

"Hello, baby. What's the dope on Sprague?"

There was no answer for a moment and Crane jerked the hook angrily, thinking he had been disconnected. Then the woman's lifeless and somehow seductive voice said, "Sprague is dead."

"What!"

"He was killed at eight o'clock last night by a hit-and-run driver."

Crane suddenly felt as though the fruit salad was disagreeing with him. He opened the glass door to let fresh air into the booth.

"How'd it happen?" he asked.

"I don't know. The Lawndale police station has a report on it. All I know is that the body was left with an undertaker named Bascom on Crawford Avenue."

"We'll look into it right away." Crane wrote the name on a pad of scratch paper fastened to a ledge below the phone. "By the way, is Mr. Woodbury in?"

"Yes. Would you like to talk to him?"

"No, thanks. Good-bye."

William Crane had begun to sweat a little. He rubbed his face with a handkerchief and then felt around in his pocket for another nickel. "What the hell!" he said aloud. "What the hell!" He dialed the third number.

Warden Buckholtz answered his private phone. "Hello?"

"This is Crane. Have you a message for me?'

"You're to meet two men in Weber's smoke shop on the corner of Randolph and Wells at three o'clock. They're friends of Connors, and they'll introduce themselves to you. Three o'clock."

"Thanks a lot, Warden."

"What progress are you making?"

"Not so good."

"You better hurry—you haven't got much time."

"Don't I know it!"

Crane returned to the table and told the others about Sprague.

Finklestein said finally, "It looks as though somebody knocked him off. I can't see any other answer."

"It's goddam funny," Williams said. "Particularly as a couple of torpedoes tried to knock us off at about the same time."

Crane had to tell Finklestein how the men in the car shot at them near the Detective Bureau. His narrative of their close escape moved him so much he ordered a double Scotch-and-soda from the waitress. Williams had the same.

The attorney was upset. "But they can't do that. First it was Grant, and then they tried for you, and now Sprague. They're bound to run into trouble."

Crane drank half his liquor at a gulp. He began to feel very slightly better. He asked, "Why did they pick this time to kill Sprague?"

"They knew he was going to spill something to us this morning," Williams said.

"How did they know that?"

Finklestein wrinkled his forehead. "By God! It does look as though somebody in our group had been talking."

"The only other person who could overhear what we say," Crane said, "is the warden." He drank the rest of his whiskey and ordered another. "But I don't think he'd take the chance of talking about our meetings. He'd be afraid of getting himself in a jam."

"Well, what are you going to do about Sprague?"

"Doc and I will go out there. You see if you can find out where everybody was between seven and nine last night." Crane accepted the whiskey from the waitress. "You might have some-body try and trace Sprague's movements. Find out what time he left the office and if he did anything unusual during the day."

"All right." Finklestein took the bill. "When will I see you again?"

"I don't know." Crane tilted the whiskey glass and ran his tongue around the edge and added mysteriously, "Maybe never."

First they went to the Bascom Mortuary at 605 South Crawford Avenue and talked to an undertaker with licorice liver patches under his eyes.

"I can assure you the deceased died from injuries sustained when he was struck by the automobile," the undertaker repeat-ed. "If you would like to examine the body, I will——"

"Never mind," Crane said. "We had an idea Mr. Sprague might have been murdered, but if you're sure he wasn't shot or stabbed, we'll take your word for it."

The undertaker was aggrieved. "I prepared the body per-sonally." He was standing under a palm tree which looked as though he had embalmed it, too.

"O. K." Crane started to put on his hat, thought better of it. "You're going to give him a nice funeral?"

"Yes, sir!" The undertaker pointed at a sign hanging on the mahogany paneled wall beside a small and even unhealthier palm. "One of our Bascom Wonder Funerals."

This sign disclosed that a Wonder Funeral, including a handsome Lincoln hearse, three automobile loads of mourners (we can augment your own mourners if you desire), the use of our private chapel with the $8000 Barton organ and the Golden Isle Quartette, could be provided for as little as $217. There was also a choice of five distinctive caskets.

"That's mighty fine," said Crane heartily. "I wouldn't ask for a better funeral for my friend here."

"If you like," said the undertaker tentatively, "we have a plan . . ."

"When I croak," said Williams, "it won't be in Chicago."

The undertaker followed them to the door. "That's all right. You can wire funerals anywhere in the United States now."

"My God!" said Crane. "Next you'll be able to have a baby by telegraph."

The district police station was a weather-scarred brick building. They walked up the rickety stairs to the complaint room and asked the desk sergeant if they could see the accident report on the Sprague death. He tossed a heavy report book at them, and they finally found the place, but it wasn't much good. Amos Sprague, sixty-seven years old, 4221 Harrison Street, a clerk, had been fatally injured by a hit-and-run driver as he was getting off a Madison Street surface car at Crawford Avenue. The body had been taken to Bascom's. The report was signed, "Wallen."

Williams was about to ask the desk sergeant where they could find Wallen when the door to the captain's office opened and Deputy Strom and another policeman came out.

"You mugs again." The deputy did not appear glad to see them. "I was askin' the captain here if you'd been out yet."

"We just heard about it," said Williams. "What happened?"

"The captain knows all about it." Deputy Strom turned and led them back into the office. "Captain O'Grady, this is Doc Williams, who used to be with the state's attorney's office, and Mr.—er——"

"Crane."

"Glad to know you." Captain O'Grady was a handsome old Irishman with craggy eyebrows and a straight back under his blue uniform with the gold braid. "Is it all right to give them what we have?"

"Sure," said the deputy. "Tell 'em everything."

"Well, it's nothing to mention, anyway." Captain O'Grady indicated seats for them, sat down behind his desk. "This Sprague was gettin' off a Madison streetcar about eight o'clock last night at Crawford. He was just nearin' the curb when a big sedan hit him. The conductor, Zimmerman——"

Deputy Strom said, "A good Ulsteman."

"Zimmerman," repeated Captain O'Grady, "stopped the street car and jumped out, but one of the two men in the sedan is already kneelin' beside Sprague, feeling of his body. 'He's dead,' says this man to Zimmerman, gettin' up. Zimmerman asks him his name, and the man says, 'To hell with you,' and he climbs in his automobile and is off before a soul can stop him."

Crane asked, "Did anybody get the license number?"

"That's a very funny thing. It appears the car had no license at all."

Deputy Strom's alert eyes contrasted with the impassivity of his heavy face. "It was dark, and the conductor and the passengers might not have been able to see the license plates."

Crane asked, "Then you think it's an accident?"

"I don't know." The deputy rubbed his chin. "I would have if you two hadn't got me worked up with your wild tales last night."

"About as worked up," said Mr. Williams, "as Rockefeller when he finds a new dime in his pants."

"Maybe I didn't take much stock in your story then, but even a copper changes his mind. Of course, we have hit-and-run cases every day, but the drivers don't usually stop at all. It looks queer. This Sprague was one of those people you had us look up, wasn't he?"

William Crane nodded his head.

"How was he involved with Westland?"

Crane told him of the old clerk's promise to supply a motive for the murder of Mrs. Westland and how they had wondered where he was during the morning's meeting.

"Does old Buckholtz let all of you meet Westland every day?" asked the deputy.

"Naw," Williams lied. "He just lets his attorney, Finklestein, see him. We wait outside."

Crane spoke to Captain O'Grady. "Don't you think the man in the sedan might have been looking to see if Sprague had any papers on him after he had made sure he was dead?"

"He could have been, all right. At least, there was none at all found on the man."

The deputy drummed on the table with staccato fingers. "What d'you think Sprague had?"

"I wish I knew," Crane replied. "If he was murdered, it must have been something good."

"This is about as dizzy a case as I ever seen," said Deputy

Strom. "Why didn't Sprague come to us a long time ago if he knew something? Why did he wait until a couple of days before Westland goes to the chair? And Grant. How does he fit in the picture? What's a cheap crook doin' with a lot of society people? It don't make any sense to me."

Crane walked to the wall and examined a picture of the veterans of the Haymarket Riot, taken in 1893. The men looked strange with their handle-bar mustaches and long blue coats and rigid helmets with the gold numbers on the front. "The only way I can figure it out," he said, "is that Grant was afraid to come to the police during the trial for fear they'd send him up for being in Mrs. Westland's building on the night of the murder. Maybe he did a job in the neighborhood that night. Anyway, he must have seen Westland leave the apartment and say good-night to his wife, and so he could be sure Westland wasn't the murderer. And when he saw that Westland had been convicted, he decided to take a chance with the police and give his evidence."

Deputy Strom shook his head, said, "As for Sprague . . . ?"

"As for Sprague, he probably thought Westland was guilty until he was called into our conference by Finklestein. The first question the lawyer asked everybody was: 'Who could have had a motive for putting Westland out of the way?' Sprague, thinking this over, suddenly remembered something that hadn't meant anything to him before. So he investigated and stepped on the murderer's toes, and got himself knocked off."

The deputy said, "All this is so if you believe Westland didn't kill his wife but was framed."

"I have to believe that because I'm working for Westland."

"I think you are on the right track, my boy," said Captain

O'Grady. "Of course I'm not for being the great detective the deputy is."

Deputy Strom was pleased. "Now, none of your blarney, Captain. I'm just a flatfoot that's lucky." He rested a hand on Williams' shoulder. "I still don't see any reason to change my opinion of Westland's guilt, but I'd hate to see an innocent man go to the chair. Is there anything I can do to help Crane or you, Doc?"

Crane said, "Finklestein is checking on where everybody was at the time Sprague was killed." He rubbed the back of his neck. "And he's going to try to trace Sprague's movements that day, but that will be tough for him. I wonder if you would have somebody try."

"Sure. I'll assign a couple of men."

"And there's one other thing." Crane looked dubiously at the deputy. "Woodbury—that's Westland's partner—has a Webley automatic just like the one Westland had. They served in the British Air Corps together. I'd like to have Major Lee, the ballistics expert, look it over. He's still got the reports on the bullet that killed Mrs. Westland, hasn't he?"

"He keeps all those reports. But I don't know how I'm going to get the pistol from Woodbury. I'd need a warrant to get into his apartment. Still, Doc Williams and I have done worse things than steal a pistol. What do you want to know about it—whether it was used to kill Mrs. Westland?"

"That and also whether it could possibly be Westland's pistol. His had a name plate on it, and Major Lee could check to see if one had been removed or tampered with."

"O. K.," said the deputy. "But I'll leave the pistol with Lee in your name. I don't want to be officially connected with this thing."

"That'll be fine. I'll get in touch with Lee tonight, and I'll let you know what he finds out."

"You will if I can get that pistol," said Deputy Strom.

"Don't worry, boss," said the man whose name was Butch. "We can handle 'em." He was a compact dark man with a nose which had been broken and badly set. His left eye was flecked with white spots; a jagged scar halved his forehead.

Crane, Williams, Butch, and another man, called Little Joe, rode west on Madison Street in a black Lincoln touring car with side curtains. Little Joe was a stocky man with a wiry clump of reddish hair on his head, some of which clung to his neck below his gray cap. He drove the touring car with a casual disregard of the force of gravity, the traffic laws, and other motorists.

Crane said, "They may not be tough, anyway."

"Listen, boss," Butch said, "they don't come any tougher than us." He was not boasting, simply stating a fact. "We wouldn't be runnin' the Teamsters' Union if they did. Ain't that so, Joe?"

"Yeah," Joe said.

Butch looked forbiddingly at Crane. "Connors musta told you about us."

"You bet he did." Wind whipped the side curtains against the body of the car and whistled across the back seat. Crane shuddered, pulled his collar around his ears. "He said you boys could muscle your way into heaven and come out with a truck-load of harps."

This was a lie, but it satisfied Butch.

"Connors would have been all right," he said, "if he could of left the coppers alone. It's O. K. to knock off a hood or so, but you oughta be careful about shootin' coppers. It makes the judge mad, and sometimes he won't let ya fix the case."

They rounded the corner of Halstead Street with a scream of rubber on bricks and smashed into the rear end of a shiny sedan just pulling out of a parking place. A large man climbed ponderously out of the sedan and stalked toward Little Joe, who was already out and examining the damage. The man's face was red, and he said:

"Why don't you watch where you're going?"

Little Joe tested the front bumper on the Lincoln with his foot, nodded with satisfaction, and started back to the front seat.

"Wait a minute, buddy," said the man. "Wait a minute. You can't get away like that." He pulled at Little Joe's shoulder.

Little Joe swung around and faced the man, balancing on his toes. His arms looked oddly long for his blunt body. "You tryin' to make somethin' out of this, mister?" he demanded.

The crimson bluster seeped from the man's face, leaving it wan and frightened. He stepped back two steps, started to say something, and then didn't. His arms bent at the elbows in front of him as though he wanted to push Little Joe away from him.

"You're lucky I'm in a hurry," said the gangster, "or I'd paste your pan for you." He climbed in the touring car, shoved in the gear, and drove off, leaving the big man standing on the brick pavement beside his damaged car.

"One of those smart guys," observed Butch.

Little Joe said regretfully, "I would of socked him, only there was a cop on the corner."

They pulled up smoothly in front of Petro's restaurant on Halstead Street, and all four of them went inside. Two Italians were drinking at the bar, each with a foot on the brass rail, and the small baldheaded bartender was drawing a stein of beer from a brass spigot. Butch paused at the door, snapping the lock so that it would fasten when the door was closed. The bartender leveled the foam on the stein with a discolored ruler, looked at them in surprise.

Little Joe addressed the two Italian customers. "Would you guys like to go home on foot or in a hearse?" he demanded.

Their soft brown eyes fearful, the men circled Little Joe, circled Butch, and passed silently through the door. Butch shut it firmly behind them.

"Wassa matter?" demanded the bartender. "What you fellas tryin' to do?"

"Where's Petro?" Crane asked.

The bartender was still holding the stein in one hand and the ruler in the other. The foam on the beer had disappeared. "Wassa matter?" he repeated. "Wassa matter you fellas?"

Butch walked around a slot machine on a tall table with twisted metal legs and reached over the bar and seized the bartender by the collar. He knocked the stein out of his hand and jerked him over the bar. The bartender's feet hit the steins left by the two Italians, sending them crashing to the floor. The spilled beer made wet ovals on the wood.

Through the chintz-hung door to the dining room came the young waiter who had served them on Monday. His dark eyes were incredulous and angry. He shouted, "Where do you guys think you're at?" His face was somber from dirt and a two-day beard.

Little Joe moved toward him. "Hello, Dago," he said.

"Wait a minute." Williams stepped in front of the squat gangster. "Choir-boy is mine."

He hit the waiter tentatively with his left hand, then let him have the right in a wide swing just below the jawbone on the neck. Knees buckling, the waiter backed against the table with the metal legs, slid down it like an actor in a slow motion picture. The slot machine, slipping off the tilted pine top, landed on his shoulder; then glanced to the floor, spewing coins over the cracked boards. Presently the waiter toppled onto a pile of nickels and lay there, glaring balefully at Williams.

Crane watched, fascinated, until Butch said, "Here's another."

It was Joe Petro. He was wearing slippers, trousers without a belt, and a purple shirt, and his fat body filled the doorway. His shirt was open at the collar like an author waiting to be photographed after he has sold his first novel, only the Italian had on stained flannel underwear over his chest. His face was expressionless. He held the chintz curtain back with his left hand.

"Stick 'em up," said Little Joe; "we wanna speak to you." He had a short-barreled .38 in his hand.

Crane stepped to the side so that the pistol would not shoot him if it went off. "You remember me?" he asked Petro.

The Italian shook his head.

"Choir-boy remembers me," Williams said, looking at the waiter; "don't you, choir-boy?"

Gleaming black eyes defied them from the pile of nickels.

Butch pulled the bartender nearer to him. "You better lie down too," he said. He twisted his wrist, sent the old man in a spinning fall to the floor.

"We won't hurt you if you tell us the truth, Petro," Crane said. "We want to know why you and your men tried to kill us last night by the Bureau."

"Yeah, tell us," said Little Joe.

Petro's fat face was the color of tallow. "You crazy," he said. "I don' know you."

"Should I sock him, boss?" asked Butch.

Crane said, "Not yet." He scowled at the big Italian. "I know you shot at us, but I want to know why."

Petro's mouth moved convulsively. "You sonabitch, get out o' here." The voice emerging from the thick neck was ludicrously shrill. "You don' pull thisa stuff on Joe Petro."

"Hit him," Crane said.

Butch hit him.

Little Joe said, "Don't lower them hands, Dago, or I'll plug you."

"Now, do you want to tell us?" Crane asked.

Hate simmered in the pouchy eyes.

Crane said, "Hit him again."

Butch put his shoulders into this one. There was a dull impact, as when an automobile hits a horse, and the Italian overbalanced, tottered back to the wall. He leaned there, blinking at them stupidly. Butch watched him incredulously. "Christ I" he said. "I must be losin' my punch." He stepped closer and drove Petro to the floor with a downward hammer-like blow of his fist.

There was a slithering sound on the nickels, and Crane turned just in time to see Williams' foot lash out at the waiter's right arm. A stiletto described a graceful arc in the air, hit the wall by the front door, and clattered to the floor. The waiter yelped with pain and clutched his wrist.

"Choir-boy wants to get shot," said Little Joe.

While they were waiting for Petro to regain consciousness, Williams drew four steins of beer and handed one to each of the others. The beer was cold, and it tasted fine. Butch drained his stein in a breath, filled it again at the tap, and then went over to Petro, saying, "I hate like hell to waste this stuff." He poured the beer over the Italian's head.

It was already dusk, and Crane turned on the electric lights. The big Italian groaned, tried to get up. Williams, lighting a cigarette, watched him interestedly. "Think he'll talk now?" he asked. He inhaled luxuriously, blew the smoke out his nose and mouth at the same time.

The old bartender was still lying where Butch had thrown him, his head buried in his arms. He was pretending that he was dead.

After the rumble of a streetcar passing outside had faded away, Crane tried again. "You might as well tell us now, Petro, because we're going to stay here until you get ready to talk."

Breathing as laboriously as a man with pneumonia, the Italian leaned one elbow on the floor and tried to ward off Crane with the other arm. Blood trickled from his mouth, and his eyes were wild. He wouldn't speak, though.

Crane, bending over him, asked the others, "What the hell are we going to do?"

"I can make choir-boy talk." Williams had retrieved the stiletto, was balancing it on his index finger. "Can't I, choir-boy?"

The waiter hissed at him through his teeth.

"No," William Crane said. "I want to get the story from Petro."

Little Joe had moved to the dining-room doorway and was looking in toward the kitchen. "Maybe the Dago's got a daughter back there," he said. "If I gave her a little . . . "

Butch interrupted him. "These spaghetti broads is poison." He reached down over the bar and pulled out a quart bottle of bourbon and a chromium-plated lemon squeezer. "I got a better idea, even if it ain't so much fun." He pulled the cork from the bottle with his teeth, spat it on the floor, and drank noisily.

Crane asked, "What's the idea?"

Butch wiped his mouth with his coat sleeve, handed the quarter empty bottle to Little Joe. "You grab the Dago's left arm," he ordered Crane.

Petro's flesh, under the purple silk shirt, was astonishingly firm, and Crane took hold of the arm with both hands. Butch, kneeling on the other side, produced a mass of brown cord from a coat pocket and unwrapped part of it around the Italian's right wrist and tied it securely to a radiator pipe. "That'll hold the bastard," he announced.

Another streetcar rolled by on Halstead Street, shook the room.

Little Joe grinned down at them, holding the .38 in one hand, the bottle, now half empty, in the other. "Goin' to show him the goldfish?"

Butch picked up the chromium squeezer. It had two long handles which gave leverage to crush the lemons. "I'll show him some goldfish he never seen before." He fitted the squeezer over the hand Crane was holding.

Petro's small eyes asked a terrified question of each one of them, and his breath made a rattling noise in his throat.

The center of the squeezer fitted nicely in the soft palm of the Italian's hand. "That's tender, ain't it, Dago?" Butch inquired. He pressed the ends of the squeezer toward each other.

Petro's hoarse screaming was loud in their ears.

As Butch eased the pressure, Crane asked, "It was you and your men who shot at us, wasn't it?"

A fever sweat had broken out on the Italian's face. He ran his tongue around his blubbery lips, looked appealingly at Crane. Butch tightened the lemon squeezer, and he said quickly, "Yeah, we shot at you."

"That's better." Crane nodded his head. "Now, why did you try to plug us?"

Petro's quivering lips mumbled the name, "Grant."

"You thought we had him put on the spot, didn't you?"

Petro nodded.

With eyes as dark as ripe olives in the dim electric light, the waiter and the bartender watched them silently from the floor. Little Joe, bored, was polishing off the rest of the whiskey.

"We didn't," Crane said. "Somebody got to him before we could find out what he knew about the Westland case. You don't think we would kill somebody we wanted to get some information from, do you?"

The Italian, still sweating, didn't answer.

Crane continued, "We want to find out what he knew about Westland."

Butch thought this would be a good point to apply pressure on the lemon squeezer. Petro moaned, "Jesus Cristo!" fell back against the radiator in a faint.

Little Joe waggled the bottle admonishingly at his companion. "You hadn't ought to have done that," he said; "just when he was going to spill his guts." He poured the remains of the whiskey on Petro's face.

Butch indignantly demanded, "How'd I know the Dago was delicate?"

A clock, striking somewhere in the back, sent five silver bullets of sound into the room. Petro struggled to a sitting position again, the blood pumping back into his face, his eyes, no longer urgently afraid, were calm with an acceptance of fate. "You will let me pray before you kill me?" he asked.

Crane said, "First tell us what Grant knew about the Westland case."

Petro's voice was barely audible. "He never tell me."

"Can that stuff," said Butch. "He musta told you. Come clean or I'll really squeeze ya with this thing."

Petro shook his head.

"Wait a minute I" The waiter sat up on the floor. "I tell. Don't hurt him again. Mannie Grant seen Mister Westland say good-night on the night of the murder—his wife, she was still alive then."

"Atta kid, choir-boy," said Doc Williams.

"Fine," Crane said. "Now tell us who the slick fellow was you had shadowing us in the hotel."

The waiter's eyes avoided Joe Petro. "That was the Chevalier."

"That torpedo!" Little Joe whistled. "What's he doing with a bunch of amacheurs like you, choir-boy?"

The waiter said defensively, "He eats here a lot."

"And he was just doin' you a good turn." Little Joe's face was villainous. "Listen! You tell the Chevalier the next time he wants to play Boy Scout to lay off white people. He better stick to spiggoties because if he don't, he'll find himself with a one-way ticket in his pocket some day soon."

Butch, kneeling on the floor by Petro, asked Crane: "Anything more, boss?"

Looking at Petro's pain-racked face made Crane feel ill. "No, let him go."

Butch attempted to twist the squeezer from the Italian's hand, then looked at it with surprise. "Christ!" he said, "the damn thing's stuck to a bone."

Crane got up quickly, made for the door. "Let them send

for a doctor," he called over his shoulder, stepping out into the street.

Firm-fleshed rays from an arc light ribboned the darkness. Williams and Butch joined him. The wind was like a damp towel on their faces.

Behind them, Little Joe paused in the lighted doorway, addressed the silent saloon.

"You wops better behave," he said, "or next time we come back we'll get a little unpleasant."

CHAPTER XII

Wednesday Night

"No MA'AM," said William Crane, "there's nothing wrong in this room."

He was lying on the hotel room bed, the telephone resting on his chest. It was dinner time, and it was quite dark outside and not noisy. Puffs of sharp cold air came through the quarter-open window. It was good to lie on a bed.

Crane spoke plaintively into the telephone. "I just want to speak to police headquarters. Do you mind very much if I speak to police headquarters?"

Shoulders hunched in amusement, Williams watched him from the embrace of an overstuffed chair. Poised in his hand was a glass of bourbon whiskey liberally laced with New Orleans absinthe.

"I don't want to speak to the manager," Crane said. "I don't want to speak to the house detective. There is nothing wrong in this room. I just want to speak to police headquarters."

The hotel operator, defeated, made angry clicking noises in the ear piece. At last another woman said, "Police Headquarters," and Crane said, "Deputy Strom."

After a series of men with sullen voices had answered on various extensions, the deputy was located. Crane asked him if he had any news.

"I got the pistol for you and left it with Major Lee." The deputy's voice came in a bull-like roar, as though he was talking on the transatlantic phone. "He'll have a report for you after supper. I'm counting on you two to let me know what you find out from him."

"We'll call you," Crane said. "How about Sprague?"

"Nothing much out of the way about him. He came to the office at the usual time yesterday, worked until six and then left."

"How'd he happen to work so late?"

"They said at the office he worked that late, or later, a couple of times a week."

"Where did he go after he left the office?" Crane asked.

"We aren't sure, but we think he called on Simmons, the butler for Westland."

"The hell you say!"

"Yeah. One of the stenographers in the office heard him call Simmons and ask him if he was going to be in about six-thirty."

"Did you ask Simmons if the old man had called on him?"

"I sent a couple of men around to talk to him, but he said he didn't see Sprague at all. He admitted he had received a telephone call from him, just as the girl told us, but he said Sprague didn't show up."

A woman and a man, talking loudly, passed by the door. Their voices came in through the transom. The woman's tone was shrill. "I don't see why I have to put up with him treating me like I was a common floosie . . . or his wife," she said querulously.

Crane grinned at Doc Williams, spoke into the mouthpiece: "Did you see if Simmons had a record?"

The deputy's voice was aggrieved. "Do you think I'm a correspondence-school dick? I did, and he ain't got any."

"What are you going to do?"

"Nothing. You can't arrest a guy because he was supposed to have talked with a fellow who was later killed by a hit-and-run driver, can you?"

"No, I guess not."

"You talk to Simmons. Maybe you can get something out of him." The deputy's voice was losing some of its power. "You can call me about him and the gun later. I'll be here at the Bureau until midnight."

"O. K." Crane hung up the receiver softly, then, after a few seconds, raised it to his ear. There was a sound such as you hear in a sea shell against your ear and then a click. "That goddam operator," he said.

"Forget her," Williams said. "They always listen in when they think you don't want them to. What's this about Simmons?"

Crane told him, then took a mouthful of the bourbon and absinthe. It tasted sweet at first, but after he had swished it against his gums, the flavor changed to anis. He swallowed slowly and exhaled through his nose at the same time, sending the sharp fumes through his sinus into his forehead.

Williams watched him. "You better be careful or that stuff will set you on your ear."

"I want to be set on my ear."

"What are you going to do about Simmons?"

Crane filled his water tumbler one quarter full of absinthe. Then he put in an equal amount of whiskey. The resulting mixture was decadently green. He sipped it experimentally, added a piece of ice. "Which do you think is better," he asked, "bourbon laced with absinthe, or absinthe laced with bourbon?"

"Listen, are you going to give up on this case?"

Crane drank again, letting the ice tickle his nose. "Green is more artistic, but brown is masculine." He found he had trouble focusing his eyes on Williams. "Give up? Give up?" He stood up, put one hand between the buttons of his shirt in a Napoleonic attitude. "The sun never sets on William Crane."

Doc Williams regretfully poured the rest of the bourbon and the absinthe into the bathtub. "You'll feel better when you get something to eat," he shouted over the noise of running water.

Crane pushed back the cab door, said to the driver, "You can wait. We're going on north in a minute."

He and Williams got in the green automatic elevator, and he pushed the button for the eighth floor.

"I never rode in so many taxis in my life," Williams complained. "All we do is ride in taxis. It makes me seasick to think of them. How far north are we going?"

Crane said, "You'll find out." He shoved open the eighth-floor door and rang the bell to Westland's apartment. He was still pretty drunk, but he had everything under control.

Simmons opened the door until the safety chain was taut. "Oh, it's you," he said. He did not undo the chain.

"Yeah, it's us," Williams agreed.

Simmons was wearing a white silk shirt, a pair of black trousers pulled snug at the waist by a broad belt, and patent leather slippers. The bright bulb in the hall made angular his brittle jaw and protruding cheek bones, but his eyes were shadowed. "What do you want?" he demanded. He looked, with the queer shadow and light on his thin face and the silk shirt and the broad belt snug at the waist, like a good Spanish painting of a bull fighter.

"We'd like to ask you a few more questions," Crane said.

Simmons' voice was harsh. "What about?"

From the void behind him came the sound of a big jazz band playing the Limehouse Blues, sweet and slow and heavily accented, as the piece should be played. Simmons turned, called over his shoulder, "Wait until I fix the radio," and disappeared.

Williams said, "What the hell's the matter with that guy? Why don't he ask us in?"

"I don't know," Crane said. "Maybe he thinks we're after the silver."

Simmons came back and peered out at them through the crack in the door. "Well?"

Leaning one hand against the door jamb, Crane asked, "What did Sprague ask you when he visited you here last night?"

"I didn't say he visited me last night." Simmons blinked his eyes. "We talked over the——"

"I know you talked over the phone, but I also know he came out here and saw you."

"Oh!" The momentary slackness of indecision on Simmons' face betrayed him. He felt it himself. "Out here . . . ?"

"Yes, out here." Crane was angry. "I want to know what you didn't tell the police."

The servant in Simmons made his voice humble. "I didn't tell the police Mr. Sprague was out here because I didn't know if Mr. Finklestein would want me to. I'm sorry if I've done wrong."

"That's all right. Suppose you tell us what happened."

Inside there was a tinkling noise as though a butter knife had struck a glass half filled with liquid.

Simmons spoke hurriedly, loudly. "Mr. Sprague telephoned me and said he was coming out to see me. He seemed very excited when he got here, and I must say very strange. He had me lock the door after I let him in, and before he said a word he went to the window and looked down at the street."

"Why did he do that?"

"He didn't say, but I had an idea he was afraid someone was following him." Simmons was speaking less guardedly, and his whole face was in the light now. "He pulled the curtains shut and came over to me and said: 'Simmons, I believe I know who killed Mrs. Westland.'"

Simmons was making the most of his dramatic opportunity, and he hissed, "Mrs. Westland," through his teeth like the villain in East Lynne.

"'I believe I know who killed Mrs. Westland,'" he repeated. "He used just those words, but when I asked him who he only shook his head and said, 'I have to make sure first.' Then he asked me some questions about Mr. Westland's gun."

They paused while the automatic elevator went by the floor. In the circular glass panel of the door, as it passed, were framed fleetingly a pretty girl's bored face, heavily painted, and the white silk scarf and black overcoat of a man in evening clothes.

When the rumble had ceased, Crane asked, "What did he want to know?"

"He asked me when the gun was taken, and I told him on the evening of the murder because I had seen it when I was cleaning that afternoon. Then he inquired as to who had been in the apartment that evening, and I told him about Woodbury."

"Did he seem pleased about that?"

"He just nodded his head. He said it didn't matter, anyway."

"Didn't matter?"

"That's what he said—it didn't matter."

"The hell!" Crane rubbed his ear. "What else did he want to know?"

"That's all."

William Crane echoed him. "That's all!" He turned indignantly toward Williams. "Sprague comes up here, asks about the gun, finds that Woodbury might have taken it, then says it doesn't matter anyway and goes home. What kind of sense does that make?"

Williams said, "Maybe our little friend here ain't tellin' all he knows."

"I swear, gentlemen, I've told you everything Mr. Sprague said. I thought it was queer myself."

Crane watched the man's eyes. "He didn't leave any papers for you to keep?"

"No, sir."

"Have you ever been in jail, Simmons?"

"Jail!" Simmons' eyes glittered venomously behind his bleached skin. "Who says I been in jail?"

"Nobody. I just asked you."

Simmons' face was completely in the shadow now. "Well, I'll just answer you. I've never been in jail—" he closed the door until the chain hung in a deep loop—"if it's any business of yours. Good-night."

Crane and Williams stared in slow astonishment at the closed door. "Got kinda tough, didn't he?" Williams observed.

Punching the button for the elevator, Crane said, "We wouldn't have learned anything more from him anyway." He jerked open the green door and added, "Not that we learned anything in the first place."

They walked out of the building in silence and climbed in the taxi. The driver slammed the door, asked, "Where to?"

"We want to go to 5123 Sheridan Road," Crane replied, "but we'll stop at a saloon on the way out there."

His arm linked with the leather strap, Williams inquired, "Isn't that where Miss Martin lives?"

"The saloon?"

"No, you dummy, that number on Sheridan Road."

"Any saloon do?" asked the driver.

Crane answered them both. "Yes."

In the saloon, after an old-fashioned, Crane telephoned Major Lee at the Crime Detection Laboratory, learned he would be back about ten o'clock. On the glass shelf back of the bar, between a fat bottle of benedictine and a thin one of Goldwasser, stood a clock. He tried to make out the time, leaning over the bar. His eyes didn't seem to focus very well, and he shook his head.

Williams said, "If you're trying to see that clock, it's nine-five."

"The hell it is! That means we only got time for two more drinks."

When they went back to the taxi, Crane blew his breath in puffs from his mouth, interestedly watched the silver mist form in the cold air. He stopped and tried to blow a circle, but he couldn't. "That's a point for the cigarette manufacturers," he announced. "You gotta have smoke on your breath to blow rings." As Williams shoved him into the cab, he asked petulantly, "Why hasn't the American public been informed of this fact? Is this a conspiracy of silence?"

Smoothly the driver started the cab and began to drive north over level pavements. The window by his left arm was open a few inches, and air from the outside freshened the warm air in the cab. Crane leaned back on the leather cushions, closed his eyes, breathed heavily, and presently fell asleep.

When they reached the Sheridan Road address, Williams shook him violently. "You're the damndest detective I ever heard of," he said. "The good ones sit up with hot coffee every night for about a week to solve a case, while you sleep every chance you get."

Crane was indignant. "Who's been asleep?" He climbed out of the cab, told the driver to wait, and briskly and somewhat unevenly entered the imitation marble lobby of the three-apartment building. A buzzer sounded on the inner door in response to his pressure on a black button opposite the name Albert Prudence. He held the door open for Williams, then followed his feet up three flights of green-carpeted stairs.

Mr. Prudence did not resemble his pretty niece. He was an old man with hair like absorbent cotton and a high-bridged nose. He had on a green smoking jacket and slippers trimmed with rabbit fur, and his shoulders were bent. Williams explained who they were.

"Come in, come in." Mr. Prudence's voice was high and frail and impatient, as though he might be deaf. "Miss Martin is home."

They made their way through a hall into a large living room with three windows. A lazy wood fire burned in a circular fireplace; subdued hooked rugs islanded the maple floor; a pair of very old pewter candlesticks, faint traces of copper showing through the powdered silver surface, were reflected in a mirror on the mantel.

"Mama, here are some men to see Emily Lou," Mr. Prudence said.

Mrs. Prudence was a big-bosomed woman with haughty eyes and hair more black than gray. She hoisted herself out of a deep chair with projecting wings and advanced toward them, a mechanically pleasant expression stamped on her face.

Her husband continued, "They're detectives for Mr. Westland."

Indecision erased the mechanical pleasure from the woman's face. Did you treat detectives as you would servants, or were they a shade better? She halted, obviously decided to take no chances. "I'll call Miss Martin," she said, "if you will be good enough to wait." Her voice was the patronizing voice one used for servants. She walked around a small spinning wheel and disappeared down the hall.

Mr. Prudence fidgeted. "Pretty cold outside," he stated.

"You bet," said Williams. "Pretty cold."

They looked at the room. Crane saw that it was Early American and wondered if the spindly chairs were antiques. He admired the lustrous ruby hue of four goblets, one cracked, and a pitcher on the thin shelves of a small cabinet built in the eight-foot paneled wall.

"Hello." Emily Lou advanced from the hall. Her skin was delicate and rosy, her hair darkly red in the firelight. "What are you two doing here?"

Crane made a valiant effort to hold himself steady, shook her hand, and said, "Just checking on that telephone call angle."

"The telephone call . . . ?"

"Yes, the one that sounded as if it came from you."

Mrs. Prudence, hovering behind Emily Lou, laughed contemptuously. "I never believed in that telephone call. Why should Mr. Westland say at first that my niece called him and then change his story and say it was someone whose voice sounded like hers?"

"I don't know," said William Crane. "Why?"

"Because he made the story up, and then had to get out of it when he saw Emily Lou wouldn't support it by lying."

"Now, Auntie Mae." Emily Lou's voice was angry. "We've had all this out before. The story of the telephone call didn't help Robbie's case anyway, so he wouldn't have any reason for making it up."

Mrs. Prudence snorted like a sea lion. "Reason or no reason——"

"Mama," her husband interrupted her, "these men want to find out something."

Crane looked at the fire with distrust. The heat was making him feel giddy. "It's this way, ma'am," he said. "If the telephone call was made, the person who made it must have known where Miss Martin was at the time. He, or she, couldn't have taken the chance that Miss Martin was with Westland at the time, or out of town, or something. Therefore they must have had some way of knowing where she was."

"She was right here with us," said Mrs. Prudence. "Anybody could have seen her come in."

"Yes, but whoever called had to be sure that Westland wouldn't call back. Once he had reached Miss Martin the plot would have been spoiled."

"Plot!" exclaimed Mrs. Prudence with fine contempt.

Mrs. Prudence's clear blue eyes were circles of wonder. "You mean the telephone here must have been tapped?"

"That would be the only way you could intercept Westland's return call, if he made one."

Mrs. Prudence said triumphantly, "But he never said he made one."

Under her disapproving eye Crane wrestled stubbornly with his overcoat, finally got it off. "That doesn't make any difference. They had to be prepared for it whether he made it or not."

Emily Lou Martin's figure was petite and nicely rounded, and she filled her apple-green dress with seductive curves. She said, "But how could anybody tap our line?"

"That's what we want to see. Would you mind if Mr. Williams looked at your telephone connections? He's an expert on wire tapping."

Williams looked mildly surprised, said, "I wouldn't—"

Crane held up his hand. "Now don't be modest." He bowed politely to Mrs. Prudence, nearly fell on his head. "If we could see the telephone . . . ?"

The telephone was in the hall they had come through and was within easy hearing distance of the living room. Williams examined it gingerly. It was like all the telephones he had ever seen, but he said, "Hmm." The others watched him interestedly.

"Somebody couldn't have come in here while you were in the back of the apartment and used the phone?" Crane asked.

Mrs. Prudence said, "There's a safety catch on the door and besides—" she snorted nastily—"we were in the living room at the time Mr. Westland said the call was made."

"I wasn't," Emily Lou said. "I was in my room."

"Maybe somebody could see her there," Crane suggested, "and in that way could tell she was in. You'd need two parties, one to tap the phone and one to see if she was in."

Mr. Prudence injected himself mildly into the conversation. "Couldn't the person have already tapped the phone and then watched from some vantage point?" He looked appealingly at his wife. "She could have made the call as soon as she saw Emily Lou was in her bedroom."

"That's a strong possibility," Crane declared. "A strong possibility, Mr. Prudence." He spoke heartily in an effort to dispel a feeling of faintness. "We'd better take a look out Miss Martin's bedroom windows. Perhaps we can spot the point from where she was observed."

Mrs. Prudence said, "Hrrmp!" She took her husband's arm, led him into the living room. "We'll let Emily Lou show the men her bedroom." Her tone implied Emily Lou had invented a new kind of immorality.

The bedroom was very feminine. Silver-backed toilet articles, a huge powder box with a rose-colored puff, oddly shaped perfume bottles, covered a low boudoir table facing a tall mirror. An open closet door was armored on the inside with shoes in individual pockets, and in back of them were rows of dresses. The wall paper was flowered to match the window curtains, and there was a mingled smell of perfume and pine crystals.

Crane opened the window and took a deep breath of the cold dry air. He felt better at once. Miss Martin, standing beside him, smelled faintly and pleasantly of lilies of the valley. The window looked into the court of a large apartment hotel built of yellow bricks. It would be possible from about fifty windows to look into Miss Martin's room. In one of the nearer windows an athletic man in green silk shorts was taking setting up exercises with a pair of dumbbells, pushing them above his head, lowering them, thrusting them out to the side. His chest was designed with black hair, his face was rapt.

Crane said, "Nice view . . . for a lady."

Miss Martin's lips curled in scorn. "I've learned the facts of life by watching that court."

The athletic man put his dumbbells down, started to take off his shorts. Miss Martin hurriedly turned away. Doc Williams, who had been standing behind them, was looking into a bureau drawer. "That your marriage certificate?"

Miss Martin picked up a framed certificate. "No, it's my mother's."

"Oh, I just saw the name Emily Lou Martin."

"My mother's name was Emily Lou."

Crane said, "We'd better look into the tapping possibilities. Where does the telephone wire go?"

"It runs along the hall," Miss Martin said. "This is an old building, and the wires don't run in the walls. At least, that's what the telephone man said when he installed it."

As they went into the hall to look for it, Williams asked, "They wouldn't tap it in the apartment, would they?"

Crane examined the place where the wire went under the wainscoting below the telephone. "Where else could they tap it? It would be next to impossible to pick out the Prudences' wire once it got into the main cable with hundreds of other wires. They'd either have to get it here, or in the basement."

"They'd have a hard time in the basement," said Emily Lou. "The janitor lives down there, and he keeps a police dog."

They went down to the basement anyway, routed an aggrieved janitor, who closely resembled Chic Sale, out of bed, and examined the exposed phone wires. They were in perfect condition.

"Nobody come down here without my knowing it," the janitor assured them, holding on to a pair of discolored pants with one hand and with the other trying to keep his unbuttoned shirt together. "The purp's here all day, and I'm here all night."

On their way up the wooden back stairs, Miss Martin explained that the dog slept in a kennel in the yard. "He spends most of his time barking at cats," she added.

In the white kitchen they found the hole where the wires went down to the basement. "This is the top of three apartments, isn't it?" Crane asked. When Emily Lou nodded, he continued, "How about the apartments below? Either of them empty?"

"They're both occupied by people we know."

Doc Williams, who had been tracing the wire along the hall like a bloodhound, exclaimed, "Hey! Look here!" His shout took them through the darkened dining room to the hall entrance. He had a piece of the baseboard off, was examining the wire. Quite obviously it had been cut at that point, then carefully spliced.

Crane bent over and examined it, shook his head. "Now that we've found something, I don't know what it means."

Williams asked, "How could anybody have gotten in here to do that?"

"Fiddlesticks!" Mrs. Prudence, hands on hips, stood watching them. "The telephone man did that when we complained about the service. He said something must have accidentally cut the wire."

"When did the telephone man come to fix it?" Crane asked.

Emily Lou's eyes were round. "He came on the day before the murder—that is the day before Mrs. Westland was found."

"Nonsense, my dear." Mrs. Prudence shook her head. "He came on the day the body was found. I remember distinctly because Mr. Woodbury tried to telephone you and couldn't. Don't you remember he had to send a telegram?"

"Yes . . . but the man I'm thinking of came on Sunday, the day before that. I was here all alone when he came. He said he had orders to test the wire."

Crane was helping Williams replace the baseboard. "You mean there were two telephone repair men?"

"There must have been. Auntie had one come on Monday, and I saw one on Sunday. What do you think . . . ?"

"The first one must have been a phoney," said Williams. "He must of tapped the wire."

"Cut it," Crane corrected him. "He must have cut it so the phone wouldn't ring in the apartment in case Westland called back after the fake Emily Lou had talked to him." He stood up, brushed his hands on the seat of his trousers. "Let's see where he could have run a wire."

Right around the corner from the hall was a curtained dining room window. It overlooked the roof of a two-story apartment building and a vacant lot. "The wire could have gone out here," said Crane.

Mrs. Prudence glared at him. "No it couldn't. We always keep these windows closed."

"That wouldn't make any difference. The man could have closed the window over the wire. You wouldn't have noticed it, particularly if you didn't use the dining room on Sunday evening."

"We don't," said Miss Martin.

"Then, when the call had been completed," Crane said, "the man could have simply jerked the wire loose, hoping that you would attribute the broken connection to an accident."

Mrs. Prudence was adamant. "I don't think the wire could

have gone out this way—not that I'm admitting there was any such wire."

Back in the hall again, bending over the place where the wire had been cut, Crane asked, "What's directly opposite this point on the other side of the wall?"

"My bathroom," said Emily Lou.

Polished green-and-white tile, as lustrous as semiprecious stones, made the bathroom dazzling in the electric light. Two fluffy black rugs ink-spotted the tile floor; aquamarine tinted glass enclosed a shower; an asparagus green tub with silver taps was coolly inviting. On a chromium shelf above the tub were a Japanese loofa; a cylinder of pine bath salts, and a nail brush. Half-a-dozen oversize towels, monogramed in green, hung from a chromium rack.

Williams walked across the floor gingerly, as though in a museum display, and examined the wall adjacent to the hall. It was unmarked. He looked around cautiously for the toilet but was unable to find it. He thought, What the hell kind of a bathroom is this?

"The wire didn't come through here," Crane said.

"It didn't come through anywhere because there wasn't a wire." Mrs. Prudence's eyes were exasperated. "Don't you think you've been bothering us long enough?" She turned and marched toward the front room.

Williams followed her, but Emily Lou detained Crane. "Is there any chance of saving him?" she asked in a low voice.

Crane turned away from the tears in her eyes. "I don't know. There's still time for something to turn up."

She let the tears run down her cheeks, looked at him un-ashamed. "I don't care," she said, "I can't be brave all the time.

I try to believe it will be all right, but——" Her carmine lower lip trembled.

Crane pressed her arm gently with his fingers. "Keep in there pitching," he said. "It means a lot to him."

In the hall she asked, "Do you think the wire means anything?"

"Well, I figured it must have been tapped here, but I don't see where they could have run their cord. It would either have to go through the dining room or through your room, and I don't see how it could have without being noticed."

Williams and Mrs. Prudence were waiting at the front door. "I hope you're satisfied," said Mrs. Prudence acidly.

"Genius is an infinite capacity for not being satisfied," William Crane replied. He bowed to Mrs. Prudence, smiled at Emily Lou, and started down the stairs. Four steps down he halted and called back, "Miss Martin, do you think Miss Brentino would know your voice well enough to imitate it?"

Emily Lou said slowly, "She certainly heard it enough when she was Robert's secretary."

Even on the second landing Mrs. Prudence's snort of contempt was audible.

As they were climbing into the waiting taxi, Williams observed, "Damn funny people."

Crane gave the address of the ballistics laboratory, then asked, "Why?"

"They spend all that money on a bathroom and then don't put a toilet in it."

"You just didn't see it. It was in a special closet."

"All right, but why do they have to have kitchen furniture in the living room?"

172 · JONATHAN LATIMER

They rode in silence for the rest of the trip because Crane couldn't think of an answer for that one.

Major Lee, the ballistics expert, met them in his outer office. He handed Crane Woodbury's gun.

"No luck?" Crane asked.

"Depends upon what you want," said Major Lee. He was a tall blond man with a whiskey-red face and a curly mustache. "This gun didn't fire the bullet that killed Mrs. Westland, although it is of the same type."

Crane asked, "There isn't any possibility that this was Westland's pistol, is there? His had a name plate on it, but it might have been taken off."

The major shook his head. "This never had a name plate on it."

Crane fingered the gun, gazed reflectively at the major's pepper-and-salt suit. "What did Deputy Strom say when you told him?" he asked.

"He said, 'That puts the bee on Westland.' I think he was worried for fear I would find this was the gun."

"He was."

"I can't say I blame him. I never thought Mr. Westland was guilty; the evidence fitted together too nicely."

"Then why did you testify for the prosecution?"

"I merely said the bullet which killed Mrs. Westland was fired from a Webley automatic. I didn't say it was fired from Westland's automatic."

"You didn't say it wasn't either."

"You find me Westland's pistol and I'll tell you one way or another in a very short time."

"*Touché!*" Crane said. "I haven't been able to find anything so far on this case." He thanked the Major and led Williams to the faithful taxi.

"Where to now?" Williams asked.

"Up to Miss Hogan's apartment to meet Finklestein."

"How do you know he'll be there? He didn't say anything about meeting us there."

"He ate clams for lunch, didn't he?"

CHAPTER XIII

Wednesday Night

CRANE KNOCKED loudly on the polished door of the apartment occupied by Miss Hogan. The giddiness from the absinthe and the other liquors had subsided, and he felt very gay. He knocked again: tap-titi-taptap-tap-tap.

Doc Williams, frowning, stood behind him. "How much was the cab bill?" he asked.

Crane was entranced with the hollow sound his knuckles made on the door. He tried, "We'll rally 'round the flag, boys, we'll rally once again," rotating his knuckles against the wood to imitate the military swirl of drums. The result was impressive. "If you only had a fife," he said to Williams, "we could do Yankee Doodle."

"How much was the cab bill?" Williams repeated.

Crane said, "Eleven dollars," and then prepared to play "The March of the Wooden Soldiers" with both hands on the door. This proved impossible, however, because the door swung open, and Finklestein, dressed in a dark-blue suit and carrying his overcoat on one arm, stood there in its place. His face changed slowly from dignified composure to intense rage.

"My God, I thought you were the house detective," he exclaimed. "What's the big idea?"

"I am a detective," Crane said with dignity. "I'm a very great detective."

"He's drunk," said Williams.

"What's the big idea?" the attorney demanded again. "What's the idea of coming up here and scaring me half to death?"

Crane pushed past him into the apartment. "Where is the lovely Miss Hogan," he asked, " . . . the lovely Miss Hogan?"

She was standing in the hall, hands on hips, a scornful scarlet smile on her lips. "What do you want?" she asked metallically. She had on black silk lounging pajamas, cut low over firm breasts, and high-heeled open sandals. Painted toenails matched her orange hair.

"You," Crane said. "I like you."

He felt that he did, too. He not only liked the smell of narcissus that came from her, but he liked her smooth tan flesh and the narrowed blue-penciled eyes and the sullenly descending curve of her lips. He looked at her, and she at him, her eyes sultry, until Finklestein came back from the door.

"Where have you been all afternoon?" the lawyer demanded. "I thought you were going to look me up."

"Too busy," said Crane. "We've been working."

Finklestein looked interrogatively at Williams, who said:

"I don't know. At least we spent thirty-four dollars for cabs."

"Thirty-nine," said Crane. "I gave five bucks to the last guy." He took his eyes from Miss Hogan, added: "Let's go sit down. I want to hear about those alibis you were supposed to get."

In the subdued light from two lamps, the living room was exotic with the coin-covered tapestries and the huge red-and-brown portrait of the Spanish boy on the terra-cotta walls, and the big windows backgrounded with city lights.

Crane dropped into a deep chair and demanded a drink.

"There's only gin," said Miss Hogan.

"Gin? That's a medicinal drink, isn't it? Like soda pop?"

"You don't have to drink it," said Miss Hogan acidly.

"No, but I wouldn't think of refusing something you recommend. In fact, I'd like to taste gin. I've heard about it so long."

She hesitated, undecided between laughter and rage, until Finklestein said, "You better make some gin bucks for all of us."

After she had crossed the red-tile dining-room floor to the kitchen, Crane asked, "How about those alibis?"

Finklestein shook his head. "They're all bulletproof. I can account for everybody at the time Sprague was run over except Simmons."

"You're sure none of them could have been driving that car?"

"Positive. Want me to tell you where they were?"

"No, I'll take your word for it." Crane swung his legs over the arm of the chair. "You covered Miss Martin?"

"Everybody but Simmons."

"I'll fix him," said Crane. "Is there a telephone in this apartment?"

The telephone, an ivory cradle model, proved to have such a long cord that Crane was able to use it without moving from the chair. He called Wabash 4747 and finally located Deputy Strom.

"The gun wasn't the one," he said.

"I knew it wasn't," the deputy replied. "It was Westland's pistol that killed his wife."

"Maybe, and maybe not."

The deputy snorted.

"Listen," Crane said.

"Yeah."

"That Simmons. You know Simmons?"

"Yeah."

"Well, listen. He just told me he saw Sprague."

"The hell he did!"

"Yes he did. He said he just saw Sprague, I mean he just said he saw Sprague. He said he lied to you."

There was a pause while the deputy sorted out this information. Crane made clutching motions at Miss Hogan, who had returned from the kitchen with fogged tumblers on a silver tray, and she handed him one. He was drinking deeply when the deputy asked:

"Did he tell you why he kept that from me?"

"He didn't tell me much, but he acted very suspicious . . . very suspicious."

The ice cubes in the glass made the bottom damp in Crane's hand. The drink had lemon juice, charged water, sugar and plenty of gin in it, and it made his mouth taste clean and fresh. He thought if they made a mouth wash of gin and lemon juice it would sell very well.

Deputy Strom said, "I think I'll pick that guy up. It won't hurt to ask him some questions."

"You better check his fingerprints."

"Who do you think you're dealing with," the deputy asked bitterly; "a bunch of nincompoops?"

Crane said, "Yeah," and the deputy hung up violently.

Finklestein asked about the gun, and Crane told him how the deputy's men had taken it to the ballistics expert.

"Too bad it didn't match," commented Finklestein. "We might have been able to pin something on him with that and his phoney alibi on the night of Mrs. Westland's murder and the fact that he's the only one who could have taken Westland's pistol."

"I don't like that guy or his girl," said Doc Williams. He was sipping his drink slowly. "She tried to tell us that the phone call Westland got that night was really from Miss Martin."

"Miss Brentino's all right," said Crane. "She's got a lovely figure."

Miss Hogan said, "Those are the dames to look out for."

Crane finished his drink, handed the glass to Miss Hogan. "Those are the dames I'm always looking out for."

Williams said, "She was Westland's secretary before he got in a jam. Why couldn't she and this Woodbury have framed something on Westland? Maybe they stole some of his stocks, or something, and then framed him."

"Why would they have to frame him?" asked Finklestein. "If they stole something from him all they'd have to do is to leave the country. Framing him wouldn't do any good, because the theft would be discovered when his estate was audited."

"Maybe so," Williams shook his head, "but there's something funny about that pair."

Crane said, "I wish you would check over his account, anyway, Finklestein. There might have been some funny business."

"All right. I'll put some auditors to work tomorrow." Finklestein suddenly sat up in his chair. "Say! That reminds me of something. One of Westland's lawyers called me yesterday and said that when Mrs. Westland's estate had been probated they found nearly eight thousand dollars' worth of stolen and counterfeit stocks and bonds among her things."

"The hell you say!" Crane thrust out his lower lip. "Could Bolston . . . ?"

"No, I checked on that. The phoney securities were listed as having been bought for Mrs. Westland when Westland was still handling her account. He was in such a jam, and besides the estate was left to him, so the attorney never did anything about it."

"Christ! Everything keeps coming back to Westland." Crane, drinking and talking at the same time, spilled gin buck on his necktie. "But I still don't think he did it."

"Who gets his money?" asked Miss Hogan. "I bet the one that gets the money did it."

Finklestein gazed at her admiringly. "You're a smart one."

"I'm always thinking of the money first," Miss Hogan confessed.

"Like a mercenary soldier," Finklestein observed.

Crane said, "She belongs to an older profession than that."

"You go to hell," said Miss Hogan.

Finklestein spoke hastily: "That Miss Martin gets all the money. He's left it to her in a will."

"Wouldn't Wharton have a chance of breaking it?" Crane asked. "He's the nearest relative."

"He might, but he'd have to prove duress, or undue influence, or insanity, to get anywhere."

"Hell, they've all got motives," said Williams. "Bolston or Woodbury could have the same reason to get Westland out of the way—to rob the office—and Simmons gets ten grand according to the will, don't he, counselor?"

"That's the main bequest."

"For ten grand a person might do a lot of things," said Miss Hogan.

Crane pointed at his glass. "How would you like to get us another little drink?" He smiled at her vivid face. "Just a touch more gin than the last one."

While she was gone, Crane related the story of the trip to Miss Martin's home. Finklestein was much impressed.

"How do you suppose anybody got into the house to cut the wire?" he asked.

"I suppose it was the first telephone man Miss Martin spoke about," Crane said. "The second one was legitimate."

"But if Miss Martin saw the first man, why didn't she identify him? You said you were sure the plot was arranged by someone close to Westland, and certainly she would know him."

"I guess he could have an accomplice."

"I suppose so. But how could they get the wire loose after they had talked to Westland? They'd have to do that if the trick was to go unnoticed."

"All they'd have to do would be to jerk it loose. They had the dining-room window open a crack and the wire would slide out. That's probably what put the phone on the blink."

Miss Hogan returned with the drinks. She gave Crane one which had in it slightly more gin than lemon juice and charged water. "That ought to hold you," she said.

Crane tasted the mixture, replied, "You're doin' better, baby." He drank about half the glass.

Finklestein watched him with reluctant admiration. "If you only detected as well as you guzzled liquor you'd be all right."

"I'm a great detective." For emphasis he waved his glass in the air and splattered liquid over his trousers. To avert another such accident, he drank all that was left. "I tell you I'm a great detective."

"Sure," said the lawyer, "you're a great detective. But what else did you do this afternoon?"

Crane told him about Joe Petro. "I didn't like to see the

poor guy beat up," he confessed, "but you can't let him go around shootin' at you all the time. I mean there's a limit to almost everything." He stood up abruptly, and the glass shattered on the floor. "I mean I'm a good-natured fellow and all that, but I——"

"Why was he trying to shoot you?" Finklestein asked. He was impressed.

Williams said, "He thought we put Mannie Grant on the spot at the night club. He was just tryin' to pay us back."

Crane leaned unsteadily over Miss Hogan. "I'm a great detective," he asserted. "You know me, don't you, baby?"

"Sure," said Miss Hogan. "I know you." She was listening to the others.

"And then," Williams said, "we made the waiter tell us what Grant had seen on the night of Mrs. Westland's murder."

"What was that?"

Crane said, "Tha's right, don't pay any attention to a great——" He tripped over the large table, miraculously caught a toppling lamp.

Williams continued, "Grant saw Westland leave this apartment, and he saw Mrs. Westland say goodnight to him. That proves he couldn't have killed her."

Finklestein shook his head. "No good as evidence now." He pushed his gold-rimmed glasses higher on his nose. "It's of no value coming second hand the way it does. If we only had Grant . . ."

"He's dead." Crane, returning from the kitchen with a glass of straight gin, screwed up his face in derision. "Hadn't you heard, counselor?"

"Has he got all the gin?" Williams asked Miss Hogan.

"No, I haven't got all the gin," said Crane. "I left some in the bottle." He collapsed on the davenport. "I'm not a hog, I'm just a great——"

The three of them left hurriedly for the kitchen. Miss Hogan took Finklestein's and Williams' glasses and poured the remainder of the gin in them. Running hot water over a tray of ice cubes, Finklestein asked Williams, "Do you think Crane's got hold of anything?"

Williams tossed a squeezed lemon into the garbage pail. "I wouldn't know. He never makes sense on a case, but he usually delivers the goods." He poured the lemon juice from the squeezer into the glasses.

Miss Hogan, leaning a perfectly sculptured hip against the white sink, said, "I wouldn't give two bits for Westland's chances. I think the 'great detective' is about as daffy as they come."

Williams said, "Aw, I wouldn't say that."

Charged water gurgled from the neck of a White Rock bottle, ran up Finklestein's sleeve. "He's supposed to be a hot shot," he said. "His agency has done some big jobs."

"He doesn't take this job very seriously, then," said Miss Hogan. "I haven't seen him sober yet."

Over the fresh drinks they discussed the case. Williams maintained that Woodbury was the guilty party, asserting he was the only one who could have stolen Westland's pistol.

"How about Simmons?" asked Finklestein. "He could have taken the pistol." He sipped his drink, added, "I don't like his looks."

Miss Hogan said she'd pick Bolston just because they didn't seem to have much against him. She suggested they see who the great detective favored. They went into the front room, but they were unable to ask him. The great detective was lying face upward on the davenport, his jaw resting on his chest, his breathing deep and regular. The great detective had passed out.

Isadore Varecha's eyes followed Westland's movements like those of a devoted spaniel. He took an orange from the wicker basket. "Onc't I sell oranges," he volunteered. He giggled a little, twitching his mouth.

Westland nodded. He had found that the little murderer cried less when somebody talked to him occasionally, and he had made a point of doing so. Then Varecha helped get rid of the fruit Emily Lou showered upon him.

"Onc't I got a girl, too," Varecha added. He stuck a discolored thumbnail into the orange peel and jerked off a piece. "I used t'give her candy." His mouth twitched, he glanced swiftly over his shoulder, then smiled slyly at Westland. "I killed her."

"What!"

"Yeah." Varecha slobbered a little. This was good! You betcha! Him showing that nice fella what a guy he was! "I push her in front of a car on Lawndale Avenue and run. Nobody even seen me." His head made that mechanical, furtive jerk to let his eyes peer over his shoulder. "Her name Anna."

The electric light in the corridor was milk-pale on the murderer's face. Hair grew in quarter-dollar patches on his chin; his neck was still raw from the attempt to hang himself. Westland watched the bubbles of spittle form on his quivering lips, asked, fascinated: "How did they get you if nobody knew it was you?"

"Ho! Ho! Dat wasn't what they got me for." This was good! You betcha! Varecha stuttered with eagerness to tell his story. "Dat was another goil. I went up to this floosie's room, see?— and give her a dollar an' she lay down and she was big and fat like she was with a brat, see? and I took my knife an' cut her open at the stomach." Varecha's face was fanatic, exultant. "You oughta heard her holler."

"My God! Why did you do that?"

"Why?" The ecstasy faded from Varecha's eyes, his thin shoulders hunched forward, he shrank into himself. His head ached now. What was this man asking him? Oh yeah. Why? He mumbled his answer. "I don' know."

Deep rumbling snores came from Connors' cell: the snores of a healthy man in good natural sleep.

Varecha reached around the cell, touched Westland's shirt with his fingers. "I ain't scared to go with you along," he said. His eyes were like those of a devoted spaniel.

CHAPTER XIV

Thursday Morning

HE COULD feel the sunlight upon his face, but he didn't open his eyes because he was afraid the shock would kill him. He had been lying on his back with his mouth open, and his throat felt like freshly dried rawhide. He tried to swallow, and the quivering movement of his neck muscles made his head throb viciously. He abandoned the idea of clearing his throat and tried to go back to sleep. In this he was unsuccessful, but he discovered that as long as he lay motionless his head didn't ache.

Indeed, he discovered that by not moving he was able to achieve in himself a remarkable sort of duality, a beautiful separation of body and mind. It was almost as if his body didn't exist—except for some minor trouble about breathing—and he was nothing but brain, functioning smoothly and splendidly, in an absolute vacuum. He pondered on this perfect state of unfleshliness for a while, thinking how unnecessary were the long fasts, the flagellations, the pillar-sittings, the cave-dwelling through which the ancient saints achieved mastery of the flesh when they could have, like himself, gained their end quite speedily by drinking bourbon and absinthe and gin.

From a contemplation of the saints he turned his mind upon himself. His first problem was to determine who he was. This would have been easy if he had dared open his eyes, but he knew better than to do that. Instead, he lay on his back and thought and thought and suddenly he remembered that his name was William Crane and that he was a detective. He then directed his precise and machinelike mind upon the Westland case.

About an hour later, Miss Hogan came into the room and said, "Hey! Are you going to sleep all day?"

Crane knew what would happen when he opened his eyes, and it did. As soon as the sunlight struck them, it seemed as though a million needles had been driven into his skull. Not only the part of his brain directly back of his eyeballs hurt, but the top of his head hurt. The pain even extended down the back of his neck.

"My Gawd! You look awful," Miss Hogan said.

She was wearing Chinese-red lounging pajamas with huge sleeves which exposed bare arms, and her hip line under the silk was muscular, and even in his extremity William Crane was unable to repress a feeling of interest. However, he said, "Go away, I'm dying."

"Well, please die somewhere besides in my bed."

Crane rolled his eyes and saw that he was indeed in bed, in a nice wide bed with fine sheets and peach-colored blankets. The top blanket had JW embroidered on it in silk thread. He looked further, exclaimed: "God! I've got pajamas on!"

"I should think you had. No guy's goin' to sleep raw in——"

He interrupted placatingly. "They're nice pajamas. They're swell pajamas. I wouldn't ask for better pajamas, even if they are yellow. But what I want to know is, how did I get them?"

"Fink and your friend put you to bed. I gave them the paja-mas for you."

"So!" He pondered for a moment. "Where are they?"

"Your friend went to his hotel, and Fink is seeing about an audit of Mr. Westland's account."

"The rats! Deserting a pal in trouble!"

"You didn't expect them to wait for you all morning?"

"All morning!"

"Yes, all morning. It's after half-past ten."

He sat up, and at once the bed began to turn on its axis. He sank back on the pillow and groaned.

Miss Hogan's teeth were like an Ipana advertisement. She thrust a glass in his hand. "Drink this and you'll feel better."

It tasted dry and bitter, but sure enough he did feel better.

"Now," said Miss Hogan, "you take a shower while I fix something to eat."

He put his hands to his head and was surprised to find it was still in one piece. "I'm never going to eat again."

Miss Hogan did not answer him. She picked up the glass and walked, neither hurrying nor lingering, out of the room. Under the sheer red silk he could see her slender legs and the ta-pering, muscular lines of her dancer's thighs.

In the black-and-white tile bathroom, because he wasn't sure how long he could stand up, he took a very hot bath first. The tub was a big one, and he sank into the slightly muddy water until only his knees and his nose were exposed. After a time he began to feel pretty good. There were three kinds of bath crys-tals—pink, green, and white—in jars on a shelf beside the tub, and he dropped two handfuls of each in the water. Such a stink presently arose that he was forced to climb out and step into the glass shower cabinet. Spinning the stainless steel handle to the point marked Hot, he let the stream nip at his back. Mist silvered the sides of the cabinet; the spray roared; water ran into his parched mouth, through his burning eyes; he burst into off-key song:

> *"Daisy, Daisy, give me your answer, do.*
> *It won't be a stylish marriage,*
> *I can't afford a carriage,*
> *But you'll look sweet upon the seat*
> *Of a bicycle built——"*

Abruptly he halted his rendition, turned off the shower. In the silence which followed he said, "Hello." The word echoed in his ears. He repeated it, "Hello." Shivering, he stepped from the cabinet, wrapped an orange and black towel about his middle and thrust his head out the bathroom door.

"Hey, tutz," he called.

Miss Hogan slouched into the hall, a Lucky Strike dangling from her sullen lips. "There's a razor in the cabinet over the wash bowl," she said. "Too bad it's a safety so you can't cut your throat with it." Her violet eyes were inscrutable.

"Listen, tutz. Will you do me a favor?"

"The name's Myrna."

"All right, Myrna. How about the favor?"

Her eyes were suspicion-shaded. "I might . . . "

"It isn't much. You just stand here and listen for a minute or two. Then tell me what you hear."

He closed the bathroom door, threw the towel on the floor, went into the shower cabinet, shut its door, and turned on the shower. When the water was running well, he said loudly, "FLASH . . . this is Mrs. Crane's boy, William, broadcasting from a shower bath on the fifty-second floor of the RCA Building in New York. . . . Here's a torrid tip from Chicago. . . . William Crane, the playboy sleuth, and Myrna Hogan, lovely leisure lady, are dunking doughnuts in each other's coffee and is a certain criminal lawyer on fire?"

He shut the shower off and, the towel wrapped around him again, looked out at Miss Hogan. "What d'you hear?"

She shook her head. "Nothing."

"I didn't think you would." He closed the door on her puzzled face, got ready to shave.

By the time he was dressed the pleasant effect of the bath had worn off. His head throbbed unmercifully, and there were pains in his neck. Also he had cut himself in three places while shaving. Examining these in the mirror, he critically decided his color was bad enough to give him an excuse to go to Florida. He dusted powder on his face and went out to the living room. Miss Hogan, curled in a chair, slim bare ankles exposed, was reading the society section of the *Herald and Examiner*.

"They don't dish up the dirt in these Hearst papers the way they used to," she complained.

He asked, "How would you like to go to Miami with me for a trip, baby?"

"Why should I like to go with you?"

"I don't know. I thought maybe you were fascinated with my brown eyes."

She looked at him speculatively through long dark eyelashes. "If you had any money, you might be the sort of mug I could go for."

"I'll have plenty of do-re-mi as soon as I get Westland off."

Her husky laugh was genuine, for once. "You've got as much

chance of doing that as I have of leading the daisy chain at Vassar."

"Will you go if I get him off?"

"Sure—that'll be an easy promise to keep." She came out of the chair with catlike grace. "How about breakfast? You'll need plenty to solve the Westland case."

"I'll be ready as soon as I make a call."

He went to the telephone and jerked out the cord to see if it was as long as he had remembered it from the night before. It was. He called Warden Buckholtz.

"This is Crane, Warden—the detective in the Westland case."

"Yeah?" The warden managed to repress his enthusiasm.

"I'd like to speak with Westland."

"What?"

William Crane was very patient. "I'd like to speak with Westland."

"You would, would ya?" The warden's curious voice, shrill as that of a harem eunuch, was incredulous. "What do ya think I'm goin' to do, page him? Or maybe you think I ought to have a telephone installed in his cell?"

Crane said, "I have to speak to him. It's very important."

"I'm running a jail, not a hotel."

There was a click as the receiver at the other end broke the connection. Quickly Crane rang the number back, spoke angrily when the warden answered.

"Listen, you fat son of a bitch, if you hang up on me again I'll call the State's attorney and tell him about the bribe you accepted from Westland. And if he doesn't want to do anything about it, I know a certain deputy chief of detectives who is itching to get his hands on your dirty neck." Rage made his head ache, but he continued, "You scramble down to the bottom of that jail of yours and bring Westland to the telephone. . . . Can you hear me?"

After a long pause, Warden Buckholtz said, "You've got me all wrong, Mister Crane. I want to do everything I can to help Westland, but I can't——"

"Yes you can. I'm at Superior 8971. You get Westland and call me back here in ten minutes. If I haven't heard from you by then I'll start calling some numbers myself."

This time Crane hung up.

"You certainly have a persuasive manner on the phone," observed Miss Hogan from the dining room.

"In another minute," he said, "I'd have lost my temper."

The coffee was steaming hot from a silver percolator. He gulped tomato juice with a spoonful of Worcestershire sauce in it, then tried the coffee. It was excellent, as black as tar, as pungent as garlic, as clear as dry sherry, as hot as Bisbee, Arizona.

"This is really fine coffee," he said appreciatively, "but I can't do anything with the scrambled eggs."

"Try just a little," she urged him.

Sunlight, peering through the windows at the table, threw her face into planes like a Cubist painting. She had a firm jaw line and a good thin nose, but you couldn't tell about her eyes, because of the exotic blue mascara. Her neck was slender, and her breasts, only partially hidden by the low curve of her red silk pajamas, were smooth and full and firm.

Pretending to eat the eggs, he watched her covertly. "I got pretty drunk last night," he said. "I don't remember going to bed at all."

"You passed out on the couch. Your pal and Fink got you into my room and put you to bed."

"Where did they sleep?"

"Both of them went home about three o'clock this morning."

He tried to balance the fork on his hand, but it fell off, struck the china plate with a metallic clang. He thought how funny it was with a hangover your hands were steady enough when they were moving, but as soon as you held still they shook. Even when he leaned an elbow on the table, the hand shook.

She watched him, disdainfully amused. "You've certainly got the jitters."

"How did you sleep last night?"

"Swell."

"Nothing disturb you?"

"No, I slept swell."

"I didn't——"

She laughed huskily. "Do you think I slept in that bed with you? I used the other bedroom. You'd remember if I'd been in bed with you."

Despite the hangover, which had begun to make the backs of his legs ache, he thought with pleasure: Here is a nice bawdy wench. He said, "I'd certainly hate to sleep through an experience like that."

She said, "Few do."

The telephone rang. When he answered it, Westland's voice sounded brittle. "Have you got something? The warden said it was important."

"I haven't got anything definite yet, but I think I may be on the trail. I've been working hard."

Behind him Miss Hogan said, "Liar." He said, "Shut up." Westland asked, "What's that?"

"I wanted to ask you a question," Crane said. "I want you to think about the phone call you received from the woman you thought was Emily Lou—I mean Miss Martin."

"Go ahead."

"Can you remember if there was anything peculiar about the connection that night?"

"You mean whether it sounded like a local or long distance call?"

"Yes, or if there were any funny noises."

There was a long pause. Miss Hogan's breath was soft on Crane's neck; he could smell Christmas Night perfume.

"I think I do remember something," Westland said at last. "It was sort of a roar, like a strong wind blowing through trees, or the sound Niagara Falls makes."

"Niagara Falls!" William Crane exulted. "Hot damn!"

Guard Galt lingered for a moment after the cell door had clanged behind Westland. His emaciated face was jaundiced, his cheeks were hollow, his eyes deep set and small under an un-washed forehead; he grinned with his saffron buck teeth like an Egyptian mummy.

"Ain't seen your friends lately," he observed.

"No?"

The guard's Adam's apple jiggled up and down, his eyes glittered maliciously. "They ain't deserted you?"

"No."

"You look kinda sick. I thought mebbe they deserted you." The guard licked his lips. "You ain't scairt, are you?"

"No." Westland spoke dully. "At least, not much."

He didn't feel very frightened; just nauseated, as if he was going to vomit.

"You'll get scairt tomorrow." The guard was watching him

intently, hopefully. "I expect we'll have to carry you to the seat, from the looks of you now." He wiped his nose with the back of his hand. "That's the way a lot of them go. They hold up to the last day, and then they turn into jelly, too scairt to do anything but snivel like a woman." He rubbed the back of his hand on his trousers. "You'd be surprised at the ones who lose their guts. . . . There was that Tough Tony Caprio, for instance—he broke up when they shaved his head, just flopped down on the floor and——"

"Shut up, you rat!" Connors stood with his face between the two bars nearest Westland's cell, his jaw rigid with anger, his blue eyes ice pale. "Shut up!" His voice was unsteady. "Before Christ, I'll have you knocked off if you don't quit prying around here."

Galt retreated a step, then said, "I was just talkin' to him. I was just tellin' him how the tough guys folded up when——"

"Get out!" The gangster shook the bars. "Get out of here or I'll come out and kill you with my bare hands. Get out!" His voice rose in a hoarse shout.

Galt retreated along the dim corridor, his face twitching as though from a nervous disease.

"That son of a bitch!" Connors smiled at Westland. His face was quite handsome now, having lost its former grossness because of the lack of food and the draining tension of waiting. "I'll get him. See if I don't."

Suddenly, looking at the gangster's composed face, Westland realized his debt to his courage and sanity, which, by their very sureness, had saved his mind just as he had unintentionally, by kindness, saved the little Jewish peddler from the gulf of stark terror. So, with the awe of a small boy, he asked:

"How will you get him?"

"I don't know—" there were white lines from the bars on the palms of Connors' hands—"but I'll get him."

In the next cell Isadore Varecha slept, uttering small cries, disjointed phrases, like a fevered child.

A few minutes after William Crane had finished talking with Westland, the telephone rang janglingly. "Oh my God!" exclaimed Crane. "Hasn't the telephone company any respect for my nerves?"

Miss Hogan answered the phone, then said, "It's for you."

It was Doc Williams. He was in the lobby and he wanted to know if it was all right for him to come up. Crane told him to come up and see.

Miss Hogan was looking out one of the windows when Crane came back into the living room; her face sullen without unpleasantness, her amethyst eyes slumberous, her full vermilion downward-curved lips voluptuous. The yellow rays from the sun made the upper part of her lounging pajamas transparent, outlined her lithe body. She did not have on a brassiere. Crane caught her about the waist, bent her backward like a tango dancer, kissed her on the lips. Immediately he regretted his action: first, because the motion started his head throbbing violently, and second, because she bit a large chunk out of his lower lip.

She looked at him, neither angry nor flustered. "Be careful, Clark Gable, or I'll spank."

The blood tasted salty and warm in William Crane's mouth. He patted the lip with a handkerchief. "My judgment doesn't seem so good this morning," he said. He admired her composure.

"Your aim is all right, though," said Miss Hogan. She moved fluidly to open the door for Williams.

"Hello, you runnerouter," said Crane.

Williams observed him with disgust. "You look like hell."

"I feel like hell." Crane daubed at his mouth with his hand-kerchief and examined it. The lip was still bleeding. "I wish I was in New York."

Williams spoke critically. "What kind of a detective are you, anyway, wishing you were back in New York? You haven't done anything in this town but ride around in cabs, try to make wom-en, and get drunk. You'd think you were on a vacation." He took a deep breath. "A good detective would have a Siamese postage stamp, a gold collar button, some peanut shells, and one of Jean Harlow's garters as evidence by this time.

"Yes, sir, by God!" Doc Williams added; "a good detective'd not only have those things but he'd say: 'Doc, this crime is a bafflin' affair, but I've solved it. A dooced strange affair it was, too.'"

"You practically took the words out of my mouth," Crane said. "Miss Hogan and I have solved the Westland case, and it's going to surprise you."

"Oh no, it's not," said Williams. "Your saying it was any-body that done it wouldn't surprise me. You could arrest the Governor and it wouldn't surprise me. The thing that does sur-prise me is that you think you know who killed the lady. I've been with you all the time and I know you haven't any evidence."

Miss Hogan, watching them noncommittally, asked, "Who did kill Mrs. Westland?"

Crane shook his head. "Tell you later."

"He don't know," said Williams irascibly. "He's just talkin'. He hasn't any evidence."

"Evidence?" Crane dabbed at his lip. "Oh, it's evidence you

want? Well, we'll get some—that is, if there's life enough left in me."

Miss Hogan eyed the place where she had bit his lip. "There's still plenty of life in you."

Williams asked, "When do you expect to begin this great search for evidence. . . . Sometime next week?"

"No, we can begin right away. Where's Fink?"

"He's going over Westland's books—and over the firm's too."

"Then I got a job for you. There's some things I want to get right away."

"Some bottles of whiskey?" inquired Miss Hogan with elaborate sarcasm.

"At that, I wouldn't mind a little——"

Williams interrupted him. "What do you want me to get?"

"First I'd like a cab—" Crane folded the handkerchief into a neat square and put it into his hip pocket—"and a stop watch——"

"A stop watch!"

"Yes, a stop watch and . . . a deep-sea diver."

CHAPTER XV

Thursday Noon

THE CAB driver was a hook-nosed Greek with a cap pulled down over his left eye. His name, according to the smudged identification card, was Nick Papos, and his age was twenty-six. He slouched in the left corner of the front seat, elbow out the open window, and his lips seemed to snarl at the inmates of each car he passed.

Doc Williams handed Crane the stop watch. "I rented it for a ten spot," he said. "I suppose you'll want an elephant next."

Crane pulled the watch out of its green felt case. "How about the diver?" The nickel surface was cool in his hand.

"He'll be ready any time we want him this afternoon. The price for him and a boat is five hundred bucks."

Crane said, "We're putting more men to work than Roosevelt's recovery program."

Pedestrians swirled about them as the cab, halting for a red light at Oak Street and Michigan Boulevard, neatly blocked off the cross walk. An elderly man with a white mustache and a red face circled cautiously around the engine, shook his cane angrily at them.

"I'll bet he's tryin' to tell us he's a taxpayer," said the driver scornfully. Yellow appeared on the traffic light; he started the cab with a jerk and sent four women into flight like a covey of startled quail.

"Didn't get a one," observed Williams sympathetically.

"Naw," said the driver; "they got a closed season on jaywalkers this year."

The cab just caught the light at Division Street, swung to the left off the drive, then to the right on Astor Street and pulled up in front of Westland's apartment.

"Leave the meter down," Crane said.

Doc Williams started to get out of the cab.

"Stay in. We're not stopping here." Crane set the stop watch at zero. "What time is it?"

Williams looked at his wrist watch. "Eleven-thirty."

"That's swell. That's just swell."

Williams regarded him with suspicion. "What's swell?"

"That it's eleven-thirty."

"All I can say is, one of us is wrong."

Crane addressed the driver. "Nick, I want to go to the corner of La Salle and Adams in the Loop. How long have you been a driver in Chicago?"

"Five-six years, boss."

"Good. I want you to take us there the very quickest way you can. I don't care what kind of roads you take, just go the quickest way."

"But we just come from that way." The driver rubbed his nose with the back of his hand. "If you want to get there so quick why didn't——"

"Don't worry about that. Pretend we just picked you up right here on Astor Street and told you to take us to La Salle and Adams as quick as you could." He spoke slowly to let the words sink in. "You don't need to break the speed laws, just go as fast as you can without getting arrested."

"You want me to start right now?"

"Sure."

Nick Papos put her in low and let out the clutch. He thought, What I care if the guy is daffy? William Crane pushed the head on the stop watch, listened with gratification to its regular ticking.

They went directly over to La Salle Street, four blocks to the west, and then turned south. At Chicago Avenue they were held up by a stop light, and on the sunlit La Salle Street bridge they got caught behind a gas truck for a minute. Williams looked out at the smoke-gray water in the Chicago river and shuddered.

"I'd hate to have to swim in that," he said. "The water looks as though it was ready to freeze."

When the cab swerved in toward the curb at La Salle and Adams, Crane jumped out. "Drive around the block a couple of times," he told Williams. "I'll pick you up in a minute."

He entered the marble-and-gold lobby of the building in which Westland had his office, crowded into an elevator, and was skyrocketed to the thirty-fifth floor. He walked up to the door of the Westland suite, examined the inscription; Westland, Bolston & Woodbury, for about thirty seconds, and then halted the stop watch. It registered 17 minutes, 14 and 3/5 seconds. He wrote this figure on the back of an envelope and returned to the street.

Climbing into the cab beside Williams, he said, "Nick, it took you about eighteen minutes to come here from Astor Street. Now I want you to take me every other possible way between the two places that you can make in twenty-five minutes.

I want you to cross the river at a different place each time, but you can't take more than twenty-five minutes for the trip."

The driver said, "How about Michigan Boulevard, boss?"

"All right. Michigan Boulevard." Crane started the stop watch.

They went north to Wacker Drive and east to Michigan and then north again across the big bridge. Crowds of people hurried in either direction along the pedestrian walks; stenographers and clerks out for an early lunch; salesmen, window gazers, shoppers: the usual line of loafers peered raptly at the empty river.

"I almost forgot," Williams said suddenly. "I checked with the phone company about the service calls at Miss Martin's place. There was a call for a repair man on the day Mrs. Westland was found, but the company has no record of a man being sent out there on the day of the murder."

"No?"

"No. The guy Miss Martin saw must have been a phoney."

"That's what we thought, wasn't it?"

The cab, making good time with the progressive traffic lights on the Avenue, passed Walton Place. Two blocks away they could see the building in which Miss Hogan was living, the red bricks bright in the sunshine.

Crane, looking up from the stop watch, said, "I wish that Hogan dame would commit a murder. I could enjoy tracking her down." He felt his swollen lip reminiscently.

"That would be one case you'd work hard at," said Williams.

Crane said, "Aw, now."

Presently the driver said, "Here you are boss, back at Astor Street."

The watch showed that 20 minutes, 31 seconds had elapsed

since they left downtown. Crane sat the hands at zero, said, "All right, back to Adams and La Salle again."

This time they crossed the river over the new, wide Wabash Avenue bridge, then swung west on Wacker to La Salle. Not bothering to get out, Crane stopped the watch when they reached Westland's office building. The time was 17 minutes, 2 and 3/5 seconds. The next trip was on State Street, and the watch showed 21 minutes flat when they reached Astor Street. The driver said they were lucky not to meet a streetcar on the busy bridge. Returning to the Loop, they took the Dearborn Street bridge and made the trip in 19 minutes, 37 and 1/5 seconds.

It was about one-thirty and Doc Williams gazed longingly at the Loop restaurants. "My God, I'm hungry," he said.

Crane spoke to the driver. "Stop at a lunch place on the way back," he said. "I'll deduct the time we stop from the running time."

They went back over the Clark Street bridge behind a streetcar. They followed the car clear to Chicago Avenue, making frequent stops while passengers got on and off, and halted in front of the Elite Restaurant and Lunch Counter, Ladies Invited, on the corner.

"This ain't a bad joint," said the driver.

"All right. Doc, you get some sandwiches and coffee," Crane said. "We'll eat them while we ride. Get Nick something too."

"Don't get me nothing with onions in it," said Nick. "I go with a Swedish broad, and she don't like onions."

Crane leaned back on the upholstered seat with his eyes closed until Williams came back with three hamburger and three American cheese sandwiches on white bread and a paper container of muddy coffee. He refused the sandwiches but drank some of the coffee from a paper cup. It didn't taste good.

The driver, holding his coffee in one hand and taking the other hand off the wheel to bite into his sandwiches, reached Astor Street safely. After deducting 8 minutes for the stop, Crane found the trip had still taken 26 minutes, 47 seconds.

"I never seen a street I'm so sick of as this one," Williams said, wiping his mouth with a silk handkerchief. "How long do we have to keep comin' back here?"

Crane set the watch at zero again. "It's up to Nick."

The driver tossed his empty cup and the oiled paper from the sandwiches into a carefully groomed front yard. A fat nursemaid, leading a brown-and-white wire-haired terrier and two small children with saucer-blue eyes, glared at him. He ignored her, said, "I guess there's a couple of ways we could go yet."

"Well, go 'em," said Crane.

They went farther west this time, over to slovenly Wells Street near the edge of Little Italy, and crossed the river with the elevated roaring over their heads. It was dark on the bridge, and William Crane said, "This is something like it," but when they reached the corner of La Salle and Adams he discovered more than 28 minues had elapsed. They returned by an even more out of the way route, and the time was again more than 28 minutes.

Parked again in front of the apartment on Astor Street, Crane shook his head sadly. "That all, Nick?"

"All!" said Doc Williams. "It's a wonder the nursemaids don't yell rubberneck at us as we go by."

The driver said, "That's all unless you want to go by the lower level of the Michigan Boulevard bridge."

"Sure, let's go that way," Crane said. He pushed the watch, closed his eyes.

Doc Williams groaned.

The pavement, when they got near the bridge, was much rougher. The cab shook and rattled, and the driver was forced to slow down to avoid several large holes. A block to the east, Michigan Avenue's sleek pavement soared upward in a gentle hill between the Tribune Tower and the white Wrigley Building, but they continued to parallel it until they were within a block of the river. Then they turned to the left and cut under the elevated highway amid a forest of cement and steel braces. They swerved around a wagon drawn by two fat horses and entered the gloomy, steel-surfaced lower passage through the bridge. Their side, going south toward the Loop, was wide enough for two cars, and a similar one-way passage, for northbound traffic, was on their left behind a curtain of steel cross braces. On their right, through widely separated steel beams, could be seen the slow river current. Although sunlight dappled the water, it was gloomy in the passage.

"This is a good way to go," said the driver, "because most people only use it when they have to. It ain't crowded, and you miss the stop lights, too."

Once across they turned to the right and ran up an incline and came out on familiar Wacker Drive. The stop watch read 19 minutes, 30 and 1/5 seconds when they arrived at La Salle and Adams.

"Any more ways you can think of, Nick?" Crane asked.

"No, that's all, boss."

"Good. Let's go back under that bridge the way we did before, heading for the Loop."

"Headin' for the last round-up," said Doc Williams wearily.

They went around and came through the underpassage again. In the middle, Crane told the driver to pull up to the right-hand side by a particularly wide opening in the steel braces.

"Have you got a good-sized monkey wrench?" he asked the driver.

"Sure, boss. Why?"

"How much will you sell it for?"

Williams asked, "What in hell do you want a monkey wrench for?"

"How much will you sell it for?" Crane repeated.

"It's a ver' good one," said the driver. "I wouldn't think of sellin' her for less'n five bucks."

"Five bucks!" Williams looked at Crane in astonishment. "I can get the best monkey wrench in the world for half that."

"Maybe Nick's attached to that monkey wrench." Crane handed the driver a five-dollar bill. "Monkey wrenches are funny. At first you don't give a damn about them, but they grow on you. Yes, sir, Doc, you can get mighty fond of a monkey wrench after a time. I can see Nick is that sort of a fellow, too."

"You're feeling better," said Williams.

The driver fished a battered wrench from under the seat and endeavored to hand it to Crane, but he wouldn't take it.

"I want you to sit here in the driver's seat," he said, "and when I wave to you from the bank over there I want you to toss it through the window and into the river."

Amazement made the driver's face moronic. "You're givin' me five bucks to toss this in the river?"

"Yes, just sit in the driver's seat and toss it in the river. Be sure it goes in, though."

Williams' face was suspicious. "You haven't got hold of any more liquor, have you?"

"Who ever heard of such a thing!" Crane stepped out of the cab with dignity. "Come on." He glanced over the railing at the gray-black water. "You give it a toss when I wave my handkerchief, Nick. D'you understand?"

The driver rolled his eyes.

A sign on the cement landing opposite the Wrigley Building said: "Ride in a Speedboat, One Dollar." There weren't any speedboats around, though; only a slow eddy of scum-green water where the projecting pier shunted off the main current of the river. Bulking above their heads to the right was the Michigan Avenue bridge, windowed watch towers at both ends; and along the rail a man and a women watched the water with detached interest. Over a floating object, halfway to the other bank, two gulls circled.

Crane's handkerchief fluttered in the air. From the obscurity of the lower driveway, like a curved pen-stroke, sailed the wrench. It entered the water thirty feet from the bridge, threw silver spray into the air. Crane ran to a point opposite it, lined up the boiling circle with a post on the other bank, and called to Williams.

"Doc, mark this so you'll remember it, will you?"

Williams said, "I can remember this all right." He tilted his hat back from his eyes. "I think you're nuts."

"Maybe I am." Crane tied the handkerchief to an iron ring fastened in the cement. "And maybe I'm not. Anyway, you get your diver and send him down here, right along this line to the other bank." He indicated an imaginary line between the handkerchief and the post on the other side.

"You mean you're going to spend five hundred dollars to get that wrench back?" Williams wailed.

"Something like that."

Williams sank weakly against the base of the bridge. "You've done some daffy things since I been working with you, but this wins the grand prize."

"Well, you can make the award later. Right now you get the diver and his boat. Have him back here in an hour. I'm going to talk with Deputy Strom."

"Simmons has a record." The deputy chewed on a cigar stub. "We found his picture and fingerprints in the Bureau of Identification."

"I'm not surprised," said Crane. "One out of every forty-nine persons in the United States have records."

"He was given six months for extortion. Tried to blackmail an old widow he was working for. She trapped him, then begged the judge to be lenient with him. I guess he'd been romancing her. He should have got a couple of years."

"How long ago was that?"

"Fifteen years."

"Nothing on him since then?"

"No. He's been with Westland ever since that."

Springs on the deputy's swivel chair groaned as he put the cigar stub on the edge of his desk. There was a line of burns from other stubs on the brown surface.

Crane asked, "Did he say why he didn't tell you about Sprague coming up to the apartment?"

"He says he was afraid he'd get mixed up in his death. He figures it would be tough for him with his record."

"He's probably right. But why did he tell me?"

"He wanted to help Westland if he could, but he didn't want to get himself in a jam."

Crane stared out of the deputy's window at the junk yards across the street. "He wants to help Westland, but he gets ten thousand dollars when Westland dies."

"The hell he does!"

"Sure, didn't you know? He's left ten grand in Westland's will."

Deputy Strom shoved the cigar back in his mouth. "Nobody bothers to tell me anything." He pivoted savagely in the protesting chair. "All I knew was that Miss Martin was the chief beneficiary."

"Why should you have known?" Crane asked. "All you were interested in was to put the skids under Westland. Why should you look around for somebody who might have had a motive for putting Westland out of the way?"

"I don't know why I should be doing it now."

"You don't want an innocent man to go to the chair, do you?"

"Innocent hell!" said the deputy.

Crane grinned at him. "What else did Simmons tell you?"

"I suppose this will be right up your alley, but I might as well tell you." Deputy Strom leaned back in the chair, swung his right foot onto the table. The heel was worn down on the outside. "Simmons let Sprague use the telephone while he was at the apartment."

"Yeah?"

"He heard him call Woodbury and make an appointment to see him at ten o'clock that night."

"So!" Crane scratched his ear. "Did Sprague say why he wanted to see Woodbury?"

"Simmons said he didn't. He said he just made the appointment with him and then hung up."

Crane said, "Simmons seems to give out bits of information as though he was having teeth pulled—one at a time. How'd you get it out of him?"

"We just employed a little—" the deputy made a depreciatory gesture with the cigar—"persuasion."

Crane thought for a moment. "Did you ask Woodbury about the call?"

"Sure. He admitted he got it all right. Said he didn't know what Sprague wanted."

"Didn't he think it was funny Sprague didn't keep the appointment?"

"He said he did at the time, but when he learned Sprague had been killed in an automobile accident he didn't think any more about it."

Crane walked over to the window. "Everything about this case seems logical enough if you want to believe everything." He watched a Nash squad car pull up to the curb. "But if you don't, it all sounds fishy."

"I don't see anything wrong with Woodbury's story."

"There isn't anything wrong with it. It just seems funny he didn't tell somebody about the appointment. If you're supposed to meet somebody on the night he is mysteriously killed, you usually say something about it."

"There's nothing mysterious about being run over by a hit-and-run driver."

"I guess not," Crane said. He slid his hat off the deputy's table.

"Wait a second." Strom rose laboriously. "What do you think Sprague wanted to see Woodbury for?"

"What did Woodbury think?"

"He thought it was on business."

Crane said, "So do I."

The diver's name was Peter Finnegan. He had on a rubber suit and weighted shoes, and he looked at William Crane with blue eyes the color of a poilu's uniform. "You want me to go down for a steel monkey wrench?" he asked. His lemon-colored hair was slick with Vitalis.

They stood on the untidy deck of the *Patricia G.*, a small tugboat which had once been painted red. A tar-smeared rope, looped over a post on the river landing below the Wrigley Building, kept them from drifting inland with the current. Smoke, transparent and almost colorless, ascended from the squat funnel.

Crane said, "I want you to bring up whatever you find in the way of steel. A wrench, or anything else. Did Mr. Williams explain where you're supposed to look?"

"Yeah. Between this place and the handkerchief over there." The diver leaned over the rail. "It won't be so tough. It's only about thirty feet deep, and luckily I got an electro-magnet that'll find any steel within a hell of a distance. When do you want me to start?"

"Right now, before it gets dark."

The diver shouted, "Charley." A small grimy man with a cap peered out of the cabin, blinked in the sunlight. The diver said, "Tell Mac I'm goin' down, then come up and handle the rope."

The grimy man hesitated. "Did you get the dough in advance?"

"Think I'm a damn fool?" asked the diver.

Patricia G. trembled as the air pump started below. The diver picked up his helmet. "Give me a lift with this, will you?"

Charley came and took the helmet out of Crane's hands. "I better do it," he said. His skin had an unhealthy pallor under the grime.

Doc Williams came forward from the stern, where he had been watching some sea gulls. "I hope you know what you're doing," he said.

Crane said, "I hope so too."

The diver lowered himself on a rope ladder into the water, then let go his grasp. He sank smoothly out of sight, pulling the air hose, the rope, and another line after him.

Charley, paying out the rope, said, "The third one's for the magnet."

In a few seconds the rope ceased to move. "He's down," said Charley. Bubbles broke the oily surface of the water, traced a path to the other bank. An inquiring gull coasted down to inspect them, discovered nothing to eat, and returned upstream to a sentry post by an open sewer main.

"You're lucky the river runs away from the lake, and not into it as it used to," said Charley.

"Why?" asked Crane.

"A diver never'd be able to walk in the silt and mud the river would deposit if it emptied into the lake. As it is, the current running from the lake keeps the bed clean and firm."

"That is a break."

"Sure, an' so is the slow current. There are plenty of rivers with currents so fast a diver couldn't stand up in them."

Now halfway out, the bubbles suddenly halted. Presently they began to return.

"He's got hold of something," said Charley.

Preceded by a maelstrom of bubbles, the diver came part way up the rope ladder. Charley unscrewed the circular glass front of the helmet. The diver grinned boyishly. "Here's your wrench." He tossed it on the desk.

Crane said, "Fine, I'm certainly glad to have it back. But—" he picked up the wrench, handed it to Williams—"I'd like you to look for something else. It should be right around where you found this."

"Mister," the diver said plaintively, "would you mind tellin' me what it is?"

"It's about the same size as the wrench."

The diver raised himself until his shoulders were level with the rail. He hooked his elbows over the wood. "So it's a guessing game we're playin'." He winked at Charley's dirty face. "Animal, mineral, or vegetable?"

Crane said, "Listen. I'd like to tell you what I hope you find, but it's better I didn't. Go down and take another look, will you?"

As the water was closing over the diver's head, a policeman leaped from the concrete pier to the *Patricia G.* He said, "What's goin' on here?"

Charley jerked his thumb at Crane. "Ask him."

Crane asked, "What's the matter, officer?"

"Matter? Look at that bridge."

All of them tilted their heads upward. The bridge was lined with spectators, rows deep, like the two-bit bleachers in a ball park.

"In another minute they'll be blocking traffic," said the policeman.

Crane made his voice authoritative. "I can't help it. We're

from the War Department, and we have to get the depth of the river at this point. Washington wants it for some harbor figures." He looked at Williams. "Bit of a rush job, eh, Major?"

Williams managed to conceal most of his astonishment. "Why . . . quite right, Colonel."

Crane continued, "However, officer, we should be finished in a very few moments. If you'd just see nothing happens up on the bridge we'll be . . . "

"I'll be pleased to, Colonel." The policeman's face was respectful. "I was in the army meself during the war."

"I'll wager you served under General Foreman."

"Yes, sir. How'd you know?"

"Just a guess. He's a damn fine soldier." Crane nodded his head and, lying, added, "Know the old boy well."

The policeman was hardly off the boat when the diver's bubbles indicated he was coming back. Water streamed from his shoulders, gurgled into the river as he raised himself on the ladder. As soon as Charley had unscrewed the front of his helmet, he said, "I guess this is what you want." He held out an automatic pistol. "It must've been down there quite a while."

Crane accepted the pistol. It had a silver plate on the side with the name "R. Westland" stamped upon it. "Just what I wanted," he said.

"Jumpin' Jesus!" Doc Williams exclaimed. "How did you know it would be down there, of all places?"

Major Lee tried the pistol's trigger. "I think we can make it shoot." He rubbed off some of the rust with his thumbnail. "But we haven't any Webley bullets."

Williams said, "Can't we buy some in a sporting goods store?"

"I imagine we can if we look around."

"Try Woodbury," Crane suggested. "I bet he'll have some."

"He wouldn't dare give them to us," said Williams.

"He wouldn't dare not to."

"What you want, Mr. Crane," asked Major Lee, holding the pistol in the palm of his hand, "is to find out if the bullets fired from this pistol correspond to the marks on the Webley bullets which killed Mrs. Westland, the records of which I have in my files?"

"That's the idea. I'd like to have a report as soon as possible."

"It won't take long . . . if we can get some bullets."

"Williams will try Woodbury," Crane said. He took the pistol from the ballistics expert. "Where could I buy a war-time Webley like this in America?"

"Buy one?" The major scowled. "There are a number of firms which handle old and obsolete weapons, but most of them stock American equipment. They sell the stuff to South American countries for revolutions, and for their armies, too. But I can think of a few that might have some Webleys on hand."

"Could you give me their names?"

The major said, "Certainly." He spent some time checking names on a long list of armament firms, then handed it to Crane.

"Thanks," Crane said. "Would you mind letting Williams know what you find out about Westland's pistol as soon as you can? He'll keep in touch with you."

"I'll be glad to."

Crane put the pistol on the major's desk and followed Williams out to the street. They went over to the Drake Hotel and sent straight telegrams to the firms checked on Major Lee's list. The telegrams read:

HAS ANYONE BOUGHT A WAR MODEL WEBLEY AUTO-
MATIC FROM YOU WITHIN LAST YEAR? PLEASE ANSWER
AT ONCE COLLECT. IMPORTANT.

DEPUTY CHIEF OF DETECTIVES ERNEST STROM,

CHICAGO, ILL.

Crane paid the astonished girl sixty-one dollars and for-
ty-three cents for eighty-two telegrams, said, "We better get to
Strom before the collect answers start coming in."

8:15 P. M.

Finklestein marched into the hotel room as Crane was pushing a pair of green balloon-silk pajamas into his zipper bag. The
attorney's lips were compressed tightly, his cheeks were flushed
over his jaw bone.

"I went over our client's accounts," he announced.

Crane lifted his comb and one of his two silver-backed military hairbrushes from the dresser. "Well?"

"He's got enough hot bonds in his possession to float a gov-
ernment loan."

Crane hesitated over the bag. "Stolen bonds?"

"Stolen and counterfeit. It looks as though he's been in every
mail robbery for the last ten years."

"Gosh! How much worth?"

"So far the accountants have been able to check on nearly six
hundred thousand dollars' worth, but we aren't through yet."

Crane rubbed the back of his hand with the hairbrush.
"That's more money than Westland's got." The bristles hurt his
skin. "How'd he get it in his account?"

"It's not all in his account. Most of the bonds have been
stuck among the securities of Westland's personal clients, the

stuff they let the firm hold to cover their trading account." Finklestein mopped his brow with a silk handkerchief. "It looks as though Westland had been buying the hot bonds from gangsters, substituting them for good bonds in accounts and then selling the good bonds on the market."

"How'd you find out about it?"

"One of the auditors happened to notice some bonds he knew were supposed to have been retired. He checked on them and found they had been stolen in the big Rondout mail robbery. The reason they hadn't been cashed by Westland is that they were listed as being stolen. So then we got hold of a list of stolen bonds from the Federal Building and checked up every bond in every account."

"You think, then, that he was buying the bonds from some gangster at about a dime on the dollar and pushing them into his clients' accounts?"

"It couldn't be anything else, unless he actually stole the bonds himself."

Crane said, "Well, it's goddam funny." He dropped the brush in his bag. "You better ask him about them in the morning."

"You don't think he'd tell us, do you?"

"Why not? He doesn't have to worry much about being arrested for stealing the bonds, does he?"

"Then you don't think he knows what's been done to the accounts?"

"I don't know. I expect he would have told us about it before this if he had. Either that, or he's guilty of his wife's murder." Crane pulled the zipper on the bag. "Maybe he just floats hot bonds between murders."

Finklestein eyed the bag. "Where're you going?"

"I'm going to Peoria."

"This is a swell time to be going to Peoria, on the night before Westland——"

"Don't get excited; it's on business." Crane fished a telegram from his inside coat pocket, gave it to the attorney. It read:

WEBLEY AUTOMATIC, WAR MODEL, SOLD LAST APRIL TO A P. T. BROWN OF ST. LOUIS, MO.

WASHINGTON ARMS COMPANY

PEORIA, ILL.

Crane explained, "That's in answer to about a million telegrams I sent out to armament firms all over the country."

"Why'd you do that? I thought it was Westland's pistol which killed his wife."

"We'll know about that pretty soon." Crane grinned at the angry bewilderment in Finklestein's pale eyes. "You see, I found Westland's pistol this afternoon."

"Found it!" Finklestein theatrically pressed a hand to his forehead. "This is getting too much for me. Where did you find it?"

"In the Chicago River."

"In the river!" Finklestein's knees folded, he sank down on the bed. "How did you find it there?"

Crane lifted his bag. "This is beginning to sound like a vaudeville act." He picked his camel's-hair coat off the floor. "I've got to catch a plane, and I'll tell you all about it tomorrow. Major Lee is going to make a ballistics test of the gun as soon as Williams finds him some bullets, and then he's going to wire me at the Père Marquette Hotel in Peoria when he finds out whether it did the job or not."

He pulled his hat from under the bed, put it on his head.

"I think I've got this case solved, and I want you to have things fixed so the Governor will give us a reprieve if we can produce some new evidence."

Finklestein said, "I already talked to him once."

"Never mind." Crane looked at his watch. "Jesus! I better hurry. The plane leaves in forty minutes. You fix the Governor and find out all you can about the bonds—where they were stolen and so on."

Bouncing off the bed, Finklestein said, "But do you know who killed Mrs. Westland?"

"I'll tell you tomorrow, when I come back from Peoria."

Finklestein pursued Crane down the corridor, tugged at his coat sleeve. "Listen, just tell me how the murderer got out of that apartment and left it locked like it was."

"Just a clever trick," said Crane. "Really quite simple."

"He must have had an extra key?"

Crane punched the button for the elevator. "There wasn't any extra key."

He stepped into an elevator. The gold-painted door blotted out Finklestein's face.

CHAPTER XVI

Thursday Night

7:30 P.M.

William Crane paid the cab driver and handed his pigskin zipper bag to a redcap. "Peoria," he said.

"You've got ten minutes," said the man. "Gate 3."

From the smart blue-clad ticket agent, Crane bought a one-way ticket to Peoria. He paid three cents for a *Herald and Examiner* and sat down in a moderne chair in the waiting room. A story by Delos Avery on the front page began:

> When Robert Westland, socially prominent broker, sentenced to die for the murder of his wife last spring, goes to the electric chair shortly after midnight tomorrow, he will walk between a gangster and a fiend.
>
> Neither of his companions are fellow clubmen.

Farther down the column it was reported that Attorney Charles Finklestein, acting for Westland, had attempted by telephone to secure a reprieve for his client, but had been unable to present the Governor any new evidence on the case. The rest of the story was a re-hash of the careers of Westland, Connors, and Varecha. Crane was reading this with interest when a fat lady in a purple dress leaned over him.

"Have you the time, young man?" she asked nervously.

"For what?"

She looked at him blankly. "I mean, what time is it?" She had a brown mole and a light mustache on her upper lip.

He examined his wrist watch. "Eight-fifty-three."

"Yes, that's the same time as the big clock up there." The fat lady shook her head in a relieved manner. "I was so afraid it had stopped." She lowered herself into a chair beside him. "This is my first airplane trip, and I wouldn't want to miss the plane, would I?"

"No," William Crane agreed.

"I'm really terribly thrilled about it." The fat lady shivered like a dish of raspberry jello. "Just imagine poor little me way up alone in the clouds. Only I do wish I knew somebody who was going too; it would be so very comforting. You don't happen to——"

"No, I don't." He rose hastily. "I'm just meeting a friend from the East. Never been up in a plane in my life. Wouldn't go up. Terribly dangerous." He retreated to the field.

The redcap hailed him. "Your plane is just pullin' in."

A very pretty brown-haired stewardess with a blue overseas' cap smiled at him as he stepped from the portable staircase into the plane. He smiled back at her, then selected a seat at the rear of the cabin so the view from the window wouldn't be obscured by the wing. Other passengers filed past him and took other seats, self-consciously trying to appear casual.

Two men in dungarees were fastening sacks of mail under

the wing. Ahead, a big twin-motored Curtiss-Condor sleeper, bound for the Southwest, was trying its engines, sending a curtain of dust across the field. The faces of people waiting to meet the New York plane were white by the fence in front of the ticket office.

The co-pilot, an astonishingly young man with red cheeks, sauntered down the aisle, paused at the door. "How about it, sweetheart?"

"One more," said the stewardess. "A Mrs. Pettibone." Her voice was sweet.

"We're a minute late already." The co-pilot was politely accusatory.

"Here she comes now," said the girl.

There was a sound of puffing, of pushing, of hands clawing on metal. "Oh, dear!" exclaimed a voice behind William Crane; "I'm so out of breath I don't have any strength left."

"You're all right now, Mrs. Pettibone," said the co-pilot.

Mrs. Pettibone's hips brushed Crane's face as she passed him. He glanced up, saw with horror she was the fat lady of the waiting room. Hastily he raised the newspaper over his face, sank down in his seat. He could visualize the stricken look which would come into her eyes when she discovered the young man of the waiting room had lied to avoid her. He realized he was in for a bad hour and a quarter to Peoria.

It was all right while they were starting, the engine vibrating the plane and the passengers stiff and defensive under the deafening roar of a motor full out, but as soon as they lifted sweetly from the ground and Chicago unrolled under them like a sparkling rhinestone evening gown, Mrs. Pettibone started to examine her fellow passengers. Crane held the paper in front of his face and, because the woman's chair was higher than his, slightly over his head.

Although this position became very tiresome after half an hour, he stuck grimly to his resolve not to hurt the fat lady's feelings. His arms ached, his shoulders pained him, he read every item on the front page five times, but he continued to hold the paper over his head.

The stewardess halted beside him, a saucy smile on her tomato-red lips. "Care for some chewing gum?" She regarded the upheld paper with frank curiosity.

"I hate chewing gum."

Lingering, the girl persisted, "Would you mind telling me why you're holding that paper over your head?"

Crane said, "I expect to use it as a parachute when the plane falls."

The plane moved steadily from one pale brass curtain rod of light to another along the illuminated airway, and finally they were in Peoria, and Crane hurried out of the cabin. His arms were very tired, but he was experiencing a comfortable sensation of having acted the part of a gentleman.

This sensation was a rare one indeed, and he enjoyed it as he waited for a taxi to swing around in front of him. He was just reaching for the door when someone tapped his arm. It was Mrs. Pettibone. She said:

"You naughty, naughty boy—playing hide-and-seek with me all the way to Peoria."

William Crane shuddered violently, leaped into the cab.

The desk clerk at the Père Marquette examined the registration card, said, "I believe I have a telegram for you."

The yellow envelope was addressed to William Crane. He slit it with his thumb, opened the folded sheet, read:

WESTLAND'S GUN NOT THE ONE THAT SHOT HIS WIFE.

DOC.

Crane said, "It's for me, all right." He followed the bell boy to the elevator and from it to a spacious corner room. He tossed the boy a quarter and, when the door had closed, opened the telephone directory. He found the Washington Arms Company in the yellow section of the book, called the number, but the hotel operator reported no one answered. Dubiously, he looked under Washington in the front of the book and was gratified to find a G. Washington whose office phone number corresponded with that of the arms company. The home number of G. Washington was answered by a woman.

She was Mrs. G. Washington, and she said her husband had gone out of town overnight, but would return by train at eleven o'clock the next morning. He would, she continued, probably go right to his office. She said her husband was the only one who had access to the records.

"It's lucky he's to be in town," she added.

Crane said, "Yes, it is."

He went down to the hotel restaurant for dinner, and although Peoria is noted for its whiskey, he drank only milk. Soon afterward, in line with this reformation, he went to bed.

11 P. M.

Isadore Varecha was sleeping like a child, and this was almost as annoying as his former sobbing. Westland lay on his back, a handkerchief over his eyes, and listened tensely and angrily to the fiend's gentle breathing. He wished he could fall asleep as simply and as easily. Instead, he stared into the whitely translucent cloth, feeling edgy and faint and nauseated, as he used to feel in college before a football game. This comparison of the sensations before a game and before being jolted to death in the electric chair was bathetic, and he smiled, but only because he was pretending to be brave and not because he wanted to smile. He would much rather have wept. He was really scared as hell.

Presently, when he could lie still no longer, he pulled the handkerchief from his face and sat up on the bed. As though somebody had pushed a stiff whiskbroom in them, his eyes smarted in the bright light. Rubbing them, he noticed a black shadow on the corridor wall opposite Connors' cell. Curiosity brought him to the front of his own cell.

The priest was standing there, his dark robe motionless, his ruddy face solemn, intently watching Connors, who was hunched over on the end of his disordered bed. Neither was speaking, and Westland received an impression they had been facing each other in silence this way for a long time. Connors seemed oblivious of the priest, his moody eyes staring past him, not looking at him, not looking away from him. The priest's scrutiny was personal and, in a way, triumphant.

As Westland stared at them, the drifting air, damp and chill, crept across his face, numbed his wrists and ankles.

Finally the priest spoke softly. "Have you changed your mind, my son?" His voice had the timbre of a bass viol.

Connors said, "No."

The priest's garments made an angry frou-frou as he walked

past Westland's cell along the corridor. His red face was grim. Westland swung around to look at Connors.

No longer veiled, the gangster's eyes were luminous with fear and regret.

Friday Morning

11:30 A. M.

When William Crane walked through the rain to the office entrance of the arms company's bulky brick warehouse for a second time, the prim, spinsterish reception clerk attempted a smile.

"Mr. Washington is here now," she said. "I'll just call . . ."

In a minute she shoved away the suspended telephone mouthpiece, announced with a simper that Mr. Washington would see Mr. Crane.

Mr. Washington was a saturnine man with quince-colored skin. He had on a purple shirt and a green necktie. He shook Crane's hand, leaning over his mahogany desk.

"Pretty bad day," he observed mournfully.

"Terrible," Crane said. "Awful."

"Rain," said Mr. Washington disgustedly.

Crane said, "Yeah, rain." He brushed some drops from his top coat, added, "Seems to me the good old-fashioned winter snow is getting scarce. Nothing but rain nowadays."

This seemed to be the right note. Mr. Washington's expression became brighter. He extracted a pencil-thin cigar from his lips, held it daintily between his two fingers. "When I was a boy I used to walk through snow as high as my head to get to school." He waved the cigar in the air. "Four miles it was, too. You don't see snow like that now."

After further conversation had exhausted the subject, Crane explained that he wanted to find out, if possible, who had purchased the Webley.

"So you're from the Chicago police," Mr. Washington observed. "I wondered what you wanted when I received that wire yesterday afternoon."

"It's in connection with the Westland case," Crane said. He didn't say anything about the Chicago police.

"The Westland case?"

"That rich broker who shot his wife."

"Seems like I read something about it, but it wouldn't be any wonder I didn't. We don't have much Chicago crime news in our papers down here."

Crane said that new evidence had made the police believe Mrs. Westland had been killed with a Webley purchased from Mr. Washington's company.

"Well, I'll be durned!" said Mr. Washington, intrigued. He thumbed through a green file cabinet. "Here's the sheet. P. T. Brown of St. Louis bought two Lugers, three Mausers, one Colt, and one Webley, all war models. Said he was a collector. The lot cost him one hundred and sixteen dollars."

"P. T. Brown?" Crane chewed meditatively at a finger. "Do you know who handled the sale?"

"No trouble about that. Only got one salesman: Oscar Havermeyer. Like to talk to him?"

Crane nodded.

They went out past the spinsterly reception clerk, who did not look up at them, and down a damp corridor and into a large room filled with an amazing and sinister collection of weapons, ranging from silver-mounted derringers to an express rifle for elephant hunting. Along racks against the walls were rows of Springfield rifles; a Browning machine gun leered at them around a glass showcase full of automatic pistols. There were guns in every direction.

Mr. Washington said apologetically, "This is only the display room. We keep most of our weapons back in the warehouse."

"You could start a revolution with the stuff you have right here," Crane said. "A hell of a big revolution."

"We have." Mr. Washington lifted a dangerous-looking revolver out of the nearest glass case. "We even supplied the guns for both the revolutionists and the federalists in one Central American country. Business hasn't been so good lately though." He handed the revolver to Crane. "Wyatt Earp's."

"The old frontier marshal?"

The revolver was a blue Colt .38 set in a .45 frame. Eleven notches slashed the sweat-darkened butt. There was no trigger. It balanced sweetly in Crane's hand.

Mr. Washington said, "He didn't mark up Mexicans." He pointed out a slim rifle with a curved powder horn hanging from the barrel. "One of old Dan Boone's bear rifles." Then, mysteriously, he bent over and tenderly lifted a tarpaulin from a bizarre mechanism on the floor. "What do you think of this?"

The thing looked like a huge coffee grinder. There was a gaping funnel on top and on the side there was a large wheel with a wooden handle. A black barrel projected from one end.

"What is it?" Crane asked.

"If Abraham Lincoln hadn't been such an obstinate cuss, this would have ended the Civil War in a month." Mr. Washington caressed the funnel. "I wouldn't sell it for ten thousand dollars. It's the first practical machine gun."

"A machine gun?"

"Sure. You turn the handle, and another fellow loads it, and it'll fire one hundred shots a minute. It was invented during the Civil War, but old Abe, who was always meddling in military affairs, wouldn't let the army use it. He called it the coffee mill."

"Maybe it wouldn't work."

"Sure it would. Abe and the generals were hidebound just as they are now." Mr. Washington gave the crank a tentative turn. "Would you like to see it work?"

"Gosh, I would," Crane said; "but I've got to find out all I can about that Webley and then go back to Chicago."

"Oh, sure." Mr. Washington gently tucked the tarpaulin around the mechanism. "I'll get Oscar."

Oscar Havermeyer was blond, big, Germanic, and dumb, but he remembered the man who had bought the Webley and the other pistols.

"Would you be able to identify a photograph of him?" Crane asked.

"I believe so."

Crane extracted four photographs from an envelope. "Is he one of these?"

Havermeyer examined the four prints, nodded his head. "Yes." He started to hand Crane one of them. "It's this——"

Crane said quickly, "Don't tell me. Show them to Mr. Washington and see if he picks out the same man."

Havermeyer presently announced Mr. Washington's choice was the same.

"Good," said Crane. "Now, Oscar, did you notice anything strange about the sale? I mean, was this Brown more interested in the Webley than in the other pistols?"

"Well, he wanted to know if the Webley would shoot."

"Ah-ha! What d'you tell him?"

Havermeyer blinked his tranquil eyes. "I didn't tell him anything. I didn't know myself. I got some bullets, and we went out to the range and shot it a couple of times. It worked fine."

"Swell!" Crane said. "Can you show me the range?"

They walked through the back of the armory and into a sunken yard. At the far end, halfway up a twelve-foot earthbank, three white paper targets were suspended. The rain, soft on their cheeks, brought out the rich smell of the fine Illinois loam, made it black and glossy. To their right, the Illinois river bent in a half moon.

Crane asked, "What's back of those targets?"

"Earth," said Mr. Washington. "Earth and clay."

"Do you remove the bullets after you shoot them into the bank?"

"We haven't for a couple of years. We don't do enough shooting to make it worth while."

Crane scowled at the sky the color and texture of a gray squirrel coat. "Have other war-time Webleys been shot into the bank?"

"No. That's the only one we had in the place. They're pretty rare in America, although I guess you could get plenty of them in Canada."

Crane strolled down the range, lifted one of the paper targets. The blue clay was pockmarked with hundreds of holes.

"I wonder if you could get the Webley's bullets out of there?" he asked.

Mr. Washington said, "You'd have to tear about six feet of bank down to get at the lead, and even then I doubt if you could tell which bullets came from the Webley."

Havermeyer's soft blue eyes were wide. "I could tell them."

Mr. Washington shook his head dubiously. "It'd take a man half a day to dig into the bank and screen out the lead." He tilted his jaw upward. "Besides, it's going to keep on raining all day."

Crane thrust his hands in his pockets. "I'd hire men to dig for the bullets and—" the toe of his shoe made a wavery "I" on the sticky earth—"I'd give one hundred dollars for each bullet they found."

As though about to whistle, Mr. Washington pursed his lips. No sound came, however. Instead, he said, "Well, business hasn't been so good . . . "

3:30 P. M.

Later in the afternoon, while the men were working, Crane sent a telegram to Finklestein. It read:

PLEASE HAVE EVERYBODY INCLUDING MURDERER AT WARDEN'S OFFICE 9 P. M.

Outside it was still raining.

CHAPTER XVII

Friday Night

THE WARDEN's big wall clock—Naval Observatory time, adjusted hourly through Western Union—said nine-twenty-two when Crane, Oscar Havermeyer, and Major Lee, followed by Williams and the diver, Finnegan, entered the office. Blue cigarette smoke shrouded the room, shadowed a confusingly large number of people. Finklestein jumped out of a chair.

"Boy!" he exclaimed. "I was beginning to think you weren't going to show up."

"I see you got my wire," said Crane. He allowed himself to be pulled over to a tall man with heavy eyebrows and a big crooked mouth.

Finklestein said, "This is State's Attorney Ross. The Governor has agreed to accept his recommendation on a reprieve."

Crane said, "How d'you do," and added, "Then all we have to do is convince you?"

The state's attorney had a slow smile. "That's all . . . and I hope you do."

Oscar Havermeyer was wearing square-toed tan shoes and the best blue suit of store clothes $15 would buy and a straw hat.

He and Finnegan backed up against the wall, stared covertly at Miss Brentino's pale face. She had on a sleek Pernod-green wool suit with a redingote coat and black shoes; her legs were slender in sheer neutral silk. Woodbury's dark head was bent attentively over her.

Crane looked past Bolston's broad shoulders to Warden Buckholtz. "Could you bring up Westland?"

"Sure." The warden struggled out of his swivel chair. "Right away." His small eyes darted a curious glance at Crane as he went out the door.

Crane peered through the smoke, saw Deputy Strom standing with Simmons against the wall, and observed, "So you brought your prisoner."

The deputy scowled. "As far as I'm concerned he's free." He chewed his short cigar viciously. "This is your party now, and I miss my guess if it ain't a flop."

Crane ignored him. He asked Bolston, "Where's Wharton?"

Finklestein said, "He hasn't shown up yet."

Emily Lou Martin was wearing a russet knit-wool dress with a red leather belt. She said, "I bet he doesn't show up." She was wearing silk stockings the color of ripe wheat, and she was perched on the warden's desk with her slender legs crossed. Doc Williams could see a seductive triangle of flesh where the silk ended far above the knee.

"Oh yes; he'll come," said Crane.

Westland arrived with Warden Buckholtz. He looked as though he had just survived an attack of malaria. His face was deeply lined; there were discolored hollows under his eyes; his skin was yellow. He managed a feeble smile. He had only two hours to live.

Emily Lou slid from the warden's desk, threw her arms

around him. "What have they been doing to you, honey?" She ran her fingers across a pancake-size circle of bare skin on the top of his head.

Westland pulled her hand away. "They shaved me. On the head and here." He showed, under the slit left leg of his trousers, a hairless leg. "I feel like a Spanish bolero dancer with these flapping pants." His voice quavered, belied his sick grin.

"We have to cut the trousers and shave the head and leg for the electrodes," Warden Buckholtz explained. "That's so there won't be a short circuit."

"Oh, my God!" exclaimed Westland. He looked at the warden through feverish eyes. "Can't you——"

"It's all right," Crane said. "It's all right."

Pushing his back from the wall, Deputy Strom said, "Like hell it's all right. Let's see some evidence."

"You'll see some as soon as Wharton shows up." Crane rubbed his chin. "In the meantime I'd like to ask Westland one question for the record."

Westland said, "Go ahead." He had gained control of himself.

"It's about your clients' brokerage accounts. Did you know they were all loaded with phoney bonds?"

"Phoney bonds!" Westland glanced incredulously at Woodbury. "They couldn't be. I bought most of them myself."

Woodbury fingered his black mustache. "They were, though, Bob. Even some of Joan's bonds in her safe in the apartment were part of the loot of an Indiana bank robbery."

"That's impossible. I don't see how . . . " Westland's voice faded away.

Deputy Strom said, "Not much you don't."

Bolston, leaning his broad shoulders against the open door, announced, "Here comes Wharton."

Wharton entered at a trot, his face cherry-red. "By gad, I'm sorry to be late, Bob." His voice was thick; he was a little drunk. "Delayed unavoidably." He patted Westland's shoulder.

State's Attorney Ross said, "It's getting late, Crane. You better start pretty soon . . . or . . . "

Crane went over and sat on the warden's desk. His knees almost touched Miss Brentino's hip. "First I'm going to reconstruct the general events of Mrs. Westland's murder, before I go into the evidence."

Deputy Strom laughed unmirthfully. "You haven't got any evidence."

"We'll see. Anyway, as I reconstruct the murder, Westland was lured to his wife's apartment by a telephone call which at the time he believed came from Miss Martin."

Deputy Strom asked, "Can you prove there was a call?"

"Listen, flatfoot," said State's Attorney Ross. "You've had your turn. Give him a chance."

"I'm just reconstructing now," Crane explained, "not presenting facts."

The deputy spat on the wood floor.

Crane continued, "Whoever talked to Westland made him mad, and he went over to his wife's apartment. They had a quarrel which was heard by the elevator boy, Tony. Then, according to Westland's story, which by the way was accepted by the police, he left the apartment at 12:40. Now the Shuttles had testified that they heard a shot at 12:10, but Mr. Bolston discovered that they had been mixed up because of the change from daylight saving time to standard time that Sunday night." Crane glanced at Bolston for confirmation.

"Woodbury and I made the discovery," said Bolston.

"The shot was actually fired, then, at 1:10, or half an hour after Westland said he left the apartment. This was interesting, but of little value to us, because we had only Westland's unsupported testimony as to when he left his wife's apartment. From the standpoint of the state he could easily have lied about that."

State's Attorney Ross nodded.

Crane glanced at the soft curve of Miss Brentino's cheek bone. "To continue with the reconstruction—after Westland left, the real murderer, who was waiting for him to leave, entered the apartment and shot Mrs. Westland. He killed her with a Webley automatic, but not with Westland's Webley, as the police believed. We know this because Major Lee has proved it by ballistics tests on Westland's pistol, which we found in the river."

"I've already talked with Major Lee about that," said the state's attorney. "Both Strom and I admit the State was wrong there."

"How do you get the murderer out of the locked apartment?" demanded Strom.

"I'll come to that later." Crane lifted a dagger-shaped paper cutter from the desk, pricked the back of his left hand with it. "He did get out, however, and on the next day he stole Westland's Webley. It had to disappear so as to incriminate Westland, but the murderer couldn't take the risk of stealing it before the crime. Its disappearance might have aroused Westland's suspicion, or he might have reported its loss to the police."

"You ought to try fiction writing," said Deputy Strom.

"Thus we have three things which implicate Westland. First, the use of a Webley in the murder and the disappearance of his own Webley. Second, the trick of locking the apartment so that it appeared as if only Westland's key could have been used.

Third, the timing of the murder so that the medical examiner would say it could have been done while Westland was known to have been in the apartment."

"This is very pretty," said State's Attorney Ross, "but what about the motive?"

"It was a double motive." Crane smiled down at Miss Brentino. "The murderer wanted to get rid of both the Westlands. He saw an opportunity to kill her and at the same time to get Westland electrocuted for the job."

"Killing two birds with a single pistol shot," Bolston murmured.

"That's fine," said Deputy Strom with heavy sarcasm. "You've certainly convinced us with a lot of fine facts. Now if you'll just point out your murderer, we'll send him to the electric chair in place of Mr. Westland."

Crane said, "I've brought somebody here to point him out." He beckoned to Oscar Havermeyer.

Miss Brentino's wide brown eyes watched the man advance.

"In order to shoot Mrs. Westland with a war-time Webley, the murderer had to buy one." Crane was talking to the state's attorney. "Mr. Havermeyer is a salesman for the Washington Arms Company of Peoria. He sold a war-time Webley to the murderer just two days before Mrs. Westland was slain."

Havermeyer's blond face was impassive.

"Now, Oscar, do you see the man who bought the Webley in this room?"

"Yeah," said Havermeyer.

"Will you point him out?"

Havermeyer strolled over to the door. His tan shoes squeaked like mice. "This's him." He jerked a thumb at Bolston.

CHAPTER XVIII

Friday Night

WESTLAND'S FACE was ghastly with disappointment, his voice thin. "You've made a terrible mistake, Crane."

The tumult had faded now, and the room was self-consciously quiet. Deputy Strom was whispering to the state's attorney.

"It's ridiculous." Bolston's jaw was outlined under skin as tight as rawhide. "I could prosecute you for this."

"No you couldn't," said Crane. "So far you've only been identified as the man who bought a Webley similar to Westland's two days before the murder."

Bolston said, "Your friend is as crazy as you are."

Crane handed the assistant state's attorney two notarized sheets of paper. "These are the affidavits of two more witnesses to the purchase. Both of them identified Bolston's photographs. One of them is president of the company; the other, his secretary. They're willing to testify that Bolston bought the gun."

"They recognized the photograph just like I done," said Oscar Havermeyer.

State's Attorney Ross folded the affidavits, thrust them in his pocket. "Bolston, you'll have a hard time getting around three witnesses."

Deputy Strom looked at him in surprise. "I thought you said——"

"Give Crane a chance to finish," said the state's attorney. "A man's life——"

"Even if I did buy the gun, which I didn't," asserted Bolston, "there's no proof in that act that I killed Mrs. Westland." He glanced at Strom's face. "Why doesn't he produce the pistol he says I bought?"

Crane said, "I can't, because it's too well hidden."

"You see . . . ?" exclaimed Bolston.

"But," Crane continued, "I can do something just as good. I can prove the gun which Bolston bought was the one used to kill Mrs. Westland."

All of them stared at him incredulously. State's Attorney Ross asked, "You can do it without even having the pistol?"

"Yes. Without magic, too. Major Lee, the floor is yours."

Major Lee looked embarrassed. "It's really quite simple." He fished two envelopes from his coat pocket. "In one of these envelopes are the bullets Mr. Havermeyer brought from Peoria. They were fired from the pistol which Mr. Bolston has been identified as testing before he bought it." He laid the envelope on the warden's desk. "In this other envelope is the bullet which killed Mrs. Westland. Its ballistics marks are identical with those on the Peoria bullets."

"You mean," asked Ross, "that the marks prove the pistol Mr. Bolston has been identified as buying killed Mrs. Westland?"

"Exactly."

Woodbury's eyes, narrowed appraisingly, were upon Bolston. "Would your evidence stand up in court, Major Lee?"

"It always has."

Strom was bewildered but not licked. "If you could go to the river and find Westland's gun, with every place in the whole city to look for it, why can't you find the one from Peoria? My guess is you found Westland's because he told you where he hid it."

"What point would Westland have in not speaking about it before?" Crane demanded. "It would have been a big help during the trial to have been able to prove his pistol didn't kill his wife."

Finklestein rubbed his nose, asked, "Well, how the hell did you find Westland's pistol, anyway?"

"It was a piece of pure deductive reasoning, and a damn good one at that," said Crane modestly. "First I assumed Bolston was the murderer and that he had disposed of Westland's pistol so as to throw suspicion on him. Secondly, as I told you before, I knew the pistol must have been taken after, not before the murder. Then I remembered Bolston had called Westland's man, Simmons, after the murder was discovered, told him the police had gone to arrest Westland, and asked him to go down to the Detective Bureau. Simmons says the call came at 11:30."

"That's right, sir," said Simmons.

"With this time fixed," Crane continued, "I looked around for some other evidence with which I could place Bolston's actions on that morning. We know he was at Mrs. Westland's apartment while the police were there, and Miss Dea and Deputy Strom both say Bolston left to go to his office sometime after eleven o'clock. As Simmons got the call from him a few minutes later, it is logical to assume Bolston phoned him from a near-by drugstore, though this doesn't make much difference."

Bolston said, "This is all surmise. I don't see why we have to listen——"

"Let him go on," said State's Attorney Ross.

"Simmons got the call at 11:30 and left the house five minutes later to go to the Detective Bureau. Bolston watched him leave, let himself in the apartment with a key he had, stole the pistol, and started for the office in his Rolls-Royce."

Westland said, "He didn't have a key." His face had some color in it now.

"I'll explain later," Crane said. "At the very fastest, Bolston would have taken three minutes to get the pistol, so he couldn't have left Westland's apartment before 11:38. But 24 minutes later he stepped into his office. Wharton, who had been waiting there for Westland since 11:30, was leaving as Bolston came in. Mr. Wharton's sure the time was 12:02 because he had resolved to wait only until 12 o'clock for Westland."

"Right," said Wharton.

"I reasoned that Bolston would want to dispose of the stolen pistol before he reached his office. He couldn't afford to have it found on him, or in his car, yet he wasn't certain the police might not take him into custody for questioning. There was a possibility someone had seen him coming out of Mrs. Westland's apartment after the murder.

"Next I tried to imagine where he'd be likely to hide it. He couldn't afford to throw it in somebody's bushes, or in the gutter, or even down a manhole, because somebody might find it, see Westland's name on it, and give it to the police. The two most likely places seemed to be the lake and the river."

Crane ran his fingers through his hair, grinned across at Doc Williams.

"Now, Bolston didn't have time to go to the lake and still make his office in 24 minutes, so I decided he must have tossed the pistol in the river. By an expensive method of trial and error with a taxi, Doc and I found there are only about six ways you can drive from Westland's home to his office and still keep within 25 minutes. You have to cross the river on each of these ways, but all but one of them take you over open, crowded bridges with a watchman's tower at each end—not very good places from which to throw a weapon that could involve you in a murder.

"The time element again told me Bolston couldn't have parked his car and walked along the river bank until he found a good place to throw the Webley away, so the choice was narrowed down to the one bridge which seemed suitable: the Michigan Avenue underpass, which is dark, not crowded and not guarded.

"Once I had decided this, it was an easy matter to pick out the most likely spot on the bridge for pistol-throwing, and to determine by tossing in a monkey wrench just how far out a pistol would go if the driver of the car slung it backhand through the window next to the passenger's seat. Then we sent a diver down with an electro-magnet, and he found both the wrench and the pistol."

"What do you say to that, Strom?" asked State's Attorney Ross.

"He probably planted the pistol there himself," said Deputy Strom stubbornly.

"If I did, I threw it in the river six months ago. Major Lee will assure you it had been under water for some time, and Mr. Finnegan, the diver, will testify it was pretty well buried in the mud."

Finnegan took his blue eyes off Miss Brentino. "That gun wasn't just trun in there, let me tell you. We'd never of found it if it hadn't been for the magnet." He spoke directly toward

Miss Brentino. "You understand about divin', miss? You can't see——"

"Never mind," said Finklestein. "There's only forty minutes left. Let Crane go ahead and tell us about the key Bolston used to get into Westland's apartment."

Bolston objected, "You mean the key he says I used."

"I mean the key you used."

In shifting his weight, Crane brushed his knees against the green wool on Miss Brentino's suit. "The key brings up the story of the telephone call. We felt that whoever called Westland would have to cut into the line in Miss Martin's aunt's home in case he called back. We went out to Miss Martin's apartment and found where the wires had been tapped just outside the dining room."

"The hell you did!" exclaimed Strom.

Miss Martin said, "Yes." Saying the word dimpled her chin. "It was tapped all right. The wire must have gone right out the dining-room window."

Finklestein rubbed his diamond ring against his lips. "You don't know who tapped it?"

Miss Martin said, "No, we don't."

Crane said, "Yes, we do." He smiled at Miss Martin's surprise. "It puzzled me quite a bit, but I happened to solve the problem while I was enjoying a hangover. There's nothing like a hangover for clear thinking."

Williams said, "Why look at me? How should I know?"

"It was really Miss Brentino who gave the clue away." He looked down into her luminous eyes. "She once asked: 'Who could best imitate Miss Martin's voice?'"

"Well, who could?" asked Finklestein.

"Miss Martin herself."

Her eyes suddenly all whites, Miss Martin fainted, slid from her chair to the dusty floor. Bolston said, "You son of a bitch," and started for William Crane. Surprisingly, Deputy Strom intercepted him, seized his arms. Westland, watching the action dazedly from the door, made no move to help Miss Martin.

Woodbury and Miss Brentino pulled Miss Martin into her chair. She moaned, drank some of the water the warden poured from a tarnished silver decanter, and then sat up unassisted. Her face was wan, her expression was preoccupied and secret.

"You must be wrong here, Crane," Woodbury objected. "We know Miss Martin didn't leave her home that evening and that the telephone is in the front of the apartment, where her uncle and aunt would have heard her if she had called."

Crane watched Bolston from the corner of his eyes, ready to jump behind the warden's table in case he got free of Deputy Strom. "The telephone is in the front of the apartment," he agreed, "but I discovered the solution. Westland told me he heard a roaring noise, like a water fall, when he was talking to Miss Martin and she was cleverly using the bad grammar so he wouldn't be sure later whether or not it was her. Well, the noise he heard was the roar of water from a shower bath.

"Miss Martin tapped the wire in the dining room, only a few feet from her door, ran the cord under the rug through her room into the bathroom. Then she shut her door, also the bathroom door, and further, to make sure her family didn't hear her, she turned on the shower full tilt. There's nothing like a shower to drown out the sound of a human voice."

Williams asked, "Then her story about a strange man comin' to fix the phone on the day of the murder was a phoney?"

"Sure. She made it up while we were questioning her. I don't suppose she thought anybody'd ever find the place where the wire was tapped." Crane stared boldly at Miss Martin. "It makes a pretty, even a seductive picture, the thought of Miss Martin standing naked in her shower and making the phone call which nearly sent Westland to his death. I'd like to have been there."

Miss Martin passed the back of her hand over her eyes.

"So would I," said Doc Williams.

"I'm sorry to say that Miss Martin and Bolston were in cahoots," Crane continued. "That's where the key to Westland's apartment comes in. Simmons told us Miss Martin was the only other person to have a key, and of course she gave it to Bolston before the murder. That's how he got in to steal the pistol."

"But why the hell would Miss Martin do that?" Finklestein objected. "She was engaged to marry Westland."

Crane looked at Miss Martin's tremulous lips. "Who knows why a woman does anything? However, I can give you a couple of pretty fair reasons. One is that she was due to inherit about seventy thousand dollars from Westland in case he died.

"The other is that she never could have married him because she was already married to Bolston."

The lawyer said, "Well, I'll be God-damned!"

"Yes, indeed. Williams saw part of a marriage certificate while we were going through her room to look for the tapped wire and—" Crane tried a lie—"we checked up on it and found it was for Miss Martin and Bolston."

Miss Martin sat upright in her chair. "I thought you prying fools saw all of it," she said.

Bolston said, "Be careful."

"They can't make a wife testify against her husband," she said, "and besides——"

"Shut up!" Bolston shouted.

Crane pivoted around to State's Attorney Ross. "I guess that gives it away, doesn't it?" He rolled his head so that he was look-ing at Bolston. "Williams just saw Miss Martin's name on the license, not yours. She said it was her mother's certificate, but it seemed a little strange that her mother should have the maiden name of Emily Lou Martin too.

"And then I remembered I had seen Miss Martin buying you neckties in Saks' Fifth Avenue. That was the fatal clue, because nobody but a newly married husband would let a woman buy ties for him." Crane grinned at the state's attorney. "You know what kind of ties a woman buys?"

Ross said, "Don't I!"

"Why Miss Martin fell for Bolston is something I can't tell you," Crane added, "but I'm sure they thought it would be nice to keep the marriage secret until Miss Martin had Westland's money. Then they could get married again openly."

Miss Martin stared at Bolston, but he wouldn't look at her. Instead, he looked out the window, his face inscrutable. Deputy Strom, still holding his arms, said, "If you can tell me the mo-tive, I'll have to admit you're right."

"The motive isn't so tough." Crane watched Miss Martin's frightened eyes. "The brokerage business hasn't been so hot late-ly. In fact, Westland, the head of the firm, had to depend on his income, yet Bolston has been living in style, with a fancy car costing twenty thousand dollars, a Japanese servant and his own apartment, a couple of clubs and lots of shows and parties. He admitted to Williams and me he had no private income, so nat-urally the question is—how does he do it?"

"Yeah," said Finklestein, "that's the question."

"The answer is Westland's accounts, which your auditors found filled with stolen and counterfeit bonds. You can buy these for a dime on the dollar in any big city if you know the right place to go, and Bolston did. Before Westland was put in jail, Bolston had been sticking those hot bonds in his own accounts, thinking, I suppose, he could leave the country when things seemed about to be discovered, leaving Westland to make good. He probably had a nice sum of money tucked away, because there's a good profit in buying a bond for ten dollars, sticking it in place of one worth a hundred, and then selling the good bond for ninety dollars profit. Do that long enough, and you're bound to make money."

Strom nodded.

"But Mrs. Westland, who kept a lot of her own stocks and bonds in her apartment safe, discovered that some of her carefully purchased securities were bad. Bolston had been handling her stock transactions for two years, ever since she and Westland separated, so she immediately suspected him.

"She called Woodbury and told him she wanted to see Bolston about some bonds, and Woodbury relayed the message to Bolston, who knew at once he was about to be discovered. This was on a Friday, and Bolston knew he would have to face her on Monday, which gave him Saturday and Sunday to decide what to do. I think he must have been contemplating a murder before this, though he may have made up his plan on the spur of the moment, but anyway he realized that if he could get both the Westlands out of the way everything would be just dandy.

"Not only would Bolston's wife inherit Westland's money, but he would also be able to remove the hot bonds and stocks from his clients' accounts and stick them into those of Westland's clients. This would make it unnecessary for him to flee the country, since people, when the bad bonds were found after Westland had been electrocuted, would be convinced that

Westland had not only murdered his wife but had defrauded his clients.

"So the Westland case turned out to be sort of an oblique murder—the slaying of Mrs. Westland to get Westland out of the way."

"But what about the killing of Grant," asked Finklestein, "and Sprague?"

"Bolston had to have Grant killed because he wasn't sure what the burglar had seen. Naturally, sitting in our council meeting, he knew all about our plans to find Grant, and later Miss Martin informed him of the date we'd made through Petro.

"Bolston got his gangaster friends to have Grant killed as he sat trying to decide whether or not to talk to us in the night club. I don't know who the gangsters were, and I don't care. That's up to Deputy Strom. Neither do I know who killed Sprague, who had evidently come across some traces of Bolston's account juggling. He tried to do a little detecting on his own, even went up to see Simmons, then made an appointment with Woodbury to tell him about it. Sprague had already warned us he was on the track of something, and Bolston, watching him at the office, probably saw he had been looking through the accounts.

"A couple of the gangsters, very likely the same friends, trailed Sprague in an automobile, ran him down when he got off a streetcar. One of them jumped out and felt of their victim, not so much to make sure he was dead as to find if he had any papers on him which would incriminate Bolston. If there were, he got them; but that's another job for Deputy Strom."

Finklestein started to ask, "But the key? How did——" He halted, goggling at Miss Martin. She had fainted again, was slowly slipping out of her chair. The state's attorney caught her and said to the warden, "You better have her taken to the infirmary."

Two shapeless matrons came and helped her out of the room. She glided between them like a sleep walker. Crane didn't watch her go; neither did Bolston.

"I'll bet she'll do some talking," said Strom.

Williams asked, "But how about Miss Brentino and Woodbury? Why did they have a phoney alibi on the night of the murder?"

Woodbury looked surprised. "Phoney?"

"The alibi was all right," said Crane. "They said they were at the Black Hawk, and we thought they couldn't have been there because the place was reserved for a sorority party. But I'm certain Miss Brentino is an alumna of the sorority and was invited to that party."

"Phi Mu," said Miss Brentino.

Crane scratched the back of his neck. "I think that's about all."

"Plenty," said State's Attorney Ross. "I'll put in a call for the Governor from my office right away. Warden, you better come with me and talk to the Governor after I get through."

"What'll I do with this guy?" asked Deputy Strom, a massive hand on Bolston's shoulder.

"Take him down to the Bureau and book him for murder," said the state's attorney.

"Before I go," said Strom, "I'd like to find out how this guy got out of Mrs. Westland's apartment if there wasn't an extra key."

"So would I," said Finklestein.

Crane said, "It was quite easy, wasn't it, Bolston?"

Bolston stared out the window.

"After Bolston had shot Mrs. Westland, he took her keys out with him, locking the door behind him. Then he returned in the morning, a few minutes after the time he knew the maid always got there, and helped break in the door. He was the last one of the little group to rush into the room, as Miss Dea told us, and while the others were looking with horror at the body on the floor, he simply placed the keys on the table with Mrs. Westland's purse and the coins."

"Well, for God's sake!" exclaimed Finklestein.

Bolston said nothing while Deputy Strom fastened the handcuffs to his wrist, made no protest when he was led away. He did not appear to be frightened.

Finklestein watched until Strom and his prisoner had left the room. "They'll have a tough job putting anything over on Bolston," he said. "He's as cool as a hunk of dry ice."

Crane was looking at Westland, surrounded by people offering him congratulations. He said, "Bolston ought to get you to defend him now, Finklestein. That would be poetic justice." Westland's face was unhappy, he looked as though he were going to be sick to his stomach.

"Not me," said Finklestein. "I got an engagement with that Miss Hogan to go to Florida."

Crane said, "The hell you have!"

CHAPTER XIX

Saturday Morning

12:03 A. M.

The priest's voice was loud and triumphant.

"I absolve thee from all censures and sins, in the name of the Father, and of the Son, and of the Holy Ghost. . . . Amen."

Connors knelt on the cement floor of his cell, his head bowed over his hands. Warden Buckholtz, in the corridor, hauled out his fat gold watch. "It's past time——"

A guard swung open the cell door. Connors arose unsteadily, followed the priest out into the corridor. Westland and Isadore Varecha, from their cells, watched them pass. Farther along was Guard Galt, pressed against the wall. His lips were wet.

The priest, holding up the silver crucifix, sonorously chanted:

"Lord, have mercy. Christ, have mercy.

"Lord, have mercy. Holy Mary, pray for him."

Behind the gliding surplice, a half-length white shadow over the black cassock, Connors veered toward Guard Galt. His fist shot out; Galt's head hit the wall, and he fell senseless to the floor. Blood gushed from his mouth.

The priest, oblivious, chanted:

"*All ye holy Patriarchs and Prophets, pray for him.*

"*St. Peter, pray for him. St. Paul, pray for him.*

"*St. Andrew, pray . . .* "

A turn in the corridor made the words in the litany indistinguishable.

Seven minutes later they came for Isadore Varecha. His face was eager; he said to Westland, "I ain't afraid as long as you're coming behind me."

"Don't worry," Westland lied; "I'll be coming right behind you."

The little fiend trotted between two jailers, did not look back. Westland waited for the lights to dim, but they didn't. The electric chair was not attached to the regular jail circuit.

Presently Crane came and put a hand on his arm. "You can move back to another cell, now," he said. "They'll probably set you free tomorrow."

Westland's face was waxy. "I'd just as soon have gone with them."

Reporters in the corridor clamored for "Just a word, Mr. Westland." Two cameramen were busy screwing flashlight bulbs in a triple holder.

Crane said sympathetically, "Don't worry about Miss Martin, fella. There's other fish in the sea just as good."

Intense blue-white light flooded the corridor as the Tribune photographer set off a gunpowder speed flash.

Westland managed a sickly smile, asked, "But who the hell wants a fish?"

THE END

DISCUSSION QUESTIONS

- What kind of detective is Bill Crane? How does he compare to other series sleuths you have encountered?

- Were you able to predict any part of the solution to the case?

- Are there any qualities of this novel that seem distinctly "hardboiled"? How does it differ from more traditional mystery novel?

- Would the story be different if it were set in the present day? If so, how?

- Did the social context of the time play a role in the narrative? If so, how?

- What role did the Chicago setting play in the narrative? Would the story have been different if it were set someplace else?

- If you were one of the main characters, would you have acted differently at any point in the story?

- Did you identify with any of the characters? If so, which?

- Did *Headed for a Hearse* remind you of any other books you've read?